UNDERCOVER
with the
HEIRESS

ALIVIA FLEUR

SPENCER & CO
PUBLISHING

A catalogue record for this work is available from the National Library of Australia.

Cover design by Evelynne Labelle at Carpe Librum Book Design
www.carpelibrumbookdesign.com

Dedication

This one is for Rachel.
When I said I wanted to set a series in a street, Rachel
said I needed a curtain-twitchy nosey neighbour who was
responsible for one of the couples getting together.
Here they are.

WELCOME TO HONEYSUCKLE STREET

In a quiet corner of London, on the north side of the river, is a little street called Honeysuckle Street.

Don't bother looking for it now—you won't find it on any map. But once, before progress was the catchword of the day, Honeysuckle Street cut a treelined path between two main thoroughfares. The street itself could comfortably accommodate two carriages passing by one another. The residents spent their days in each other's company, or spotted one another on walks, or attended balls and gatherings together. A few errant children played games, and the odd elderly neighbour watched from behind twitching curtains, muttering about *young people these days*.

An enterprising developer had purchased the entire row on the north side of the street, cleared it and erected in its place five terrace townhouses. Five stories high, modelled on the Belgrave style and as similar on the outside as they were on the inside, which is to say, apart from the inhabitants, they were identical.

Five villas, each four or five stories high lined the opposite side of the street, mostly built at some stage during the reigns of the past kings named George.

And king of it all was a grey cat with a white-tipped tail named Spencer.

Spencer lived at number 6, the house in the middle of the street on the south side. It was rumoured that the old lady who occupied the house had been a lover of the Russian Tsar. Others said she had made and lost several fortunes in the American West. Others said that she had scrimped every penny she earned as a washerwoman and made a sensible investment during the last financial downturn. No one knew for sure. She didn't receive callers. She didn't make house calls.

She passed her time in the company of her beloved cats. At the end of each day, she stood on the porch and called them in. 'Mittens! Georgiana! Jimmy! Spencer! And no matter if they were curled up in the last ray of sun, or stalking along a limb, the little cats would run at the sound of her voice.

All except Spencer.

When he didn't return home, the old lady would wander the streets, calling and calling, 'Spencer! Spencer! Time for tea!' Later, when her hearing faded, she took to banging a pot with a spoon. When it suited him, Spencer would emerge, saunter his way to the house in the middle of the street, where the old lady would scald him but later, when sat by the fire, Spencer was still allowed to curl up and sleep on her lap.

When the old lady died, and unable to locate an heir, the authorities boarded up the old house. The furniture was pilfered. And after applying at kitchen doors, the kittens found new homes.

All except Spencer.

Spencer continued to patrol his street, hunting mice and chasing away noisier, bossier toms who might encroach on his territory. In return, the residents of Honeysuckle Street would find a scrap for him. Miss Delaney's cook left him the joint from the roast on Sunday. Miss Hartright put out a saucer of cream each night after her aunt had turned in. Mr Babbage put out a slice of cold ham, and not to be outdone, Mr Hempel left out two. The Caplin care-taker snuck him a biscuit, and in the evening, Miss Abberton left the downstairs window ajar so that he could squeeze himself inside and curl up by the furnace, even though he always managed to get by cook and took the best chair in the parlour instead.

Each morning and evening, Spencer sat on the decaying porch of the house in the middle of the street, silently surveying his charges. He kept watch on their comings and goings, their petty feuds and their longing looks over fences. He knew them all, sometimes better than they knew themselves.

Welcome to Honeysuckle Street.

WHO LIVES ON HONEYSUCKLE STREET?

Lady Iris Dalton, Director of Spencer and Co Travel
Number 5
Mrs Crofts, President of the Society for the Promotion of Civic Morality and the Adherence to Proper Values
Number 6
Vacant block mostly inhabited by Spencer, King of Honeysuckle Street
Number 7
Petunia Hartright, choir leader
Elise Hartright, assistant to Lady Iris Dalton
Number 8
Dalton family town residence, currently being renovated for Spencer and Co Travel
Number 9
Benton Hunter, Diplomat, currently abroad
Number 10
Townhouse forming part of the Osborne dukedom, currently unoccupied

CHAPTER ONE

9 June 1876

Nine inches was the perfect length. Three inches the perfect width.

Phineas aligned his ruler with the edge of the page and drew a sharp red line along its length. He waited a moment for the ink to dry, then slid the ruler across so he could mark out the next column. He set the square edge against the bottom of the page. Checked its position. Readied his pen.

'Babbage!'

Martins, the supervisor of clerks for the new accounts sector at Empire Savings and Loans, hollered at Phineas from the door, his head turning as he glared across the room. He strode between the desks and took each corner at an angular jerk. Clerks perched on stools cowered into their ledgers, all of them focusing hard on their numbers but tilting their heads just a little, no doubt to witness the approaching telling-off. All of them grateful that, today, it was not them.

Phineas pressed his pen against the ruler's edge. Blood-red ink leeched from the nib onto the page as he dragged the pen along the wood. It really was an excellent piece of equipment. A ruler like this was stable. It had a smooth, flat base that didn't shift with the pressure of his pen but still allowed him to see the existing margins without losing track of the other columns on the page.

It was also flimsy enough to snap with a determined flick, yet sturdy enough to plunge into a man's throat without splitting.

Not that Phineas had much need for violence.

Not these days, anyway.

Martins tapped Phineas's desk. 'Beaverbrook tells me you were late.'

Phineas slid from his stool to stand in some form of contrition. He'd forgotten the difference between a conciliatory and a bored expression and hoped that his slight frown and set mouth conveyed some hint of penance. 'I may, perhaps, have been delayed a little,' he said. 'The streets were busy.'

In reality, he had been at a board meeting for Spencer & Co. Travel. The damn thing had gone on for far longer than necessary. He probably could have antagonised Lawrence Hempel a little less. Then he might have arrived at the bank on time.

Martins crossed his arms over his chest, his flat palms tucked against his side, lifting his chin so that he could look down his nose. The man had been promoted from amongst the clerks a little over a month ago, and he seemed intent on lording his newfound power over his subordinates rather than using his experience at their level to ease their day. Yet, the light coating of dust on the tip of his boot showed he still buffed them himself at home, and his trouser hems had been tacked with an experienced yet inattentive hand, as they ran at an uneven angle. As Martins blustered something about *managerial expectations*, and *punctuality is an indicator of commitment*, Phineas gathered other fragments of information about the man. A black button that was a slightly different size to the others. A loose thread. A stiff collar. A perfectly trimmed moustache.

'What do you have to say for yourself, Babbage?'

What did he have to say? In another life, another world, he would have so many things to say. He would look Martins square in the eye. He wouldn't even blink as he delivered his assessment. *They gave you a promotion but not much of an increase in wages to accompany the extra duties, but you took it anyway because you value status over quiet stability. The dust on your shoe shows you take a different route to work, which means you've moved. You no longer have your shoes cleaned by a boot-spit, and the smudge on your collar suggests you shine them yourself, at home. Your wife still sees to your laundry and mending, but she takes no care, as she's exhausted from seeing to the extra work from the boarder you've taken on so that you can afford the rent on rooms over a shop on a slightly better street. The rose tint that saw her accept your proposal has faded, and she's wondering what else there is in a future with you, as after three years there is still no babe. While you blame her, she can't help but wonder—what if it's you? And there's one surefire way she can find out the answer, and he's leasing your spare room...*

'Well, Babbage? I'm waiting.'

Phineas straightened as he met Martins's hard stare. Martins's nostrils flared slightly.

'It won't happen again,' Phineas said.

Martins grunted what he likely thought was a manly dismissal. He sounded like an old dog growling into a dream of better days. Then he spun and stomped from the room.

As Phineas slid back into his seat, the bank clerks around him settled back into their worship of the pen. They called them the kings of the clerks, and in their own way, he supposed they were. Paid a little more than other clerks, working in clean offices, and perched on stools that were their thrones—there was no chance of a maimed leg, like on a construction site, or a hand crushed between crates, like on a loading dock. This bank was smaller than Barclays or the Bank of London, but it still offered enough opportunities for promotion, which gave their trivial lives a little hope and aspiration. Something that they lacked as they trudged the distance between Clapham and here like a morose, conformist, black-suited army, only to drown in the mundane repetition of column after column.

Thank heavens he wasn't one of them. He was just a man passing through, gathering information. And now that he was certain there was nothing else to learn here, it was time he moved on.

The other clerks sunk back into their ledgers, focusing on the mind-numbing tedium of tracking income, orders, and papers. Phineas flipped back through the pages of the ledger he'd been working on and scanned the columns before his eyes settled on a few inconsistent numbers. A four that should have been a six. A problematic two. He checked the company name at the front of the ledger, then scanned the room, searching for the clerk who was responsible for updating these accounts. No, it couldn't be. He'd had such hope for the boy. Phineas inspected the pages again, scooped up the heavy tome, and folded it into the crook of his arm to cross the room. He slid the ledger onto Taylor's desk.

'Would you mind checking my figures, sir?'

Taylor paused mid pen-stroke. His ash and grey eyebrows furrowed. 'I'm tired, Babbage. And it's been a long week already.'

'Just check my figures.'

His figures were fine, of course. Precise. Never a number wrong, never a sum out. There were no errors when it came to his calculations of pennies and pence. The phrase was code for an anomaly in the columns, a shuffling of money from one account to another, or an odd withdrawal. Usually an indicator that an employee, surrounded by all that wealth, had decided to take a little for himself.

Ever since the days of the Bank of London's financial catastrophe, many banks kept a few men on the floor to oversee the books in a way that went beyond tallying columns. Sniffing out scams and swindles or unusual financial activity, they allowed the bank to deal with an indiscretion before it got out of hand. It wasn't about the money—it was about maintaining public esteem and confidence. Men like Phineas and Taylor received no glory for their work, just a few more notes in their pay packet.

But looking for signs of fraud did make the monotony more tolerable, and for Phineas, it also gave him an extra motive to keep his distance from his colleagues. He didn't want to hesitate if he needed to rat out a man.

Perhaps that was why he'd let himself become embroiled in the lives of his neighbours in Honeysuckle Street—it gave him something of substance to do and tested his brain instead of seeing him stuck in the paper-pushing tedium of columns and rows and margins.

Taylor leant forwards and studied the page, his gaze lingering on the suspect transfers. 'Who?'

'New lad, Robinson. Only a few pounds, but more than what most start with. He's still young. A shake-up might be enough to set him straight.'

'They all start small. That's what gives them courage. You know the rules.'

'Of course I know them. I wrote them.' Phineas tapped at the column. 'It's too clumsy to be committed. His mother's sick. Maybe a reminder that a long-term position will do her more favours than a short-term windfall will be enough to steer him straight? Look at the boy. Newgate would break him.'

And not just mentally. Physically, too. Robinson was all twig, his limbs as spindly as the legs of the tall stool he perched on. He took a sheet of blotting paper and laid it across his work with focused particularity. Given time, he'd make a good clerk, and if he found someone to share his life with, he'd likely not be too miserable about it.

Taylor watched the lad over the gold rim of his glasses, then rolled his eyes and sat back. 'Make conversation with him before he leaves. See if you can nudge him into line. But one penny more, and I'll report him up the line. Then they can deal with him.'

With a dutiful nod—as if he really was a clerk speaking with a slightly more experienced clerk, and not a bank-employed spy sniffing out fraud before it got out of hand—Phineas folded the ledger closed. He was about to slide it off the desk when Taylor thumped another tome on top of it.

'My turn. Check my figures, Babbage.'

Phineas's fingers brushed over suede leather as he traced the bright foil stamp on the cover. The Argonauts Trading Company must be an important client. A new one too, judging by the brightness of the marbled paper on the inside. Phineas flipped through the pages, scanning each row.

'They used to be Abberton & Co.,' Taylor continued. 'Changed the company name last year and brought in a new board member. Some buy out.'

'It was a takeover, and a bastard one at that. Are they in trouble? They deserve to drown for what they did.'

Abberton & Co. had been the company run by his neighbour Iris and her father, Albert. She'd hidden her father's illness from the board and had gradually taken on the work herself. The board had only noticed when she'd been caught in a scandal, and when her father's declining mental state had become known, they had voted to strip the Abbertons of their position, claiming that the company could not be associated with a woman with a reputation. While Iris had found her feet with a new business that Phineas and many of the neighbours on Honeysuckle Street were investors in, the loss must have been hard for her to take. How were those buffoons faring now, without her?

'They're not in trouble,' Taylor said. 'Quite the opposite. What do you know about them?'

'Abberton & Co. were a trading company,' Phineas explained. 'Abberton imported high-quality goods and sold them to London businesses. He ran a tight business, but never a greedy one. He always said he was happy working in the middle.'

'Argonauts are aiming far higher than the middle. They're looking to open their own department stores, modelled on the Whiteley, only bigger. They'll use all their export chains, but without a middleman. They plan on charging the same prices and keeping the profit. A modest share offer to the public to fund construction of the building, the promise of fantastical returns... the usual. They've asked the bank to sell on their behalf and extend their credit.'

'Not using the Stock Exchange?'

'They're too small for the exchange. And given the offer, my hunch is that they're hoping to encourage women investors who have a harder time finding a broker willing to represent them on the floor. And who might be excited by the prospect of shopping.'

It was a risky move, but if it paid off, likely to be highly profitable. It might elevate the company from its place as a wholesale supplier to a household name. *If* it paid off.

Phineas glanced over each page, searching for the telltale smudge of an erased number or a wobbly line that revealed a hesitant hand. For all their grim muteness, the numbers on the page held as many tells as an amateur at cards. But each number had been written with confidence, every sum was correct, every column ran straight. So precise it could have been his own work.

'Who's the new board member?' Phineas asked.

'Lord Richard, one of the Marquess of Hanley's sons.'

'Compulsory aristocrat?'

Taylor chuckled. 'Likely.'

There wasn't a board in England that dared to sell shares to the public without an aristocrat on the board. For reasons he'd never understood, the stamp of a noble increased public confidence and made investors more willing to open their purses. But then, the average man or woman didn't see the books that *he* saw.

Phineas scanned the list of investors. The regular mix of toffs making side investments, pretending they didn't need new money, and new money trying to make more money, in the hopes of impressing the old money.

Phineas slid his finger over the page in a snake trail.

'Nothing out of place. Everything is in order.' Phineas turned another page. Lists of income and expenses, withdrawals and deposits, taxes and wages. He flipped the book closed. 'All in order.'

'Nothing else?' Taylor remained impassive.

'Nothing.'

'And yet?'

Phineas tapped the cover. And yet. 'Too perfect. No one in here does work like that. Except me.'

Taylor leant back in his chair and nodded. 'That's it. Couldn't quite spot it myself. It's been nice working with you, Babbage. I'll miss your eye, but more so your logic. Which way you headed? North? East?'

'South. Very, very south.'

Back at his desk, Phineas lined up his pens, rulers, pencils, and inks like usual, as if it was just another day coming to an end. Around him, clerks tucked umbrellas under their arms. They were completely unnecessary beneath the blazing June sky, but every clerk in London brandished one like a sword, even Phineas. He gave his desk one last tap in a mute farewell.

Monday he'd send a note to say he was unwell. In a week, another letter, to ask for extended leave. A month later, he'd notify the managers that he was moving for his health. They'd barely remember his name by then. They barely remembered it now.

And he'd be long gone, with fathoms of sea and sky and land between him and this city.

Clerks filed out, eager to get home to their small dwellings over shops. The ledger sat unattended on Taylor's desk. Phineas hesitated. He should at least find something to tell Iris, given that she was a stockholder in the company, to warn her of a problem if there was one. He opened the book once again, searching for some other clue. He flipped through the pages one by one but saw nothing out of place except for the overwhelming perfection.

Curiosity will do you no good. You can't keep getting involved in these people's lives. It's time to move on.

Phineas closed the book, clutched his umbrella, and set off home.

Chapter Two

The first one had been the four-leaf clover. The second a teacup, followed by a frog. After that, the robin. Or had it been the fox? She had almost a dozen lucky charms now, and after the first few, she struggled to keep the order of their arrival straight in her memory. It had been almost a fortnight since he'd sent anything new. What might the next one be? Rosanna turned the last charm he had sent—a butterfly—on its link to better appreciate the pink enamel. It was so pretty. So perfect.

'Rosie! Are you listening?'

Rosanna jerked out of her daydream to look up at her father. He was leaning over the opposite side of the desk, looming over a large map of southern England.

'Of course I am,' she said. 'I heard every word.'

'So your suggestion is...?' Her father raised a suspicious brow. Never one for indictments, Lawrence Hempel had a way of leading his children into the depths of their own lies or attempts to evade detection. When he suspected them, he never made accusations. He only fed them more rope to see if they would hang themselves on their own falsehoods.

Rosanna scanned the map. Before her thoughts had drifted, he'd said the words *further expansion*. They had two hotels in London, and one in York. This one, where they sat ensconced in the warm office, the original Aster, was the most luxurious and exclusive of them all. His hand half concealed Wales...

'Brighton,' she said with ready confidence. 'It's become increasingly popular as a holiday destination. The pier is a marvel. The fried fish is excellent.'

'Not too popular with the middle and working classes? Toffs like to be ahead of the game, not alongside it.'

Rosanna drummed her fingers on the table. 'It is popular with all strata of life, but old and new money like to be seen. If it were me, I wouldn't want to go to all that hassle to holiday somewhere quiet, just to be with the same people I could meet at a house party. I'd want *lots* of people to see my new frocks and finery, especially if I were new to society and hoping to make an impression.'

Her father's gaze narrowed. His lips moved as he muttered to himself while his finger traced first a line from London to the coast, then from Bath to Brighton. He knew every railway that fed in and out of the city, the small roads that were comfortable by carriage, and the inns along the way... every point of comfort, or possible discomfort, that might thwart a journey. He nodded, grinning as broad as a roof beam. While he'd let his children hang themselves, as a man raised roughly by the streets, he also appreciated a cunning mind that found a way of escaping when almost caught. Especially when the slip of the noose was handled with finesse.

'I'll make enquiries and begin canvassing suitable locations for renovating. Johannes!'

Rosanna's brother, working on a desk in the corner, stayed hunched over the stack of cyan-coloured plans. He withdrew a pencil from behind his ear and, in a mimicry of their father, muttered as his fingers walked across the page.

'Johannes.' Rosanna leant across and lightly touched his shoulder, and he jolted as if scalded. 'We're going to look for a new hotel location. In Brighton.'

'I was lost,' he said, answering a question no one had asked. 'Wait... Brighton? The sea?'

Rosanna smiled at her brother's absent-mindedness, even as her father tutted and rolled his eyes. The two men were so similar at times. But while her father planned business empires, her brother was far more concerned with aged wood, clay, and days gone by. Two years her junior, Johannes loved buildings and architectural plans. He came into the hotel office to work on his designs and ideas, claiming Number 3 was too noisy to focus. His well-worn copy of John Ruskin's *Seven Lamps of Architecture* was never far from his grasp, and he poured over it, seeking inspiration for his own grand designs. He preferred to carve a balustrade or hand-tile a mantelpiece rather than instal something produced in a factory. He relished the flourish on a window moulding or a well-crafted brass handle, but after devoting himself to his studies, he had yet to find a position with a firm that was prepared to take on the gentle giant and his passion for the mediaeval, the gothic, and the handmade.

Johannes said he lacked opportunity. Father said he lacked bite.

'I'd like you to take a train and scout Brighton to find a suitable property for conversion,' their father said. 'Put all that ridiculously expensive study to use. At least tell me how much it will cost to stop the right building from falling down once we start renovations. I want something old and grand and opulent. New won't suffice. It should make the hobs think of their glory days, not remind them the world is moving on. Make sure you check the footings. I don't have the patience for another Park Lane.'

'I don't want to check footings. I want to create my own buildings,' Johannes grumbled as he bent back over his plans and papers.

'One must design pavilions before one can build castles. Brighton. Or find yourself steady employment and a means to support yourself.' Their father threatened Johannes with homelessness at least twice a week, although they both knew he'd never follow through.

Johannes frowned, his sharp yet achingly precise mind working through a reply, one that might not form clearly in his mind until the moment had long passed.

Just go, Rosanna mouthed.

The office door opened. Rosanna sat on the far side of the table away from the door, leaving the lower half of the room obscured by the desk. A giggle entered, followed shortly by another. Unmistakably her younger sister Nova, eight years old, followed by Amadeus, Ammie for short, her ten-year-old brother.

Father's sternness cracked in an instant. A playful grin tugged his lips. 'Is there a ghost at the Aster, opening doors and sneaking into my office?'

The giggles became louder as they shifted from the door to behind the couch, but before Father could sneak around the table to intercept them, Mama came into the room. Her face drawn, her eyelids heavy, her blonde hair roughly pinned, she held little baby Hazel tight against her chest. The baby squirmed, squawked, then let out an ear-splitting cry. Father changed trajectory and met Mama at the door.

'We thought we'd get some fresh air. And Nanny Abigail needed some peace so that the younger children could sleep.' For all her subtle elegance and her soft meekness, Wilhelmina Hempel never apologised for interrupting her husband, and he never looked annoyed. No matter the moment, her arrival always shifted his body with relief. Like he had been waiting for the sun to rise, and now she was here, his day could begin.

Father eased the baby from Mother's shoulder and tucked her against his own. The little bundle squirmed before calming against him with a snuffle.

'Probably just too much excitement.' Father swayed a little, then kissed Mama's forehead. 'You should rest.'

Mama, her mouth still pressed into a worried line, brushed a finger against the baby's cheek. 'I'm trying to sleep when she does. Which is never.'

It had started like this with Garnett, all those years before. He was never quiet until silence was all there was. Rosanna had only been ten at the time. She had never known a sadness so suffocating and thought her entire body would break. Ever since, Mama never seemed able to settle into her babies until they could confidently toddle across a room. As if the danger had passed, rather than increased.

Rosanna startled as her sister bounded up before her. Nova held out a small white box tied with a thin pink ribbon. 'You got a present, Rosie,' she said. 'I think it's from your friend, Lord Richard.'

Rosanna took the box with forced composure, even though she wanted to rip the ribbon off and throw the lid aside. If she was going to be a lady, she needed to be calmer and control her impulses. Instead of fussing, she sat the box on the table.

'If you marry Lord Richard, will I have to call you Lady Rosanna, or can I still call you Rosie?' Ammie climbed over the back of the chaise longue from behind it and slid onto the seat.

'If she marries a marquess, she'll be a marchioness, not a lady,' Johannes said.

'He's not a marquess, only his son. The third one. She would be Lady Richard, not Lady Rosanna,' Mama said with tired patience.

'I don't care who he is, I'm not calling my sister *lady*,' Ammie announced, slipping onto the floor with a bump.

Nova pressed her spectacles up her nose as she pushed her head into the small pocket of space between Rosanna and the table. 'What's your guess? I think it's a flower. Ammie says a dog.'

Rosanna pulled the tie and unthreaded the knot. 'It will be nothing so pedestrian as a flower. It will be something exciting, like a hot-air balloon, or a—'

Rosanna peered into the box. Nestled inside, snug against a white cushion and fixed with white thread, sat a gold charm. He ordered them from Paris, he said, from a little jeweller on the Champs-Élysées.

A daisy.

'It's perfect,' she declared, and placed the box on the table.

'But you said—'

Father, speaking low as he patted the baby's back, looked at her brother. 'Johannes, take Amadeus and Nova to see Grandpa Robert. He's in the kitchen, stuck with a terribly hard task. He needs help.'

'What's he doing?' Amadeus asked nervously.

'It's not for the weak or the faint of heart. I hear he's been taste-testing new flavours of iced cream all morning.'

Johannes stumbled as the younger Hempels pushed past him to tear down the hallway, giggling and shouting out guesses of what flavours they might find before their high voices faded.

'For heaven's sake, this is a hotel. Remind them to be quiet? Please?' Father looked to Johannes. 'And ask Pierre to send up tea and coffee.'

'Will do,' Johannes said, then took off after Ammie and Nova at the same pace. He loved ices as much as the children, if not more.

Mama stifled a yawn against the back of her hand. Father guided her to the couch, and after a small show of resistance, she relented and settled against the cushions. By the time the tap at the door announced the trolley of tea and coffee, Mama's eyes had closed, and her breath had settled into an easy rhythm.

Father gently eased back into his seat. He pressed a kiss against baby Hazel's ear. 'This marquess's son seems quite taken with you,' he said.

'He does,' Rosanna replied. She made busy at serving the coffee and tea, pouring his how he liked—strong, black, and bitter. She took her tea weak and with a slice of lemon, as a lady should.

'Is that the life you want?' he asked.

'Why wouldn't I want to marry a lord?' She placed his coffee on the table before him, then settled into her seat.

'I can think of a thousand reasons. But my reasons are not yours.'

How to explain to her father who'd had nothing, less than nothing, when he fell in love with Mama? Johannes was the only one of her siblings with the faintest of memories of those early days when life had been filled with less financial certainty but so much joy. When the Aster had rarely been full and never in demand. But as the years passed and the quiet hotel empire grew and life became more comfortable, her parents' love had never waned. It had only grown stronger.

It seemed a cruel twist at times that she'd been raised to see what love, true love, should be, and yet have to negotiate a world where money twisted a man's affections in the time it took for her to be introduced. Even her friendship with Elise—her friend whose reputation had been thoroughly ruined by her sister's scandal—raised little more than an eyebrow in deference to Rosanna's family name. Her first year in society had been a sharper education than any she'd endured at finishing school. She'd learnt how to keep interested gents at a distance while she waited for them to show a greedy hand. How to read a man who saw her dowry as his for the sponging off, and not as her own income for her own self. A man who might turn cruel once they said *I do*. And they always revealed themselves—with a word, a slip, a comment. She saw through them all.

But Lord Richard had been different. He sought out her conversation. He listened to her opinions. He enquired about her work with Father and asked about her siblings. She'd met him in the dining room of the hotel when she'd been discussing the menu with Grandpa Robert. The young lord had interrupted and suggested adding *duck a l'orange* in the winter, when citrus was at its best, and then apologised. It had all been so casual and enchanting. Small conversations had extended into long ones, and with her father's begrudging permission, into chaperoned walks. A few days later, the gifts had started arriving. First, the bracelet had been delivered, glimmering against a soft white cushion with its thick gold links in beautifully crafted ovals. A week later, a four-leaf clover charm had been delivered, and when Lord Richard next accompanied her for a walk, he told her he'd picked it because it reminded him of how lucky he felt to have met her by chance.

Lord Richard, third son of a marquess, had a solid education, his own prospects, and he didn't need her money.

Surely, of all the places to begin a marriage, that was as good as any?

Chapter Three

Phineas clicked his pocket watch open, compared the hands to those on the large grandfather clock on the opposite side of the room, then snapped it closed.

They were late. As usual, everyone was late.

His chair creaked as he leant against the carved back. The noise split the quiet of the former dining room, now transformed into a cluttered meeting space for Spencer & Co. Travel, located on the ground floor of Number 4, Honeysuckle Street, across the way from his own tower of peace. Footsteps tapped on the floor above while voices and laughter occasionally bubbled down the hall and into the room. The investors' board for the boutique travel company met here every Tuesday morning to discuss business. Supposedly, anyway.

Phineas turned in his seat to check the door. One of the staff bustled past, singing, then paused.

'Are you early, Mr Babbage?' Gena, failed actress and housemistress of Number 4, leant into the room.

'I am precisely on time,' he replied with a huff.

'Oh, I think you're early. If you were on time, everyone else would be here! Would you like some tea? I've got the kettle boiling.' Her apron tails flicked out of view as she hummed away.

Phineas drummed his fingers along the edge of the table and checked the clock again. They were all most definitely late.

Of all the streets in London, all the places he could have established himself while he carried out his search, what had possessed him to imagine *this* as the ideal location?

At the time, he'd thought he'd struck gold. The combination of self-made men with working class sympathies living right alongside nobility with links to parliament and power, not to mention the independent women with connections and influence on both, had made him think that here, he'd be able to discover everything he needed to know. He would feel London's pulse. In a city where a connection and a name counted more than a man's own mettle, this place should have been the perfect base. He couldn't pay the deposit to secure a townhouse fast enough.

The reality of Honeysuckle Street? A mishmash of neighbours who found themselves embroiled in scandal, nobles who suffered their privilege as a discomfort, and diplomats without tact. So many petty squabbles and embarrassments... and somehow, he found himself at the centre of every little thing. Aiding a scoundrel. Assisting in what might be interpreted as treason. A baritone in Petunia Hartright's choir. In a neighbourly feud over windows. In friendships and squabbles. And now, on the board of a travel company, even though he hated going anywhere.

The sooner he finalised things and moved on, the simpler life would be. Today, he'd tell them he needed to sell his stake in the company. Not that he needed the money, but so that they wouldn't be suspicious and weren't left with a difficult loose end to tie off. Arley had caused enough upheaval. Then he could walk away, and the only weight on his conscience would be the one he'd brought to London—Imogen.

A nudge against his leg broke his thoughts. Phineas peered under the table. Spencer sniffed at his boot. The grey cat with the white-tipped tail usually prowled the detritus of what had once been Number 6, but since the building had been levelled years ago after that messy incident with the Hartrights—another debacle Phineas had somehow found himself part of—he spent more time lounging in parlours and stalking kitchens to find the best scraps. Phineas checked the door that led into the hallway. Quiet. He leant down and scratched between Spencer's ears. The feline rewarded him with an easy purr.

Independent. Taking what he needed. Giving in return only when it suited.

Wherever he found himself next, he'd be more like Spencer. He could even take Spencer as his new name, as a reminder to remain aloof. First or last?

There was plenty of time to decide.

A scrabble of voices bounced down the hallway. Phineas straightened in his chair and brushed the cat away. *Finally*.

Odette Delaney wafted into the room, as light as the melodies she was so renowned for singing. She lived in the large palatial villa directly opposite his own house, where her ostentatiousness made up for his reserve. Rumour and speculation always buzzed around Odette. This season, it was a Bulgarian prince who attended all her performances. As usual, nothing stuck, although her neck glinted with a new emerald choker.

Odette settled beside him at the table and Elise followed, sitting in the chair on his other side. Rosanna Hempel took the place opposite. 'Father is an apology,' she announced.

Phineas took a breath as a taunting greeting half formed in his mind.

Rosanna levelled him with a look. 'Don't start, Babbage. Not today.'

A flash of concern flicked through him. He almost inquired further, but stopped himself before he gave his worry voice. He needed to leave, not become involved. The entire point of provoking the friendliest man on the street was to avoid getting too close to him and his family. To stay aloof and not be bombarded with pitying dinner invitations.

When he'd first moved in, Phineas had barely taken a headcount of the Hempel brood. They had blurred into one, only distinguishable by their varying heights and hairstyles, always dressed with a touch of red. Gradually, the older children had emerged into adulthood through debutante balls or graduations, and only then had he bothered to learn their names. After a little over a year of sitting across the table from Rosanna, he'd learnt more than her name—he'd learnt her measure.

From a family established as reliable new money, and with an impeccable polish from governesses and finishing school, Rosanna would never be described as a society diamond but as a catch. For nobles scratching at the bottom of the family coffers, she had the potential to become a wife who would repair estates and not embarrass them, and for those with money and aspirations to move in better circles, she offered inroads to a new world with connections and proper etiquette.

He'd expected her to be plucked by some baron or even an earl in her first season. Yet, Rosanna had remained firmly unmarried for four years while continuing to hold her position on the society stage without a whisper of criticism. In clubs and coffee houses where he sat concealed behind papers and blank expressions, men spoke of her not as a has-been, ageing against ballroom walls, but as a challenge to be conquered.

Phineas met her penetrating glare. Fierce green eyes, almost black hair and sun-kissed skin. Without a doubt, Rosanna was not yet married because it didn't suit her to be.

'You have a new charm from Lord Richard?' Odette asked in her light accent that sounded French to most people but wasn't.

Rosanna suppressed a smile. 'A daisy,' she said, and extended her hand across the table, the trinkets at her wrist tinkling.

An uncomfortable prickle ran down Phineas's spine. 'Lord Richard? The Marquess of Hanley's spare?' he asked with less finesse than he'd like.

'Third son.' Rosanna twisted her wrist while Odette gasped and tapped at each charm. 'Not that it's any concern of yours.'

Phineas forced his face into a mask of composure as his mind searched and stumbled through the threads to make some semblance of sense of them. The new board member for Argonauts, the company with the perfect ledgers—that had been Lord Richard, hadn't it?

'How did you meet Lord Richard?' he asked, hoping he sounded nonchalant.

'He stays at the hotel,' she quipped. 'Because it's the best in the city.'

'No, no, no, no, no. This can't be happening.' Puffed and frazzled, Iris, the Viscountess Dalton, their company head and the brains behind everything, marched into the room and thumped a box onto the table. A thick wad of brochures spilled across the polished wood.

'Iris, it's not so bad.' Her husband, Viscount Hamish Dalton, heir to the Earl of Caplin, followed her into the room.

'Not so bad, Hamish?' She swung to face him. 'Not so bad? Austria. The tour is to Austria. Austria–Hungary, to be precise, but with a focus on Vienna. *Art, Architecture and Arias*, it's called. Travel by sea and train, visit some old churches, listen to music, look at paintings, and return within a week.' Iris snatched a brochure from one of the stacks and shook it out with such force that the paper snapped the air. She held it out without looking, as if she'd read it a million times before. 'Australia. It says Australia.'

'There are only a few letters different...' Hamish offered. 'Just the two, really. An A and an L.'

'And thousands of leagues and a lack of marsupials in where the trip will take them! People will notice.' She threw the brochure into the air, then fell into the vacant seat at the head of the table. Her assistant, young Elise Hartright from Number 7, snatched the paper as it floated down. She folded it and placed it on top of the pile.

Hamish knelt beside his wife. He pushed a stray curl from her forehead. 'Iris, you need to sleep.'

Iris shook her head. 'There's so much to do, and no time to have them reprinted.' Her voice petered out into an exhausted whimper. She hung her head, her body hunching with the effort.

As if none of them were there, Hamish knelt on the ground and pressed his cheek against Iris's. Her face contorted with grief before she leant into him. She bit her knuckle as she scanned the room.

'Sleep,' he repeated, this time more gently. 'These aren't due to go out until tomorrow. We'll work something out.' Hamish rose, yet kept hold of Iris's hand. He turned to the group. 'Albert's been having bad nights. He mostly remembers Iris, but not always the rest of us. Iris is doing her best, but it takes its toll, and... and together, we'll come up with some solution.' A slight panic contorted Hamish's expression as his gaze flitted across the empty seats to the few investors who'd bothered to turn up. 'That's what we said a few months ago. We stand by one another, no matter what. Didn't we?'

'I can fix it by hand. I have excellent penmanship,' Phineas said, just as Rosanna said, 'I can correct them.'

Their sincere tones petered out awkwardly as they turned to one another in horrified realisation. They'd spoken at the same instant. He took a breath, ready to withdraw his offer, but the light in Iris's eyes stilled him.

'Maybe I could rest for a few hours. Elise might help, too. If you all work together, it will be so much faster. You could be something of a... a...*team* even.' She looked from Phineas to Elise and Rosanna, a tired smile curving her lips. 'Gena will chaperone, if required,' she added, almost as an afterthought.

'I'd like to see him try anything that requires chaperoning,' Rosanna mumbled.

And that, apparently, was the end of the meeting. Odette left amid a flurry of excuses about princes and testing acoustics. Hamish helped Iris from her chair and led her from the room. At the door, he glanced over his shoulder and mouthed a silent *thank you*.

Phineas flopped back into his seat. With one sentence, he'd fixed himself more firmly to this place. He should be packing. Scratch that. Should be burning his papers.

'How lovely to be doing something together,' Elise said. She pulled a high stack of pamphlets from the box and placed it before Phineas.

'Delightful.'

'Fabulous.'

Rosanna glared at Phineas, her gaze hard and unflinching as she unscrewed a pen lid. 'When the viscountess awakes, she should find the task complete.'

She drew a brochure towards her, struck at the offending letters, then pushed it to the centre of the table. 'We should focus on working fast. We'll set up a line. Elise, you unfold the brochures and pass them to me. I shall fix the letters. Mr Babbage can fold.'

He would not be folding for anyone. 'The focus should be on accuracy. Viscountess Dalton does not need to wake to another debacle. I'll be neater if I work alone.' He pulled his pen from his coat pocket, unscrewed the lid, and snapped it over the end.

'I think the focus should be on the A and the L,' Elise hesitated. 'There's no need for speed or—'

'I can be correct and work quickly. I can do anything I set my mind to,' Rosanna replied.

'You may write any kind of gibberish fast. But will your penmanship be readable? Will potential clients be able to read what you have altered? Or will you be sending them to Albania?'

'Care to make a wager?' She'd continued working as they'd been talking and stacked another brochure on top of the small pile. 'I can complete more than you and be precise.'

'I don't gamble,' he sniped back. He took a brochure and made the small change.

'Just your pride for the stakes, then,' Rosanna said. She grabbed another brochure, moved her pen over the page, then pushed it aside.

He should be focusing on the information about Lord Richard. He should be sitting calmly and listening to Rosanna and Elise chat and gossip while he combed through their words for information. He should be keeping his distance.

Yet her little pile grew, and when he paused to study her corrections, they were accurate. She was going to beat him. She'd go into the world believing that she could do anything.

Which was an incredibly dangerous proposition.

For her or the world?

Undecided.

Perfect little rich girl, getting everything she wanted, believing everything about herself that she'd ever been told. Someone had to teach her a lesson.

'You have a wager, Hempel,' he said, and pulled a pile towards him. 'But make no mistake. I will have your pride.'

Chapter Four

Rosanna inspected her nails. She'd be wearing gloves this evening, but if Lord Richard had a ring, she'd have to strip them off, and she couldn't present the son of a marquess with ink-stained fingers.

Becca, the lady's maid who saw to the older Hempel daughters, tapped at Rosanna's waist. 'Deep breath now. Ready?'

Rosanna inhaled, rolling her shoulders back into her practised posture and drawing in her stomach as best as she could. A slip of boning pinched her waist as Becca tightened the cord. Breathing deeper, Rosanna gripped the edge of her dresser and inspected her shape in the mirror. Her breasts pushed higher over the lace trim when the corset compressed her ribs and cinched her waist.

'Tighter, Becca. I'd like a more fashionable silhouette.'

'Pfft. There's nothing wrong with your *silh-u-ette*. It might not be as fine as some of those ladies who flit about like little birds, but they don't have kettle drums like you.'

'Becca!'

The older lady chuckled. 'If you insist. One more go.'

As Becca tugged the corset cord even tighter, Rosanna checked the back of her hands. Was that an ink spot or a freckle? She licked her thumb and rubbed. The dot smudged, and she wiped until she eradicated it. She should not have let herself become so easily frustrated. At least she'd won and had shown Babbage that she could be both fast and precise. He'd scanned her work with an odd expression—something between confusion and admiration—and tipped his head in a kind of stoic concession of defeat before taking his leave.

Behind her, Becca tied the cords into a bow. When she finished, Rosanna sank onto her stool before the dresser mirror.

'I'd like my hair styled in this fashion.' Rosanna pointed at an etching in an open magazine. 'With the beads and the feathers.'

'Yes, miss.'

'And I'd like my peridot earrings, the ones with the pearl drops that my sisters gave me for my birthday last year.'

'Yes, miss.'

'And don't tell Mama, but a little rouge.'

'Yes, miss.'

'And I will wear my blue dress. The one with the hand-painted flowers and the lace.'

'*Yes*, miss. You told me that's what you'd like this morning. And after lunch. I've had it all pressed and ready for you for hours.'

'Sorry, Becca. I'm just nervous.'

'You, nervous? I haven't known you to be nervous since I first came through the front door. I'll never forget. Starting a new job, thinking it would be a lazy dream. Just a regular family done good who wanted some help looking the part. Wasn't I in for it, finding a firebrand spit of a girl telling me how she liked things to be, and only six years old.' Becca shook her head, smiled, and picked up her comb. 'It's all in hand, don't you worry. You focus on looking your elegant best for that poor young man who seems to be so smitten with you.'

'Becca!'

Becca chuckled as she set to work, pinning Rosanna's long brown hair into place.

'I want everything to be perfect.'

She had to be perfect. *Everything* had to be perfect. Because today, if he asked—and he seemed so close to asking... If he asked today, she had decided that she would say yes. She would not change the conversation. She would not encourage interruption. If he said, *Be my wife*, she would say, *I will*.

She'd be a lady. Independent. A fashionable figure in society. The woman who had everything.

A thump and a squeal came from the hallway, followed by a shout from Beatrice. 'Keep your stupid things on your side of the room!'

Rosanna took a slow breath. She would not be flustered. She would not get angry and let her face flush. She would not break a sweat. Not today.

'Mama says I cannot play on the stairs,' Nova argued, her light young voice serious, pleading for understanding from her older sister. 'And there isn't enough space to line up all the carriages on my side of the room.'

'Johannes!' Elliot called from somewhere further down the hall. 'Come to the courtyard. I made a new batch of pin-wheel firecrackers, and I want to test them.'

'Becca!' Beatrice swung the door to Rosanna's room open. Becca jolted. Rosanna winced as the comb scratched hard into her scalp. 'Was my lilac dress pressed? I'm going to be late for my dramatics club.'

Rosanna grasped the edge of her stool and twisted around to face her sister. 'Do you have knuckles?' she snapped.

Beatrice looked down at her fingers. 'Of course.'

'Use them! Knock first!' Rosanna hated the return to childhood frustrations with her slightly younger sister, but she also found immense comfort in her anger. Thirty minutes, just thirty quiet minutes was all she asked for. So that she might dress and prepare herself to meet with Lord Richard on what might be the most momentous day of her life. Could she not have a small sliver of time? Of quiet?

'But if I'm late, I'll lose my place in the tableau,' Beatrice pleaded.

Rosanna met Becca's gaze in the mirror. 'Finish my hair. Then help Beatrice find her dress. Come back afterwards and help me finish dressing.'

Becca worked fast, remembering the feathers but forgetting the beads. When done, she scampered from the room and across the hallway.

Rosanna picked up the string of seed beads and tucked them into her braid. For as long as she could remember, Rosanna had been responsible for dressing herself. It was only in the last half a dozen years that the long hours of building, opening, and running the three Asters had brought in substantial returns and drastically altered the family's fortunes. The changes in their lives had been fully realised about a year before she debuted, at the slightly older age of twenty. Rosanna had entered society as if she had always been a woman with confident wealth behind her. No one bothered to examine how things had been before. No one knew that Becca had first been hired as a general house mistress, and that her mother didn't keep her own help, and that Rosanna and Beatrice had dressed themselves and braided one another's hair for their first encounters with society. No one seemed to care.

The house echoed with the steady *bong* of the clock in the hall.

'Heavens.' Rosanna leapt from her chair and pulled open the door to lean into the hallway. 'Becca! Are you coming back to help me with my dress?'

Johannes's and Elliot's light laughter floated up through the stairwell, and Nova clattered past, her hair streaming behind her. But no sound announcing Beatrice or Becca followed. The last *bong* rang out loud. Seven o'clock.

Lord Richard hated to be kept waiting.

'Blast and drat it.' Rosanna huffed to herself. 'Just one night. One night without noise and hassle and drama. Is that too much to ask? Obviously, yes.' She pulled the bustle from where it had been laid out on the bed, stepped into the cage, then pulled it up over her bottom. She fastened the belt at her waist before checking herself in the mirror. Satisfied it hung straight, she snatched her cotton petticoat and tugged it over her head. A button caught on her hair.

'Miss!' Becca called from the door. 'Look what you've done. Why didn't you wait for me?'

Becca tutted and tugged at the petticoat until it lay smooth. Rosanna raised her arms as Becca gently angled the dress over her head. While Becca fixed the buttons, Rosanna fanned beneath her arms. Should she add a splash more rose water? Or would it be too much and she'd smell like she had marinated in it? The clock struck half past. No time, there was simply not enough time. Becca cinched the ribbon at Rosanna's waist.

'Thank you!' Rosanna called as she yanked the door open and raced down the hall.

A quick glance to make sure she didn't collide with anyone descending from the upper floor, and Rosanna clutched the banister to set off down the stairs. Above was the nursery for the younger children and where Becca and Nanny Abigail slept, while this floor was firmly the domain of the older Hempel children. Six of them, aged between eight and twenty-three, distributed between four rooms. The hallway on their level always had a slightly dishevelled look, with wallpaper faded from little hands trailing its edges, crumbs from biscuits smuggled from the kitchen ground into the carpet, and the endless shouts of fights or games bouncing off its walls and doors.

Rosanna turned the corner into the next stairwell. From somewhere down the corridor, baby Hazel squawked, and her mother hushed. Rosanna turned the next corner.

'Rosie, was your friend a lord? Or a count? I forget.'

On the landing, Rosanna shot a look into the drawing room to locate the owner of the voice. Amadeus had contorted himself to fit into the window ledge, his back flat against the wooden frame, knees to his chest, and feet in the air. His hair hung on end with his face upside down.

'Not now, Ammie, I'm late! He's waiting for me outside.'

'I'll let him know you're on your way!' Amadeus swung himself upright, all lanky limbs and elbows. He levered up the window, pushed it ajar, and stuck his head through the gap. 'She'll be down in a jiffy, lord sir countliness,' he shouted.

'Ammie! I'm trying to be proper!' she scolded.

Ammie shrugged, swinging himself to turn upside down again.

The door at the bottom of the stairs opened, and Nanny Abigail stepped into the entrance. One hand clasped the unsteadily toddling Thaddeus while the other ushered a red-caped Ottile across the threshold.

'The Misses Hartrights are out front,' Nanny called up to her, her focus steady on the children. 'Talking to that lord chap that keeps sending you boxes. I think Miss Petunia was trying to recruit him into her choir.'

'Oh, dear heavens, they are meant to be chaperoning us, not talking about singing.' Rosanna skittered down the final staircase and paused before the door. She shook out her dress, fanned herself a little, then paused. Were her cheeks flushed? Was her skin blotchy? She took *one, two, three* calming breaths. Just like they taught at finishing school.

Just like a lady would.

Tonight, if he asked, she would say yes.

She'd have her dress made by House of Worth.

They'd be married in the cathedral closest to his family estate.

She'd pick a date in autumn, when the leaves changed and set the oak trees ablaze with colour and the cooler wind made walking more pleasant.

They'd honeymoon abroad, in Paris or Lucerne.

They'd spend the London season in a townhouse in Mayfair, or by the park.

And all of it would be a world away from the madness of Number 3, Honeysuckle Street.

Rosanna heaved the door open and stepped onto the landing. She swayed for a moment, waiting, but Lord Richard remained deep in conversation with Miss Petunia.

She coughed.

Coughed again.

Elise tapped her aunt's arm, and at the interruption, Lord Richard looked up.

He wore a sharp grey suit and a stiff top hat in the same shade. A lush blue cravat that matched his eyes and his waistcoat. He stroked his thick sideburns, the same shade as his strawberry blonde hair, then nodded, as if convincing himself of a thought he'd had, but up until now was uncertain of.

Perfect. Everything would be perfect. She was going to be a lady.

'Miss Hempel.' Lord Richard removed his hat before replacing it on his immaculate mop of hair. 'Are you disposed to take a turn about the park?'

Chapter Five

Of all the cities Phineas had visited, travelled to, and moved through in a blur of dark corridors and scuffled conversations, London was by far the one he detested most. The fog that suffocated the buildings. The pompous pretentiousness. The swarming hordes that streamed in from the country, from the uppers to their genteel townhouses and the lowers to the slums. Both ends of the spectrum of life's lottery clogged the streets with filth and congestion all the same.

He couldn't wait to leave.

And yet this morning, when he'd planned to send a note to the office to begin his steady extraction, he had hesitated. He'd eaten jam and toast under Felix's slightly perturbed expression. While Spencer the cat finished lapping his morning saucer of milk, Phineas had donned his hat, tucked his umbrella under his arm, and set off to the bank the same as he did every working day.

In the subterranean office at the bank, Taylor had barely raised an eyebrow at his arrival. Over the course of the day, Phineas had inspected the ledger again, but he still couldn't find anything amiss. Later that afternoon, he'd slipped into the office of one of the more senior clerks and pulled the folio for Lord Richard's accounts. All had seemed healthy until...

There it was. A renegade zero, clumsily added to the end of a return, a casual shifting of the man's fortunes from precarious to flourishing. Funny how nothing could change everything.

Someone was hiding something. But who, and from whom?

And what did his churlish neighbour have to do with it?

Because for all her fire and contempt, he felt sure Rosanna and the Hempels were ignorant of Lord Richard's deception. Lawrence may have been light in his attitude to the law when young, but he was too devoted a father to risk his family's well-being in a scheme. He was also comfortable enough with his fortunes that he did not lust after more.

Phineas crossed the thoroughfare, making for the path that cut through the park near Honeysuckle Street. Summer had found London, and this year it had decided to be kind. The ornamental plums and cherries had grown lush and thick. Robins and larks hopped from branch to branch, couples hovered at the edges of the pond where ducklings—not fully grown, but not chicks any longer—nipped at one another as they bobbed on the water or waddled along the edges. The devout, seeking the solace of evening mass, gathered in a small group outside the church. He spotted Mrs Crofts amongst them, clad in black and surrounded by some of the pastel ladies from her society. Since the duke had left and she'd lost her patron, the Society for the Promotion of Civic Morality and the

Adherence to Proper Values had lost many of its members. Good.

A sudden shift in the ambiance slowed his step. Had the wind changed direction? No—the chatter of the birds overhead had also altered its tenor. A prickle raced across Phineas's skin. He scanned the park. Something was happening somewhere, some kind of disturbance not yet noted by people. Petunia Hartright and her niece, young Elise, hovered by the pond. The older Miss Hartright enthusiastically gestured as she spoke to a mother with her daughters—possibly trying to recruit them into her singing troupe.

A little further back, in the shadows, a couple stood immersed in deep conversation. Their heads bowed together, perhaps too brazenly for this time of year when the sun didn't dip until almost nine o'clock and sunsets went on forever. Phineas ground to a halt, then squinted. That was his neighbour Rosanna, speaking with a man at least a foot taller than her. Could it be the infamous Lord Richard, the man with the wayward zero?

The young lord shot a look at the Misses Hartright. Then, with a gentle nudge, he guided Rosanna deeper into the gardens, into the shadows, behind the hedges. Now there was a scoundrel's move if ever he'd seen one. They moved completely out of his line of sight, except for a flash of blue fabric as they ambled behind the hedges that edged the sunken garden. Was the young lord trying to make a scene, to create a scandal and force a betrothal? He'd not be the first to resort to such a desperate move. With access to family wealth like that possessed by the Hempels, the errant zero could be fixed firmly in place.

Served her right for being so damn arrogant and headstrong. A wave of nausea chased his flash of anger, followed by a rush of shame at his own vehemence. If Lord Richard only cared for her money, the marriage would not be a happy one. How many women had come into the bank, bereft and heartbroken, desperate to regain some control over their meagre finances once they learnt the professions of love had all been a lie to get to their purse? A life of misery was a hefty price to pay for a little youthful confidence.

Phineas set off again, altering his path to keep Rosanna and the lord in view as they moved into the sunken garden. He could just stomp in loudly and pretend he was taking a different route from his usual walk home. If he was wrong and it was only an innocent detour as they strolled along, lost in conversation, there would be no harm done. He would give her something new to scowl about. Because he might be wrong...

When was he ever wrong?

His foot hovered over the step leading into the garden. Wait. Someone else was down there.

'Mr Pennington wants his money. Now. Today.'

Pennington.

A confluence of hot and cold, of elation and dread, collided and swarmed inside Phineas so rapidly that he had to shake his head to clear the pounding in his ears. It couldn't be. After all these years... Pennington, here? He'd traced the man relentlessly, hard on the heels of a few scant clues as he desperately tried to locate the villain who may have abducted Imogen. Years of walking the streets, of listening out in clubs, of scanning names at the exchange, and this was the first time he'd heard anyone other than himself utter that name. He'd known Percival Pennington—thief, smuggler, and loan shark—had come to London. For all these years he'd just *known* it. And now, on the other side of the hedge, was a chance to find him. This lord, this ridiculous man with his sights set on his uppity neighbour would lead him straight to the answers he needed and perhaps to the elusive man himself.

Phineas pulled back, crouching between the hedge and the edge of a fountain. Cool drops of mist settled against small slips of exposed skin, and he wiped them away. He shuffled closer to the hedge and leant in, his ear straining to hear the voices which were muffled by foliage and water splashing into the pond.

'I don't know what you're talking about,' the lord stammered, his voice heavy with concealed deceit. 'I don't owe anyone money.'

'How dare you!' Rosanna. Did the woman not know when to hold her tongue? 'You clearly have mistaken us for someone else. This is Lord Richard, son of the Marquess of Hanley, and he is not in debt to anyone, especially not a grubby, no-good rogue. If you don't leave immediately, I will—'

Her words morphed into an indignant cry, harsh, hurt, and shocked. The backhand came so casually that its smack against Rosanna's cheek surprised even Phineas. A hard knock, full of malice and disregard. Rosanna staggered, then fell back into the bushes. The man leant forwards, grasped her dress, and tugged her face close to his.

'You his chit?' he snarled.

Rosanna touched a finger to her lips. Even through the shadow of foliage, Phineas saw the bright smear of crimson blood.

'I... his what?' she stammered.

'He said his chit had his money. Pay up...' The man flexed his hand, then bunched it into a fist. 'Or you'll learn what happens when people don't meet their deadline.'

'I don't have your money!' Lord Richard shouted, his voice trembling.

Phineas grasped the edge of the fountain and hauled himself up. It had been so long since he'd been faced with an altercation like this, with a man who wasn't just angry, but who might *hurt* someone. What to do? How to help? What had the corporal taught him, what had they said when he was in the army? He slunk around the edge of the garden. As he ran, he loosened his umbrella, then popped it open with a half-shout by the pond. Ducks and swans scrabbled into the air, quacking and honking as they took flight. A few people shouted and scurried out of the way. The Misses Hartright looked around, and Petunia called, 'Rosanna? Miss Hempel? Where are you?'

Angling through the walkers, Phineas staggered into the garden, shouting and cursing at ducks. He expected to find the three of them—the man, the lord, and Rosanna—but when he closed his umbrella, the only other person in the garden was his churlish neighbour. She pushed herself up from between the snapped branches of the hedge and cried out, 'Lord Richard? Help me stand.'

Phineas caught Rosanna's hand and hauled her to her feet. She stumbled into him. With a loud ripping noise and an anguished shout, she threw her arms around his neck and sobbed into his shoulder. 'I was so scared,' she cried. 'Thank heavens you were here.'

Phineas stiffened. Rosanna snuffled. He gave her a few light taps on the back.

'Did he hurt you?' Phineas asked stupidly, softly, even as the bright red mark across her cheek screamed the answer.

She looked at him, blinking, as if trying to pull him into focus. 'What? You? Where is Lord Richard?'

The confused fury in Rosanna's eyes darkened, then shifted to horror. An unmistakable gasp and a tutting came from over Phineas's shoulder.

'Mrs C-crofts,' Rosanna stammered. 'This isn't what you think it is.'

'I don't believe it! Or should I say, I do!' Mrs Crofts's voice cut through the hum of the park. 'You have been at inappropriate activities. Inappropriate! I have invited your mother to my meetings and suggested she bring her daughters, but like the rest of the street, she ignores my offers of assistance. And now look at you. Caught alone with a man! Compromised! Ruined!'

'There was another man—'

'Two men!' Mrs Crofts's voice shifted higher, fuelled with self-importance and indignation.

'Not in any problematic way, not...' Rosanna took a step away from him. Her hand clasped at her torn dress, and she touched the swell of her lips. 'He said a name, he said—'

Phineas grasped her wrist and pulled her close. 'Don't say that name. Don't say another word.'

'But she thinks we were together!' Rosanna exclaimed.

'This will make the papers,' Mrs Crofts continued. 'Take my word for it. I will see that it does, as an example to other young women on the dangers of immorality. And of parents who give their daughters too much freedom! I will send a special edition of my newsletter. I will hold an emergency session for my society next week, and everyone will attend to learn the dangers of licentiousness, freedom, and—'

Phineas turned around slowly. Mrs Crofts looked at him, her mouth contorting through various vowels, but her voice lost. One of her pastel society ladies rushed into the garden, then another. Bloody hell, now there was an audience. Rosanna's gaze darted between them as she tugged at her dress.

'Rosanna here is in no way compromised. She just caught her dress,' he said.

Mrs Crofts raised a condemning brow. 'Mr Babbage! I expect terrible behaviour from Mr Hunter or even Lord Dalton, but you? You cannot lure a lady into a garden for nefarious purposes.'

'I didn't, I was just—'

'Nefarious! You must get married.'

'I am not going to marry Miss Hempel.'

Mrs Crofts took a menacing step forwards. 'It is one thing for a woman on my street to be up to mischief, but two people will ruin my society's reputation. And after that messy business with the ballerina, I am afraid I have no choice but to insist you marry, for the reputation of Miss Hempel and the street itself!'

Phineas sucked air through gritted teeth as he tried to assemble his thoughts. He needed to learn what Rosanna knew. He needed to keep her safe from Pennington and get her away from whatever mess Lord Richard had landed himself in. More than anything, he needed some quiet. He needed bloody Mrs Crofts and her pastel ladies to stop muttering and Rosanna to stop protesting her innocence beside him.

'Mrs Crofts!' he bellowed, and the crowd quietened. 'You have guessed our surprise. We are indeed engaged. We have just been too busy to make the announcement.'

Rosanna shot him a hard look. 'We most certainly are not.'

Phineas laughed. He'd not done that for some time, so at least no one would guess it was forced. 'Darling, there's no need to be shy. Everyone will hear about it soon enough.' His voice dropped low, and he pulled her close. 'Everyone. This cannot go to the papers. I need to find Pennington before he finds you. Marry me, just for show. When I find him, I'll leave. Your reputation will remain unscathed, and you will be of no interest to him if you aren't connected to Lord Richard anymore.' She squirmed in his grasp, but he held firm. 'Unless you can think of an alternative solution?'

Rosanna peered over the heads of the crowd to the garden beyond. 'Lord Richard?' she whispered, soft and yearning. Then, with a bitter pout, she pinched her eyes shut. He waited for her to stomp her foot and rage, but she raised a trembling hand to her bright red cheek instead, pinned a smile to her lips, then nodded. 'We are ever so happy,' she gritted out.

'You are?' Mrs Crofts asked, crestfallen.

'We are.' Rosanna slipped her hand around his elbow. Phineas patted it. The crowd deflated, then scattered.

When they had gone, Rosanna grabbed his coat-sleeve and tugged him to face her. She kept her smile, but her voice scratched through her throat, coarse and heavy with indignation. 'This will be sorted. I will not stand it. I will not marry you, Babbage. I would rather die than be your wife.'

Phineas found his same forced smile. 'Interesting choice of words, Hempel. Because that may very well be the crux of it.'

Chapter Six

From the time she could toddle, Rosanna had known the church at the far side of the park close to Honeysuckle Street. Old, solid, and unchanging, its grey cement walls were ornamented with sandstone and wrought iron. With a grey slate roof and a spire topped with a simple cross made of two practical bars, the church buttressed the park with quiet confidence. The world around it changed constantly. Trees grew, lost their leaves, and blossomed in the spring. The first home she had known, a small, rented cottage with a large garden, was knocked down, replaced by the row of five townhouses and the tower of rooms which gradually filled with a swathe of siblings and noise. People moved in, then moved away. Some only came for the season. Throughout all the upheavals, even the demolitions, the church had remained a permanent, unchanging fixture of her young life. Every little Hempel babe had their head dipped and blessed by the minister here. Her parents had married here.

And now, she was getting married here too.

To a man she barely knew. Who had spent the past seven years antagonising her father for no obvious reason. Who had somehow secured the best house in the row, even though her parents had paid a deposit. Who looked at her now with no affection, no kindness, not even disdain. Just rationality.

The hectic conversation as he'd directed her back to Number 3 still rung in her ears, a week later. *Did you ever see Pennington? Did Lord Richard mention him or borrowing money from him? What is their arrangement? Does he stay at the hotel? Don't fucking argue, Hempel, this is serious.*

People will do things you can't imagine for money.

He had no solid answers as to why Lord Richard had been accosted, just that they might return and hurt her if they could not find him. If she didn't marry someone, her reputation would remain shattered. In the closed study, as her father had downed three whiskies in ten minutes, she'd held back tears about her split lip, her swollen cheek, and the screeching accusations from Mrs Crofts. Meanwhile, Babbage had rattled off that he worked not only as a clerk, but something about fraud, and that he'd been looking for a bad man and that man had made a threat against her. He'd said that name over and over, *Pennington*, and every time he did, her father swallowed a glug, then topped up his glass. Then, almost as an afterthought, Phineas had turned his sharp eyes on her.

'You work at the hotel.'

She had only been able to nod.

'After we're married, you will continue to work there.'

In less than a week, he'd procured a special licence, and this morning, as the sun rose over a tired and smog-soaked London, a small congregation of family and neighbours filled the church. Elise stood beside her, as none of her sisters had debuted yet, so none of them could serve as her maids in waiting. Little Ottile sat on the church floor as a flower girl, picking petals from her basket. She sniffed one, bit it, then scrunched up her face in disgust.

'It's ridiculous. Compromised women thinking they must marry to cover it all up. Just be compromised,' Elise muttered beside her.

Rosanna would give anything to tell her friend the story, but Phineas had sworn her and her parents to secrecy. *If we move fast, it will be over before anyone asks too many questions. Draw up whatever paperwork you like, this isn't a ruse. Hilarious, Hempel, I don't need her money. You want to wait for Lord Richard to explain? He's in trouble, and you don't know Pennington like I do. I don't need the attention; I need to work. Once I find Pennington, I'll be out of your life. Out of everyone's.*

'Flafoo,' Phineas said, then held out his hand.

Rosanna blinked hard, shook her head, and tried to bring Phineas into focus through the gauze of her veil. 'I beg your pardon?' she asked.

'I do,' Phineas repeated. 'I need your hand. For the ring.'

She'd sat in this church twice while waiting for a wedding to take place, but neither had actually happened. Maybe the trend would hold. Maybe, as with Elise's sister, the church doors would fling open, and Lord Richard would shout his objections and explain that it was a terrible misunderstanding, that he didn't owe the bad man money. And he would fall to his knees and beg her not to marry someone else.

Light flickered in the antechamber.

An omnibus rumbled by.

The doors remained closed.

Rosanna slapped her palm into his. As he pushed the simple gold band over her knuckle, it pinched the skin. She tried not to flinch. 'I do,' she said, not even knowing if it was the right time in the sermon to say the words. 'For better or *worse*, I do.'

'You may kiss the bride.' The words echoed at a distance in the vicar's monotone. He snapped his book of common prayer closed.

Phineas twisted a little to face her, his feet shuffling. He pinched the edges of the veil and raised it, and the world cleared as she looked to the man who was to be her husband for the next few weeks. Dark hair, clean shaven, wearing a simple suit with a white flower in the button... What an uncommonly ordinary-looking man. He was not even taller than her, but at least he wasn't shorter. His lips twitched. Was that a smile? Babbage didn't smile. A few little creases formed at the edge of his eyes. They fixed her with certainty, their dark brown shade almost black in the diffused church light. He leant in.

'I don't want to do this,' she whispered. 'I don't want to be married to you.'

And now he smiled properly. A small dimple indented each cheek, an incongruent softness to his hard demeanour. 'The feeling is more than mutual, Hempel.' His lips barely skimmed hers before he squeezed her hand and they turned towards the congregation. A smattering of applause followed them as they left the church. Outside, pigeons scattered along the path, taking flight with a flustered coo.

Rosanna clomped down the stairs, indignation filling her chest. 'What do you mean, *more than mutual?* I am a fine bride for someone like you. Your social standing will not suffer.' She hadn't broken her fast, and her stomach grumbled.

Phineas grabbed her elbow and spun her to face him. He took a few strained breaths. 'You think this is about your blasted reputation?'

Rosanna met his glare. 'Where is the carriage?' she asked, accentuating each word.

'The street is there.' He gestured towards the wall of Number 1 and the stark white of Odette's palatial villa that formed the bright entrance to the street. 'It's a sunny day. We can walk. You can show off your fancy dress.'

'Fancy? There was no time for a fancy dress. And no modiste would even consider an urgent appointment once they found out who the groom was. This is the dress I debuted in, three years ago. I will not walk from the church and become a spectacle for ridicule.'

'Sorry to inform you, Mrs Babbage, but your husband does not own a carriage. But if you will not walk, perhaps I can offer a solution.'

He was only her height, but he moved fast and was strong. Before Rosanna could swat him and turn away, Phineas had grasped her around the middle and thrown her over his shoulder. Rosanna squawked and screeched, and as he spun, the horrified faces of the congregation flashed in and out of view.

'Hungry?' he asked, then set off across the park. 'I believe the wedding breakfast is at Number 3.'

She pounded, she grumbled, she hollered. Still, Phineas did not relent. He only gripped her tighter, and when she began to screech, he slapped her bottom before calling out to some walkers in the park, 'It's a family tradition. From up north.'

As he jogged across the road, his shoulders dug into her stomach, and each lurch up the front stairs of Number 3 jolted her head against his back. Here, he deposited her on the landing. 'How was the carriage ride, milady?' he asked with an exaggerated curtsy. 'Would you like me to carry you over the threshold?'

Rosanna floundered to find her footing and stumbled, bumping hard against the door. Fury, black and ugly, coursed through every vein. 'How dare you make a spectacle of me.' She flung the front door open and stomped through the entrance. 'How dare you mock me and treat me so terribly.'

It felt incongruous to have undertaken a momentous event—marriage—only to then step over the threshold of her childhood home. The house breathed with familiar freshness and warmth. Tempting tendrils of the scent of bacon, bread, coffee, and tea curled in the air in the entrance. She paused before the mirror. Curse him—a pin had loosened, and a thick lock of hair bulged on one side. She would not sit at her wedding breakfast with her hair such a fright. Of all her dreams, this one she would salvage. Where were her brushes, her combs? Rosanna scanned the line of trunks and cases that filled the hallway, then crouched and slid the leather strap from a buckle.

'What's all this?' Phineas flicked his fingers, then turned to glower at her. 'Three cases, four trunks... And what is in all these boxes?'

'My things,' she replied. 'You can send over one of your staff to collect them while we are at breakfast.'

'You can bring one case.' He raised a finger in demonstration. 'Anything more is superfluous.'

Rosanna raised herself to standing. 'I am not repacking.'

'This isn't a pleasure jaunt, and it is in no way permanent. You don't need all of this. If you forget anything, you can just walk over and get it.'

She stamped her foot. 'I do need them, and I will have them, and you will not presume to tell me otherwise!'

A racket of voices and little feet banged up the front stairs, and a noisy stream of her smaller siblings filled the entrance. Nova and Amadeus skipped inside with barely a glance at them, while Ottile, always in a world of her own creation, danced over the tiles as she sang a song about pikelets and scattered petals over the floor. Frozen with an icy resolve, Phineas's hard stare did not shift.

Beatrice paused in the doorway. Elliot and Johannes stopped behind her. All of them stared, mouths slightly agape.

Phineas took two steady steps, not once breaking eye contact until he stood before her. The edges of his mouth set firm, and his nostrils flared.

From his light brown hair, parted to the side, to his simple black suit and smooth chin, Phineas Babbage was the most mundane of men. Even his eyes were a grey the same shade as a slate roof. Despite his ordinariness, she recognised a callousness in him, like the man who'd struck her in the park had displayed. And with a tumble of realisation, she understood his speed and his insistence.

Her new husband wasn't a counter to those men.

He was like them.

And he understood them in a way that, perhaps, she didn't.

'I'm going home,' he said flatly.

Her brothers and sister, still in the doorway, stepped aside to flank his exit. Phineas walked between them, nodding once as he passed her father. Silence fell.

'Rosie.' Her father spoke gently but firmly. 'You have to go with him.'

CHAPTER SEVEN

As the crow would fly... Well, a crow wouldn't bother to fly, it would merely hop the short distance from the door of the Hempel household to his own. Stamping down the stairs, walking past the bay window full of Hempel faces pressed to the glass, up the stairs and sliding the key in the lock before barging into his home like some criminal—he'd not exactly covered a momentous distance. It did not even take a minute.

It felt like a million miles.

He'd known Hempel had a temper. Had opinions and preferences. What surprised him was that they inched their way under his skin and turned like corkscrews, niggling him to irritation, when nothing and no one ever got to him.

Phineas stepped into the replicated entrance of his own home. He wanted to slam the door shut; he wanted to shout into the street, *Well, fucking die then*. Instead, he crossed the room and placed his hat on the entrance table.

As he shrugged off his coat, Rosanna trounced in. 'You don't have to be a shrew,' he spat.

She drew an indignant breath. 'I'm not a shrew. I'm a woman. A young woman in a demanding city that has certain expectations of how I look and present myself. And if you expect me to help you—'

'I am helping *you*—'

'You can make me more amenable by fetching my things so that I can dress and groom myself in the way that suits me!'

Phineas slung his coat on the hook as his irritation grew. His chest tightened with each breath, and although he tried to expel each gulp of air between pressed lips, his ire wouldn't settle. 'I'm so sorry to inform you, *milady*, but the world no longer gives a fig what you look like. You think they're going to put you in the society pages? Mrs Babbage, wife of the unknown bank clerk, stuck a feather in her cap today. Or better again, how is this—recently married, she wore her second-best dress for her burial. Shame they couldn't have a viewing, because after they hauled her body from the Thames, she was such a goddamn mess—'

'Stop it!' Her entire body went rigid with her shrill screech. She tugged at the finger on each glove, huffing as she did so. 'I am still myself. I am still a woman who likes to change her morning dress.' She slapped her gloves into her palm. 'You may be planning to leave, but I will need to carry on after all this. And I would like some consistency between who I was and the person I will need to become.' She untied her bonnet and pulled it from her head. Then she paused, her arms stretched mid-air as she scanned the walls. She turned to him, fury and confusion in her eyes.

He only had one hook. He'd never had need for two.

His discontent mumbled something like, *Should be grateful I'm helping you at all*, but it was quickly silenced by the shame that rushed from his toes through his entire body. For all her sharp bravado, Rosanna was not a worldly woman, and in the time it took for an angry man to smack the back of his hand against her cheek and tear her dress, her life had been upended. Every dream she'd ever held dear had fled—as fast as the heels of the man who'd promised her a shining future, only to run at the first test of character. For Phineas, there would be a future beyond this. For her, it wasn't so simple. Even with her reputation somewhat restored, she'd be marked by this moment for years. Was it any wonder she was angry?

'I'll get you a hook.' Phineas pointed at the wall, then shoved his hands into his pockets. 'I would like you to be comfortable while you are here. I know this isn't what you planned for yourself. But it is important. And better than the alternative.'

In the dim light of the entrance, her green eyes had grown large. Full of fear and worry, they shone like they had that night in the park when he had allowed himself to be swayed from his path. Rosanna fidgeted with the gold charm bracelet at her wrist. Its jingling filled the entrance, the melody a counter to their angry breaths.

'Lord Richard gave you that?' Phineas asked with a nod, even though he already knew the answer. He'd long ago learnt how to read the sweep of a longing hand, of a delicate movement attached to a gentle memory.

She nodded as she spun it, her fingers caressing each little charm.

'It's not real,' he said.

She jerked her head up, and her gaze landed on him, as sharp as a blade. 'It is. He buys them from a jeweller on the Champs-Élysées.'

'It's a good imitation. Good plating. It would still have cost him. Just not what you imagine.' Phineas crossed the room, caught in a mix of guilt and fortitude. There was no reason to tell her, to remove her from the certainty of her cocoon of truth and love. But she lived in a city built on a bedrock of the lies of men, and they were often exposed through the jewellery and gifts they lavished on their wives and mistresses. It was far better she learnt the truth now, from him, than she discover it for herself after he'd gone.

He took her hand. Unlike in the church, she let him draw her a little closer. He spun the chain. 'The clasp is always the giveaway. It doesn't have a proper lock. Middling forgers rarely think to protect from theft. Why would they?'

Such soft hands... Perfect for a lady, the sort that she'd been on the verge of becoming. Her skin was unmarked by the harshness of life that her parents had endured, but despite its inexperience of physical labour, it still held memories. All of a person's memories could be found in their hands. In rough callouses, in nicks and scars—and in Phineas's case, in the sweep of a blade across his palm. A scar that marked him as more than a blank slate.

Her expression morphed from a hateful glare, turning inward to sadness and confusion. 'Why would he lie? Why not just buy silver? Or from a London jeweller?'

Phineas shrugged. 'Embarrassment. Understanding the importance of appearances. Wanting to stand apart from other men. Not every lie has a malicious seed.'

The summer flush had faded, and the barest hint of rose pink grazed her cheeks. The mass of white lace and silk washed the normally healthy glow from her complexion. Her gaze darted from the chain on her wrist to the wedding band on her opposite hand. Then she looked beyond him, searching, thinking. She was quick. A spark of admiration lit inside him as he followed her shifting expression, as her nimble mind drew together fragments of memory, whispered promises and polite exchanges. He did not know their detail, but he knew the shape of them, all reflected in her eyes as she came to the unwanted conclusion herself.

'He wanted my money.' The words dragged out coarse, each syllable so dry and brittle it snapped short in the air. 'Right from the start. I was second to it, wasn't I? I spent years wading through men chasing money. Twenty-three, almost twenty-four years old, and I've not had one proposal because I would not allow the courting to continue once I spotted a fortune hunter. But I missed him.'

He nodded. False sympathies and lies had no purpose between them. She raised her chin and took a defiant breath, but he saw through her like glass. She was hurting. And she'd be no use to him if she stayed hurt.

'Felix,' Phineas called over his shoulder. A few short toe taps, and Felix, slightly ruffled and with his top button unfastened, appeared. 'Can you fetch the whisky?'

'Sir, it's not Christmas. And it's eleven in the morning.' Felix shot a look at Rosanna as he fastened his top collar button.

'It's *her* Christmas.' Phineas pulled his face into an expression which he hoped looked conciliatory. He didn't smile often and wasn't sure his muscles were arranged right. 'And can you rustle us up something to eat? We left the wedding breakfast in a bit of a rush.'

'Toast?' Felix asked. 'You haven't asked for anything other than toast in more than seven years.' He turned to Rosanna. 'You like toast, ma'am?'

Rosanna shook her head. 'Not particularly.'

Felix frowned. 'We only have bread in the pantry and few cooking implements, save a toasting fork and a few plates and pans. I doubt there's even an egg. *For years* I've been waiting to use that kitchen. And now a request, and no notice. With some warning, I could have at least stocked something other than butter and jam.'

'Head out, then!' Phineas waved a hand at the door. 'Find some cheese. Ask a neighbour.'

'And in the current state of the street, who do you suggest?' Felix shot back.

Phineas bit his lip as he counted out each house, numbers one through ten. 'Miss Delaney. She'll understand, be generous, and have a stocked larder. Don't go to her door though, head straight to the kitchens. She has company.'

Felix shot Phineas a disapproving look, then grumbled down the shadowy hallway. He re-emerged a moment later, wearing a flat cap and a coat. He continued muttering about *toast* and *time* until the door closed and silenced his complaints.

'I usually take breakfast on this level, in the room that overlooks the courtyard.' Phineas tipped his head at the hallway. 'Do you know the way?'

Rosanna studied the blank walls as if she hadn't heard him. Her eyes darted left to right like she was reading, and with an uncomfortable jolt, he realised she was reading *him*. She turned in a slow circle, and once she had canvassed every inch of his unwelcoming entrance hall, she stepped through the door and into the corridor.

He followed her as she moved confidently through the lobby, past the staircase, then into the short strip that led to the dining room. A confection of white silks and lace, Rosanna glowed luminescent against the dull walls which were devoid of memories. He'd never bothered to change the paint in any room. Never called a decorator, never even instructed Felix to coat a wall in green or yellow or hang a boring painting of the Thames. He'd never attended to anything more than basic furniture, filled the rooms that had use to him with the essentials, and gone about his life.

And why would he? He hadn't planned to stay.

Not for seven years.

Seven years.

'We also eat our meals in this room,' she said as she stepped into the dining room. The small breakfast table sat central, and she paused before it. 'Our table stretches the entire length of the room. Mama had it made after Ottile was born. Father constantly bangs his chair against the wall when he stands to cut the roast or to help one of the younger children master their knife.'

She looked left, then right, and in her sway, he followed the length of the table in her thoughts. Despite never having seen it for himself, he could draw it in his mind: long and filled with love and life. And although he was looking at the back of her head, with her hair tousled by their escapade across the park, he felt her gaze as keenly as if it were concentrated on him, slow and lingering.

How curious that she moved with such familiarity, yet was a stranger. How easily he could read her life, although he had never set foot inside the house next door apart from this morning.

Strangers, occupying identical spaces, separated by a double row of bricks.

'On the rare occasions I eat dinner at home, I do so in the library,' he offered. 'It's a little nicer. Perhaps we could dine there?' And before she could agree—or more likely, disagree—Phineas crossed to the small sideboard to open the cupboard, retrieved the decanter of whisky and two glasses, and headed back to the front of the house, towards the library with the window that overlooked the street.

The glasses clinked as he sat them on the table. Rosanna's dress rustled as she followed. She paused in the doorway for a long time. When she finally entered his favourite room, he had just poured himself a second glass.

She had divested herself of every society pretension that had survived the journey across the park. No veil, no gloves. No charm bracelet. She slouched into the chair beside him, and when she crossed her feet at the ankles, her stockinged toes poked from beneath her dress hems. She took the whisky he'd poured for her and placed it on her chest. Then, like him, she stared into the cold hearth. The silence between them sat hard and angry, the air tense with frustrations and questions. Phineas took a hefty swig.

'I can't touch your money,' he blurted out. Rosanna turned her head but otherwise stayed unmoving. 'I thought you should know. Your father has the best solicitors in London. You'll keep everything when we separate. Even if I wanted to, which I don't, I'd not be able to claim a penny. This really is just for show.'

'You said many things to Father the other night. He wouldn't have agreed to your plan if he didn't think it mattered.' She clutched her glass between her palms as she stared into its depths. 'Why must my life be upended?'

Phineas pressed his glass to his temple. 'Clerk is not quite the right word for what I do. Nor is spy. But then, neither are far from the truth of the work I do for the bank.'

'Which bank?' she asked.

No one had bothered to ask him before. 'Empire Savings and Loans. It's a small outfit, funded by a man who made his money speculating on shipping routes, here and in America and Canada. Not as grubby as some places, but large enough to attract people who think they might be able to beat the system, or clerks who think they can sneak a bond here, transfer a few pounds there. My job is to look for problems in the books. Anomalies that might be a sign of fraud. I report what I find. Usually, the managers find a way to keep it quiet to preserve the bank's reputation. Public trust and all that.'

'That man said Lord Richard owed a man named Pennington money. What has that got to do with the bank?'

'Your Lord Richard is a recent addition to the board of Argonauts Trading, formerly Abberton & Co. That's why their books caught my attention,' he explained, inwardly chastising himself for his curiosity. 'They've changed direction since they removed Iris and Albert from the board, and they're seeing spectacular returns.'

Her face brightened a little. 'Lord Richard didn't need my money?'

'*Too* spectacular. It's a sign that someone is manipulating the figures. Maybe someone in the bank, maybe someone inside the company. Two things are going on, but through Lord Richard, they're connected. I think Lord Richard borrowed money from Pennington to buy his seat on the board, and now he's come to collect. For some reason, Lord Richard can't pay.' He spun his glass in his palm. 'Pennington has no mercy. He'll use anyone to get what he wants.' He looked to the calotype of Imogen, captured in sepia by a photographer in Edinburgh, now framed on the mantlepiece. 'I've come across Pennington before, although I've never met him. He was at the centre of another problem I was looking into a long time ago, at a different bank. An enquiry that went bad.'

'Who is she?' Rosanna asked.

'Imogen. She was providing us with information. One day, she went missing.'

'And why would Pennington know where she is?'

Phineas downed his last inch in a gulp. 'Because she was his wife.'

Imogen Pennington, who'd come into the Edinburgh National to ask questions about her accounts, had been dismissed by everyone as a woman who should leave her husband to manage their financial affairs. Phineas had instead made her tea and given her space to tell her story. Through her, he'd learnt that Pennington had a stock trade in smuggling, false tickets, opium, bootleg liquor, and cruelty. Over time, he'd discovered that fraud and corruption riddled the entire bank. And when Imogen had come in one day with a bruised cheek, he'd known he had to get her away. Stupid him—he'd thought he could protect her. He'd secured false documents and booked tickets abroad so that they could both start anew. But when he'd arrived at the bridge where they'd arranged to meet on Christmas Eve, he'd only found wheel ruts in the snow.

Phineas poured another glug into his glass. 'I know it's not the best plan, but it was all I could think of in the moment. If Pennington thinks Lord Richard can't touch your money, he'll likely leave you alone. Thwarting Mrs Crofts was a bonus.'

Rosanna shot him a conspiratorial smile. 'She did look disappointed, didn't she?'

'Crestfallen. I walked down personally to invite her to the wedding. She said she had a prior arrangement.'

He smiled to himself while Rosanna settled into the corners of the chair and laughed, loud and deep, her mirth filling the room. Had these walls ever heard such pure joy?

The front door shuddered, and Felix hollered into the hallway.

'In here,' Phineas called.

For all his grumbling on departure, Felix was jubilant on his return, grinning like a schoolboy who had caught his first frog. He held a stuffed basket with two hands. 'I have caviar. And dried fruit. And cake. And ham. And look at these...' He juggled the bundle against his hip to retrieve a box of bread squares. 'Just like toast, only very small, and very crunchy. And *champagne*. Such delicacies. I'll need to plate them. I'll need to—'

Felix had an overinflated sense of loyalty, which made him perfect as the only household attendant at Number 1. He'd always been diligent and set everything how Phineas liked it, which meant the same things in the same order, every day. But with this slight alteration to his duties, the man had practically... Phineas squirmed with discomfort... he had *blossomed*.

'An indoors picnic needs a blanket,' Felix muttered to himself. 'And proper flutes. And little plates for pips and crusts.'

As Felix scurried out of view, Rosanna's eyes followed him with curiosity before she fell back against her chair, laughing. 'Your poor manservant has been starved for stimulation. I hope he doesn't expect me to change into dining dress.' She scooped up her glass and took a swig, then coughed and pinched the bridge of her nose. 'Sweet mercy, it burns.'

Phineas sniggered as he poured his third dram. 'That's how it gets rid of the parts that hurt.'

Rosanna blinked fast until the moisture in her eyes cleared. She raised the glass again and tipped it back lightly. Her cheeks hollowed a little as she paused, thinking, tasting. Savouring. When she swallowed, her neck elongated with the action, revealing a supple stretch and grace. A man with less control might imagine kissing that neck.

Thankfully, he was a man with control.

With a satisfied swish of the glass, she settled back inside the chair, her eyes glimmering with the flush of inexperienced drinking. 'All this time, right under our noses, you've secretly been a sneak. Why a bank? Why not work somewhere more exciting, like for the Crown or at Scotland Yard, as a detective? You could track down some proper criminals.'

'Fraudsters *are* proper criminals. They may not hurt people like thieves or murderers do, but the damage is there just the same.' Phineas shook his head when Rosanna raised an unconvinced brow. 'Do you know how hard it is to pin cheats like Pennington down? Complacency is their weapon. Boredom is their weapon. Numbers are everything. *Money* is everything. It shows weaknesses, loves, priorities, indiscretions. You can learn almost anything about a person if you can trace their receipts.'

'But people can write anything in a ledger. Do you know how many Mr and Mrs Jones and Smiths stay at the hotel? Even for a common name, it is *frightfully* common. And a room at the Aster is not cheap.' She took another small sip. 'Truth be told, it's a bit underwhelming. I thought we'd be posing at parties, then rifling through drawers looking for incriminating evidence.'

'To begin with, *we* will not be doing anything. *You* will be posing as a dutiful wife.'

'While *you* will be a doting husband who cannot believe his good fortune—'

'And *you* will continue to work with your father because that's the kind of progressive, open-minded husband I am—'

'Because your salary is not nearly enough to keep a woman such as myself, and I must work to supplement your income—'

'Because your father is oddly liberal, and because rich businessmen with home-grown empires and a healthy respect for society may indulge their daughters working aspirations so long as they remain useful and powerful and don't tread on too many toes!' Phineas inhaled with a small gasp as he reached the end of his outburst. No one got under his skin. Rosanna Hempel would not be the first. He took a slow sip, forcing calm into his demeanour. 'I need you to look for names in the guest register. I'll give you a list.'

'And then I'll search their rooms?' She leant forwards again in her seat, and the light sparkle returned to her eyes. 'Looking for clues—'

'No! You will come home and tell me that they are staying or have in the past. I will take things from there.'

'I thought life here might be a little bit more exciting.' Rosanna sat back with a *humph*. Alcohol-induced honesty infused each word. 'But life will be the same, except I'll be stuck with you instead of my family.'

'Don't you have excitement? Singing in the park. Riding your horse. Spending time with all those ladies you so desperately want to impress,' he snapped. This was why he never drank, except at Christmas, ensconced before the fire with only Felix and Arley for company. Although this year, he would only have Felix.

Phineas shook his head. This year, he would have no one. He wouldn't be on this bloody street anymore.

'Interests and excitement are far from the same thing,' she said. 'You said I was in danger. What if that man comes after me, regardless?'

'I suppose I could show you some tricks.' Phineas set his glass aside, stood, and beckoned for her to do the same.

Rosanna leapt from her chair. She tensed and raised her hands as if waiting for him to strike, but at his chuckle, she lowered them and flicked him a contemptuous glance.

'No need for dramatics,' he said. 'The first trick is simple: be dispensable. Forgettable. As nondescript as possible. Every group in society has codes. Basic marks of belonging, if you will. Don't just dress like a clerk or a lady, or whatever you are trying to be seen as. Study their mannerisms and habits. All clerks carry an umbrella, even when there's no sign of rain. All members of Miss Hartright's singing troupe wear mittens. Never muffs.

All members of Mrs Crofts's society wear pastels, even though she wears black. Wilhelmina Hempel always has her children wear a touch of red, a habit the older children continue, although I doubt most of them realise they do.'

He nodded at the hem of Rosanna's skirt. She frowned, began to object, then paused as she gathered a swathe of fabric into her arms which revealed a bright line of red stitching along the edge of her petticoat. She shook her skirts out again and planted her fists on her hips.

'You say all this as if women do not spend their lives trying to blend in. I imagine every case in the country would be solved if you had a force of ladies on hand. What else?'

'Listen to feet.'

She scowled at him, unimpressed.

'On floorboards, on carpet, on the street. Different types of shoes make different sounds. A man with a limp sounds different to a woman who has been dancing all night, who sounds different from a tired maid or a man intent on harm. Knowledge is power. You can learn a lot about a person from how they walk and the boots they wear.'

She looked down, and he followed her gaze to the floor. Her stockinged feet poked from beneath her skirts, and when she wiggled her toes, they both giggled. The pair of them, total lightweights with drink. Barely a few glasses, and they were both foxed.

'I have a hole in my stocking,' she confided in a loud whisper. 'What does that say about me?'

A soft vulnerability peeked from behind her fierce expression, coupled with a deprecating tug at her lips.

Phineas dragged his gaze over the soft silk of her stocking to the errant hole. Little crescent moons had formed around it, threatening to stretch and run the length of her shin. Such a small thing. What might it say?

While you try to play the part of a proper rich girl, you are likely too busy at life to maintain the perfection you wish to project. Or maybe you put others before yourself, but in a way that you hope doesn't show. You can handle discomfort and only complain to buttress yourself. On the whole, it says that there is more to you than dresses and the opinions of others. And even though you value them so much, if you can find the courage to trust your bravado, there is more in store for you in life than those insipid doves you are so intent on impressing could imagine.

Like a pawing letch, like a common lusting rake, Phineas took too long to draw his gaze from her toes to her eyes. He always saw too much without seeing, and his imagination filled in what her silhouette merely hinted at.

Delicious thighs.

A lovely round arse.

Eyes as bright as a fresh spring leaf.

'It says I need to find you needle and thread so that you can mend it before it catches and tears.' He'd wanted to sound flat and dismissive, but instead he spoke in a rasp of a whisper.

'I once read a book where a man made another man pass out with just his fingertips.' She touched him just below his ear. Phineas inhaled to suppress the delicious prickle that radiated out from the pressure, which was a mistake because her wrists smelt of lilies and hope. Now he had to contend with the urge to breathe her in fully instead, to kiss her just to see if she tasted as sweet. She pressed her fingers more firmly into his muscle. 'Can you show me how to do that?'

'I fear the male sex would revoke my membership if I equipped a woman like you with knowledge like that.' With a shoulder shrug, he broke away from her touch.

'Just one little weak point,' she insisted. 'An Achilles heel. Men have all the power. At least let me know I could if I wanted to.'

'To begin with, there is no magic point in the neck that will incapacitate a man. But when you are smaller than your attacker...' He contemplated her again. Blazes be, she was precisely his height. 'The trick is to be agile and unpredictable, not so that you can defeat them, but so you can run away. If an attacker were to grab you, what would you do?' He clasped her wrist and spun her so fast that she swayed a little, then fixed one arm firm around her middle, with her back pressed to his chest.

Rosanna squawked and struggled. 'Let me go. You can't just grab me like that with no warning.'

Phineas held firm. 'No man intent on harm is going to warn you. *Breathe*. Your fear is their power.' She remained tense. 'I'm trying to teach you. If I were your attacker, you could do lots of things to distract me. You could bring your heel down on my toe, right on the edge. You could raise your arms and slip down, out of my hold, then pick yourself up so that you can run.'

He was about to release her when her heel cracked against his toe. As he tipped his chin to curse at the ceiling, she raised her arms, whacked his nose with the back of her hand, then dropped to the ground and sprung free from his hold. Phineas staggered back a few steps, steadying himself against the bookshelves.

'I did it! I saved myself,' she cried, her voice bright with elation. 'Oh—did I hurt you?'

Phineas shook his handkerchief from his pocket and pressed it to his nose. The room glistened where he blinked through the sting, and for a moment through the haze of pain and whisky, Rosanna became the only light in his library. Her old white dress gleamed, her dark hair hung loose around her shoulders, but above anything else, her smile could have lit the candelabras. An unselfconscious mix of youthful innocence and mastery radiated from her, the same energy that had been lost to him so very, very long ago. With a stab of greed, he wanted to draw her to him and keep just a little for himself.

Then his gaze flicked to Imogen on the mantlepiece.

And all emotions, good and bad, died.

'I'll show you to your room,' he said. 'I'm tired.'

Phineas trudged up the stairs. Her skirts rustled as she followed, but he kept looking straight ahead. On the first floor he flicked a switch for the gas lamps, and their low light hummed into the corridor.

Rosanna peered up into the stairwell. 'At home, I'm higher. My room is on the fourth floor.'

'I thought you'd want a proper space with your own washroom.' He strode into the room and gestured at the small sink in the little cupboard behind the door. 'I sleep directly above. Felix set things up for you. You should have everything you need.'

She must have picked up her boots in the hallway because she dropped them to the floor. Bits of dust and dried mud scattered over the rug. He winced. Rosanna scanned the room from floor to ceiling before tapping the foot of the simple steel bed.

'Wedding night or not, I hope you have no intention of staying.' Her words rang bold, but she knocked her knuckles against each other in a nervous jitter.

He needed to reassure her that while she was here, he'd make no marital demands. Lawrence had not expressly said as much, but it was implied that Phineas would respect her independence. She would be mistress of herself. And this marriage was not real or meant to last. Genuine fear had coursed through her when he'd taught her how to evade a captor, and a little of it flittered across her face now. If they were going to get through this, he needed her secure and a little trusting. He should say something... affable. Even comforting. So he took her by the shoulders and looked her square in the eyes. 'I am not interested in you. In your body. In that way.'

And with a breath that felt like regret, he turned away and left her alone.

As he trudged down the stairs, a lurid fantasy danced through his imagination. It teased at his foxed edges and squeaked through the gaps in his slightly soused defences. Of tumbling onto sheets together and frantic kisses, of lips and fistfuls of flesh and hair and stolen breaths, of her crisp green eyes and her warm skin and fallen garments. It taunted him all the way to the ground floor. There he met a slightly downcast Felix who stared into the empty library with a tray balanced in his arms.

'She's in her room.' Phineas brushed past him. 'Take it to her.'

Phineas picked up the crystal decanter and swirled its contents. Liquor loosened everything in him—his thoughts, his memories, his control. It was why he normally only allowed himself one day a year to seek oblivion. He opened the window and tipped the bottle. Amber whisky glugged as it splashed against the hydrangea leaves.

He could not allow that to happen. He could not lose control.

There would be no more drinking while Rosanna Hempel lived in his house.

CHAPTER EIGHT

In her parents' household, Rosanna would not be allowed to have magazines, brochures, and booklets spread out before her at the breakfast table.

But this was not her parents' household.

It was hers.

'What do you think of this pattern, Spencer? Do you think it would suit my rooms?' Rosanna slid the catalogue towards the cat that perched on the upholstery of one of the sensible wooden chairs which surrounded the small circular table.

Spencer leant forwards, flicked an ear, and narrowed his eyes.

'I agree completely.' Rosanna pulled the magazine back before herself. 'It's gorgeous.'

Rosanna flipped to the next page of the catalogue, then studied the walls. This room could handle flocking, but gilt would catch the morning sun. Although a nice wood block, heavy in greens and blues, might make the space feel a little less sparse and more welcoming.

Felix stepped into the dining room. He held a plate of neatly piled toast in one hand, and, behind it, a small dish covered with pots of jam. Two steps before the table, he staggered to a halt.

'Hello,' he said, not looking at Rosanna, but over her shoulder. 'Who are you?'

'I'm Letitia,' said Letitia. 'I work here.'

Felix gave a slightly bemused titter, then knocked his free hand against his chin, as if admonishing himself.

'Letitia is our new house mistress,' Rosanna said, not looking up as she flipped a page. 'She will be managing the day-to-day activity of the house along with acting as my lady's maid. She will help the cook Jean with menus and trips to the market and ensure that Lovelace is ready for my morning ride. She will also consult with Hugh.'

Felix jerked as he looked from Letitia to her. 'Hugh?'

'A household needs a butler,' Rosanna replied.

'But a butler is head of the household,' Felix said.

'Would you rather be butler?' Rosanna asked.

'I cannot imagine Mr Babbage allowing a stranger to tend to his dress each day—'

'Valet it is. All the staff would appreciate your assistance in learning the layout of the house, where dry goods and food are stored, coal for the fires, and other daily conveniences.'

'Conveniences?'

Rosanna huffed and rolled her eyes. 'Are you a parrot? Please show everyone around.'

Felix slid the jam onto the table, followed by the toast, warily eyeing the plate piled high with croissants as he did so. 'I... I can show you the lower levels? And the kitchen? Would that be helpful?'

'I'd love to see them,' Letitia replied. 'I've never been in a house with so many stairs before.'

Felix tittered again, and the two of them set off. At the door, they pulled up sharply. 'Morning, sir,' Felix said, his voice suddenly deep and brusque.

'Morning.' Phineas stepped back, his stoic expression disappearing into the shadows of the hallway so that only the shape of him remained. Felix and Letitia scuttled from view before the man whose ring clasped her future re-emerged. He held a copy of *The Times* and folded it in half while he turned to observe Felix and Letitia's departure. 'Who the devil was that?'

'Letitia. Our house mistress and my lady's maid.'

'Our... Excuse me?'

Rosanna flicked another page, leaning in to examine it more closely. Johannes was right, William Morris designed *such* delightful wallpaper. This one of jewelled birds and bright pink flowers would be perfect in her bedroom. 'This is no longer the house of a bachelor. This is a married man's home, which means it is a married *woman's* home. Felix cannot help me dress each day or see to Lovelace.' Rosanna couldn't help but beam at what she'd accomplished on her own in such a short time. 'We have a full staff. Viscountess Dalton recommended everyone.'

'Viscountess Dalton?' Phineas groaned. 'Everyone in her employ is a failed actor or performer of some type. Number 4 is in a state of constant chaos.'

'Letitia was training to be an acrobat before she broke her wrist. She's been told she'll never swing again. Poor thing. She's quite sad about it. The prospect of steady employment has buoyed her spirits incredibly.' Rosanna raised the teapot and poured a cup for Phineas, then for herself, just like Mama would have done.

Phineas dropped his paper to the table. When he spoke, his voice rang low and serious. 'You can't just bring people in. I need to check their backgrounds.'

'Then check them. But I can't imagine the streets of Soho and audition lines around theatres are places where miscreants and criminal masterminds gather, all plotting how they can make their way onto the staff of Phineas Babbage.'

He was not a man for obvious tells, but there... in the squint of one eye and the slight tensing of his shoulder, she could see he was thinking. He took an easy breath, then turned to her with a sharp look.

'What if they talk?'

'They're *actors*.' She waved at the air, licked a finger, and turned another page. 'No one will believe them.' She slid the catalogue across the table. 'What do you think of these curtains?'

Phineas lowered himself onto a chair and put a piece of toast onto his plate, then looked up. 'It's cold.'

'Toast is so proletariat. Have a croissant. Our new cook Jean is from France. Learnt from her grandmother. They are the best pastries you've ever tasted. Try one.'

Phineas pushed the catalogue away and shook out his paper to scan the headlines. 'You do not need new furnishings. You will be here for a few weeks. Maybe less. These are sufficient.' Phineas gestured at the windows without looking at the heavy black lengths that half covered them. 'And I prefer toast.'

Rosanna had just been about to lick her fingertip again, but at Phineas's instruction, she paused, the point of her tongue wetting her lower lip. A dash of something flashed in his eyes. Was it humour? Anger? Or discomfort, maybe?

Find their weakness, he'd said. Had she, perhaps, found his? What a *delightful* discovery.

'I am a newly wed wife,' she countered, sitting a little straighter as she assessed him for a response. 'I will not receive callers to an austere home with limewash walls. You needn't fret. I have sufficient funds in my own accounts to cover the expense. Just sign them off like a doting husband would.'

'No curtains.' He twisted in his chair. 'Felix! Fresh toast!'

A shape appeared at the door, and Phineas's shoulders relaxed, but he quickly tensed again. Hugh, recently appointed butler, tugged his fringe in a deprecating move that betrayed his origins in the countryside.

'Excuse me, miss. Milady. My miss lady, my Lady Babbage, there are many trunks in the hallway. And hat boxes. What would you like me to do with them?'

'Oh, my things!' Rosanna laughed and clapped her hands together with glee. 'Have them brought up to my room. It's at the end of the hall, on the floor directly above this one.'

Hugh bent into a perfect stage bow. He backed out of the room slowly, rolling his hand the entire time, then, just beyond the threshold, turned and dashed out of sight.

'No curtains,' Phineas repeated. A twist of anger contorted his cheeks and narrowed his eyes. 'No new staff until I've cleared them. And toast, not bloody croissants. I do not like croissants at breakfast!' He snatched a pastry from the pile and, in some bizarre illustration of his point, tore off an angry mouthful. As he methodically chewed, his jaw lost its tension, and his eyes fluttered just a little.

'Delicious, aren't they?' Rosanna said.

Phineas looked down, grumbling as he spotted bits of pastry on his shirt. He slapped the croissant onto the plate, where it bounced, only to roll over the side of the table, leaving a trail of thin tan flakes in its wake. He pointed an accusatory finger. 'No redecorating my house, Hempel. It is completely unnecessary.' And he rose from his chair and stomped down the hall, his footfalls echoing.

'People will judge me,' she called after him. 'They will say I am lacking in taste. I will not have gossip suggest that I was a wife without style, and that my husband left because I did not create a comforting home.' The only answer was silence. Rosanna dashed to the door and leant into the hallway. 'I *will* have new furnishings, Phineas Babbage, or you will find yourself without a conveniently placed wife!'

The front door banged shut.

Rosanna returned to her chair.

'That settles that, then,' she said, and picked up her catalogue once more.

Morning shadows cast by the tall townhouses enveloped the carriage house and stables. Although the overhead sky blazed a brilliant blue, a cool breeze nipped at the small patches of exposed skin between Rosanna's sleeve cuff and her riding gloves.

All her life, she had never been alone. There had always been siblings and noise, and then nannies and governesses and chaperones and someone to watch over her. But today? Today, as a married woman with the veneer of a husband who felt nothing as bothersome as jealousy, she was, perhaps for the first time in her life, free.

Rosanna moved beneath the carriage house arch and into the stable. A familiar nicker greeted her. Lovelace, her head hanging low over the open half of the stable door, nudged Rosanna's shoulder and puffed a humid, straw-scented breath over her cheek. Rosanna pulled an apple from her pocket. Lovelace nudged her, then nibbled at the peace offering.

'I'm sorry we didn't go out yesterday. I was busy with that bossy man. Did you miss me?'

Her horse grumbled something like denial as she crunched the apple. Rosanna rubbed Lovelace's nose. 'I didn't miss you either.'

Mr Brown, groom to her parents' carriage horses and the only man Rosanna would trust with Lovelace, led the horse from its box and passed her the reins. 'Do you need me to fetch the mounting block from next door, miss? I mean, ma'am? I looked, but Mr Babbage doesn't seem to have one.'

Rosanna shook her head. With a firm grasp on the saddle leather, she slipped her foot into the stirrup and swung herself up, her thighs flaming with the effort. She adjusted into the seat, then tucked her leg around the pommel to sit side-saddle. Her skirt tugged at a buckle until she loosened it and tucked the navy fabric to the side. Horseshoes clipped against the cobblestones as Elise, already mounted side-saddle on her own mare, Starby, pulled to a stop before the stables. She arched a brow, and the expression contained so many more questions than whether it was ladylike to mount a horse without a block.

Rosanna had met Elise not long after the townhouses had been built and the neighbours had moved in, the same Christmas that Elise's sister had caused the scandal which so thoroughly destroyed the Hartright family's name. A blonde waif full of light and laughter, the self-declared spinster spent her time assisting Viscountess Dalton with Spencer & Co. Travel, helping her aunt with her choir, and as a member of numerous committees and fundraisers—although she had never been drawn to Mrs Crofts's society. Only a little younger than Rosanna, Elise was her counter in every way, which was likely why they had become such firm friends.

'I was surprised by your note.' Elise reined in her horse. 'This is an unorthodox start to married life. You aren't travelling?'

'Phineas cannot obtain leave,' Rosanna replied.

'From the bank?' Elise asked, disbelief edging her words.

'You know what they're like.' Rosanna clicked her tongue. 'Lovelace. Walk.'

Rosanna led the way along the narrow alley that ran the length of connected carriage houses behind the row of townhouses. An uncomfortable wedge of guilt tore through her stomach. She shared almost everything with Elise. But Phineas had been adamant—the more people who knew the reality of their arrangement, the more opportunity there was for slips of information to leak out. Beyond themselves and her parents, no one was to know, at least for the time being. As far as Elise and her siblings knew, this was a pragmatic marriage of convenience, forged to protect the fragile family reputation. What they whispered when she was out of earshot, she could not guess, and in truth, did not want to know.

Between a lull in the traffic, they took the road at a trot. In the park, Elise settled into riding beside her. Rosanna kept her gaze straight ahead as she trawled through familiar conversation topics. From upcoming gatherings to trips to the modiste to complaining about her sisters, all subjects seemed redundant today. Instead of their easy, companionable silence, the quiet air between them felt awkward and stiff.

'What's it like?' Elise asked, her words jumbled almost into incoherence.

'Number 1?' Rosanna asked, surprised by her friend's abruptness. 'The same as Number 3 and Number 7, only with no wallpaper. Incredibly bland, but not for long. I have plans.'

Elise twisted her grip on the reins. 'Not the house. Married life. You know. *Intimacies.* I was too young to talk about it with Charlise. Both of us were too innocent. I've never had a confidante I could ask before. I'm curious. What is all the fuss about?'

Babbage's ever so casual dismissal rung in her memory. What did he mean that he wasn't interested? What about her did he find so displeasing? Was it her hair? Her stature? Her shape?

Her?

'It's tolerable,' Rosanna said.

'I've known many women whose lives have been upended because of *it*. My sister, then Iris. I would hope it's more than *tolerable.*'

Rosanna neatened a few stray strands of Lovelace's mane. Elise knew her too well and would spot a lie. 'Have you progressed past a trot with your tutor?'

Elise flushed. 'We are moving fast, yes.'

Rosanna raised her crop and levelled it at a statue on the far side of the park. 'First one there and back to the start of the street wins.'

'Aunt Petunia says I shouldn't. Says it isn't ladylike.' Elise shifted in her saddle. 'Wins what?'

'The glory. What else?' Rosanna tightened her hold on Lovelace's reigns. 'On my mark. *Go.*'

After her ride, Rosanna left Lovelace with Mr Brown. She worked with Letitia to pick colours for each blank room, selected fabric swatches for the curtains, and reviewed the week's menu. She made appointments with decorators and ordered her own linens and new crockery for immediate delivery. After lunch, she wrote letters, ordered stationery with a new monogram, and sent out calling cards. The house hummed with activity, the way a house should.

By mid-afternoon, Rosanna sat and waited for callers in her parlour, the front room overlooking the street on the same level as her bedroom. No one came, save for Spencer, but as Elise had said, most people probably assumed she'd be travelling. Beatrice would be busy at dramatics, and Mama with tending to the baby. Best to wait until she'd had the rooms decorated before hosting too many visitors, anyway.

Jean sent up tea and small cakes, and Rosanna sat on a chaise by the window and ate three of them without having to fight off her siblings.

Independence was lovely.

And lonely.

After tea, Rosanna searched the library for a novel, but finding none, pulled out a book on military manoeuvres. Finally, before five o'clock, she went to her rooms to dress for dinner. When the clock struck six o'clock, Rosanna made her way to the dining room, taking the stairs at a skip. Phineas's enquiries might have progressed. Maybe he'd uncovered a clue, and tomorrow she could help him investigate.

In the dining room, the small circular table sunk into the large expanse of dark shadows. Her parents rarely ate apart from their brood, and meals stretched the long length of the table. Rosanna pressed her palm to the whitewashed wall. Had they removed her chair to make more space? Or was it sitting empty? It was Wednesday, so they'd be eating chicken. Had Amadeus taken all the gravy? Did Nova sneak her spoon for peas, refusing to persist with her fork?

In her own dining room, opposite sides of the table had been set, as she had directed. She rearranged the cutlery into the right order. She'd need to speak to Hugh about that.

Rosanna rushed to stand by her seat as footfalls drifted along the hallway.

'Good evening, Phin—'

Hugh stepped into the room. He held a single plate in his hand. He bowed with that same exaggerated subservience, and when he straightened, a slice of carrot slipped and dropped onto the rug.

Rosanna took her seat. Hugh placed the meal before her. She looked from the roast potatoes to the empty place where Phineas had sat for breakfast, and then to Hugh. 'Is Mr Babbage not returned?'

'Felix informed me that he never dines at home. He returned when you were changing. He is already in his room.'

'He returned home without coming to see me?' Rosanna picked up her knife and fork. She hadn't dressed to impress *him*, but she had dressed in anticipation of company. He couldn't even take a few minutes to greet her? She cut into the poached chicken, sawing until the blade squeaked against the plate.

'Hugh, why are you not using my new crockery?' Rosanna lowered her cutlery until it clinked against the porcelain.

'Err...' Hugh scuffed his toe and stared at the forlorn chunk of carrot lying on the rug.

'Has my bed been made up with my new linens?' she asked.

'The master said they were...' Hugh bit his lip in thought. '*Superfluous to the needs of the house.*'

'Superfluous to the needs of the house?' Her voice started low but amplified as her ire grew. 'Superfluous? We shall see about that.' Rosanna stood so forcefully that her chair fell against the floor. Then she barged down the hallway, letting the momentum of her anger fuel her ascent up the stairs. How dare he leave her to languish, and how dare he dictate her expenses to her. 'I am mistress of this house. I have a reputation to uphold. And I would like to lie on proper cotton, not on some threadbare old bachelor sheets in a stingy bachelor bed.' She thumped on his door. 'Phineas!' she called.

No answer.

She thumped again. Rosanna twisted the knob and threw the door open. It clapped against the wall, then shuddered.

'Phineas!' she shouted as she strode inside. His room was fitted out with the same simple bed, the same stark black and grey blankets, and the same sparse walls.

A light clink came from behind her.

Rosanna spun to face the small wash closet. Its door stood open, and in the mirror propped over the basin, Phineas's icy steel gaze met her own. Thick white strips of scarred flesh stretched across his exposed back, forming a tangle of remembered agony which she'd only read about in adventure novels but had never seen herself—the scars left by a whipping. He held a shaving blade in one hand while the other pressed against his cheek to hold the skin taut. Thin droplets of water clung to his extended neck. One slipped, then traversed the valley of his collarbone. Another avoided the depression and snaked its way over his pectorals, then ran fast along his side to be absorbed by his trousers.

Rosanna blinked and followed the thin sheen upwards, to just a few inches below his armpit.

D.

Not a smooth tattooed line or an odd scar, no. The letter D had been stamped into Phineas's skin as a mosaic of dots, each small cyan pinprick staining his skin, the unmistakable brand of—

'A deserter? You deserted the army?'

Phineas closed his razor and placed it on the dresser beside the basin. He took a towel from a rail and patted it against his cheek.

'But deserters are court-martialled and sent to prison. Usually, they're transported, and—' Her breath caught in her throat. 'You're a convict?'

He raised one eyebrow. No, he wasn't that old. He couldn't have served a sentence and lived here for seven years...

'You're an escaped convict? Where from? How are you—' Rosanna pressed her palm to her mouth as she inhaled. 'You're on the run. I was going to be a lady, and now I'm married to an escaped convict and a deserter. I would have been better off ruined. I would have been—'

Phineas slapped the towel onto the bench and turned. In two small steps, he crossed from the basin to the door. He stretched his arm to rest his elbow against the doorframe, and as she stammered her fears, the D elongated and deformed with the changing contour of his muscles. Heavens, he was lean. The firm lines of his pectorals tensed a little, and the slightest defined line of strength stretched from just below his ribcage through his centre, ending at his belly button. A thin line of dark hair trailed from there to beneath his waistband, his skin supple and smooth.

Rosanna took a rattling breath, then dragged her gaze back to his.

'Is that all, Hempel?' he asked, and before she could squeak out a reply, he slammed the door closed.

Chapter Nine

'How's the happy groom?'

Phineas kept his eyes focused on his ledger. 'Happy,' he replied in his usual monotone.

'You sound happy.' Taylor chuckled. 'I thought married life might treat you a little better.'

Was happy the word to describe life with Rosanna Hempel in his house? A week into it, and he doubted his logic in trying to keep her alive. The staff hummed or sang incessantly, his wife used the same knife for raspberry jam and marmalade, inevitably mixing the flavours, his courtyard smelt of horse, and Felix had started wearing cologne. His life had become a circus.

'It's tolerable,' Phineas quipped.

Barely.

Not all of it was intolerable, though. Jean, the cook, had been raised by her French grandmother, and while the squawking she called singing left no doubt as to why she hadn't secured a role on the stage, the croissants she sent to the table each morning were exceptional. Hours later, he could still taste the wafers of pastry dissolving on his tongue. And when she wasn't goading or sniping, Rosanna simmered with a measured happiness in the simple things, then accelerated without notice into an abundance of emotion. A daisy growing between the cracks in the courtyard brought forth a small smile. The delivery of new gloves made her coo with joy. And the day before, when he had returned home to learn that her brother Johannes had helped her to wallpaper her bedroom, she had beamed with unconcealed pride at their accomplishment. No faux modesty with Rosanna. She expected praise where she earned it, even if it did give her wrinkled hands and wispy threads of glue in her hair.

Those moments were a little more than tolerable. Damn himself, they were delightful.

'Only tolerable?' Taylor chuckled. 'Most men in this room would give their good hand for a night with what's yours for life. In this second, I think they'd be happy with five minutes.'

Taylor's gaze flicked over Phineas's shoulder. Instinct made him turn his head.

How she had got past the clerk in reception and made her way to the entrance of this dingy hollow of despair and penmanship, to the dregs of the bank, to its most emasculated workers, to men who wielded pens as pens, never mightier than the sword... He couldn't imagine. Perhaps that dress had done the convincing for her. Lace knitted a web of desire and envy over cotton, the ivory fabric underneath overlaid with vibrant, embroidered flowers—claret red, magenta, saffron yellow, and deep teal, all linked by emerald leaves and vines. The contrast of innocent lightness and mature darkness was the perfect complement to her sun-warmed, honey skin. Just that morning, during her inane prattling at breakfast, she had announced that she was dispensing with laced corsets, bustles, and petticoats, claiming them pointless now she was a married woman. *No point dressing to impress when I am unobtainable. I've always wanted to try the styles of artistic dress—now is my opportunity.*

Phineas had to stifle a moan. Thank the heavens for the artistic dress movement.

Both decadent and minimal, like Rosanna herself, her dress gathered beneath her breasts before falling in a gentle drape over her figure, its hem an inch from the floor. Forest green thread sat stark against the soft swell of her bosom. As she took a slightly puffed breath, the fabric pulled taut. Phineas traced the path of a vine to distract himself, but the soft fall of her skirt over her rounded hips and the voluptuous line of her legs were no less distracting.

With effort, he blinked hard, then scanned the room. Could the other clerks not be more discrete with their ogling? She was his *wife*.

'Phineas!' Rosanna called, and raised one gloved hand in greeting before launching into the room at a half skip. Her skirt flipped with her momentum, and when she stopped short before him, a delicious breath of roses and sunshine filled the air between them. 'I had hoped we might have lunch together.'

'Lunch?' he asked.

'I missed you,' she said, swaying slightly like the coquette she wasn't.

Did the room sigh?

'I've been at the hotel all morning,' she continued. 'I was on my way home and thought you might be available.' She turned to Taylor. 'Only for an hour. If it's acceptable. I promise, I won't make it a habit.'

'Taylor isn't my supervisor—'

'Of course,' Taylor interrupted with a grin. 'How could we deny a newly married man such a request?'

As they left with all eyes in the room on them, Phineas couldn't tell if he wanted to crow like a rooster or punch every man in the face. He settled for shoving his hands into his pockets and reminded himself that he had no right to do either.

She wasn't his to fret over.

Outside, shards of sun forced their way between heavy clouds and soot. Scattered puddles along the pavement glistened with fragments of the sky before patches of cloud obscured the light and doused everything in a deeper grey.

'I would have waited until this evening, but as you dine elsewhere and I never know if you're at home or not, I thought it best to find you here. I didn't want to wait until morning. And I didn't want to disturb you in your rooms. Again.'

The road clanged with midday activity. Newspaper boys called out headlines, horse hooves clapped on the stones, hawkers shouted for attention, and boot spits kicked dirt into the air as they drummed up business. How extraordinary it was that, even surrounded by so much noise and bustle, silence could settle between two people and make the short distance between them brittle and cold.

'I'm not an escaped convict.' Phineas addressed the stones, barely catching the slight tilt of Rosanna's head in his direction from the corner of his eye. 'My stepfather bribed the judge. I served a year, then was released.'

'But you *are* a deserter?' she asked.

'The ink doesn't lie.'

'Was it worth it?'

Her question caught him off guard. He'd never thought of worth or value to his absconding, just the deep conviction that he was right to do so, and that those who punished him for it were wrong. Spying on resistance groups and men suspected as being enemies of the empire—it had sounded noble when he'd been promoted, but the reality was that he watched peasants and labelled them as threats when they did not show enough deference. The rash choice to leave the army despite having promised to serve for the rest of his life had set in motion an entire train of events completely out of his control, each one crashing into the next moment of his life. Being caught. The whipping. The sentence. Sharing a cell with a forger. Fashioning himself a new name, and then another. Every necessary moment had converged into the ordinariness of walking the streets of London with Rosanna beside him, with her white bonnet concealing her long dark hair and a too-heavy smudge of rouge across her cheeks.

'I have many regrets, but not that,' he replied. 'I loved every damn second before I was caught. If I could have that time over, I would do it again.'

Keeping the beat with his step, Rosanna slid her hand around his elbow. Her body hummed with nervous energy, raw and bright. 'As intrigued as I am by the transition from convict to clerk, that is not why I came to see you. You'll never guess who from Argonauts Trading is staying at the hotel. Right now. This very minute.'

Phineas chewed his lip. 'Mr Vincent.'

'Oh.' She deflated a little. 'I thought I had done some proper sleuthing. But it seems you know everything.'

'I just weighed the information at hand and made a logical deduction. The other men reside permanently in London. Mr Vincent does not.'

'And I suppose you won't be at all surprised to know that last night he dined with one of the names from your list. A Mr Redgrave.'

Phineas spun so fast that Rosanna stumbled. He wasn't accustomed to having a lady on his elbow, and he had to grab her arm to catch her before she fell. 'The crooked solicitor is at the hotel? Did Collins and Sanders join them? Are they meeting again? Have they requested a private dining room, or will they be in the main area?'

'Why don't you come and see for yourself?' Rosanna asked as she straightened.

He shoved his hands into his pockets. 'Because I'm supposed to return to my desk in an hour. And I don't undertake field investigations. Not anymore.'

'Not anymore? That's an interesting titbit.'

Typical. His directions on jam, she completely ignored. But *now* she listened to him. She played at adjusting his collar and smoothed his lapels. 'Mr Babbage, you are a recently married man who has not gone away for his honeymoon. You have a wife with a divine new dress, and an entire roomful of clerks who are aware that she misses you terribly. I think it would be suspicious if you *did* return to your employment this afternoon.'

Phineas's temples pumped with energy at the scenario Rosanna spun to life. And she was right. If he was properly married to her and she had turned up at his workplace dressed as she was to beg a lunch with him, he would whisk her home for a completely different type of meal. He wouldn't care a jot for the lecture he'd receive the following day.

'I've seen your ledgers.' While she rubbed an imaginary smudge from his coat, he stole another sweet breath of her. 'Would you like to see mine?'

Lawrence Hempel may have staggered a bit on landing, but after an awkward lunge into the world, he had found his feet. The Aster was nowhere on the scale of other more well-known hotels like the Langham, but it offered something they didn't—boutique exclusivity, discrete entrances, exorbitant prices, and an attentive owner and manager who could pre-empt every comfort and set every trend. Hempel understood the rules concerning old and new money in London society, but more than that, he was an expert navigator of the grey area in between. He made the upper classes feel at ease, as if they were visiting a dear friend, yet he protected his employees with the vehemence of a mother hen. He paid them in line with union requests, plus a shilling per week more. He lived his life in comfort but was never ostentatious. His staff loved him, the guests respected him, and yet he spent time with neither outside these walls. His wife, family, and a few well-chosen friends were his world.

Which was why Phineas had deliberately baited him and kept him at a distance. Friendship with a man like Lawrence would only lead to disaster.

Rosanna stepped into the hotel foyer. As she crossed the tiled entrance with the name *ASTER* boldly inlaid in a black and white mosaic, her posture shifted from stiff to comfortable. She nodded at an acquaintance on the staff and greeted an impoverished but aristocratic guest with a broad smile and a slight curtsy. Like her father, Rosanna understood the veneer between living in opulence and servicing its facade. Her family was likely richer than many of the clientele, yet she knew how to make them feel that their fortunes were reversed.

Stepping behind the front desk, she glanced at Phineas and beckoned him over with a scowl. As he sidled in beside her, she opened the reservations book and ran a gloved finger down the columns. Her eyes darted across them rapidly, and he followed the delicate curve and snip of the slight upturn to her nose, observing the plump swell of her lips as she mumbled names to herself. She wasn't pretty in any conventional sense—Rosanna was too full of life to be anything so mundane. In London society, pale skin, visible veins, and fragility were lauded, whereas Rosanna radiated strength and sunshine. The slight bunch of muscles at her dress sleeve, along with the light dusting of colour and the spray of freckles across her nose, spoke of a busy life pursuing something other than ornamentation.

'It was here. Right here.' She turned another page in slight frustration, then paused. 'There. That's it. Mr Redgrave and his wife, room 204. Oh, here they come!'

Mr Redgrave, a man in his mid-fifties, yet carrying the air of someone twenty years younger, stepped into the foyer, accompanied by a woman of maybe thirty years of age. The pair nodded at the desk, then headed for the stairs.

'His wife will likely know secrets,' Rosanna whispered. 'Information. She might let something slip or have something incriminating in her possession. I could speak with her. She might—'

'That's not his wife.' Phineas followed the bustle's sway as the pair ascended the stairs and the gathered swathe of fabric disappeared.

'I am not mistaken.' She flipped a few pages of the hotel's guest register and tapped at another entry for a few weeks before. 'There they are again, Mr and Mrs Redgrave, in the second-best suite.'

'Redgrave's wife is fifteen years his senior. She was a widow, and he flattered his way into her fortune. I am telling you, that is not his wife.'

Rosanna's brow creased. She flipped through the pages of the book, as if searching for evidence to prove him wrong.

'Good job, Hempel. This is even better. It's his mistress.' Phineas couldn't help but grin. 'Is there any chance, Mrs Babbage, that you would like to re-enter society?'

Chapter Ten

She was officially a spy.

Practically a spy.

Kind of like a spy. Doing things very much akin to the type of things that a spy might do.

Just because it was something she had undertaken a dozen times before didn't make it any less spy-esque.

Because today, she had a purpose beyond gossip and making small talk with the guests. She would ask questions in the hopes of finding answers within the answers. Layers of meaning. Nuance.

Phineas had been very specific with his instructions. *Find out how he's spending money on her. Does she have her own accommodations? How often do they travel? Any new jewellery, special gifts, has he been visiting a little less than she'd expect? Then we'll know if what they're up to is making money. Are they here for a short stay or for longer? Who else does he meet with? That should give us a place to start.*

Mother had never liked to mingle with the guests, but Rosanna had relished the invitations at every opportunity. When younger, she'd convinced her father to allow her to accompany him to work. She had always chosen her best dress, kept her shoes clean on the journey across town, and scrutinised her nails in the hopes that the guests would ask her to join them in the dining room. She'd been something of a little doll at their tables—the trussed-up daughter of the man who made their London stays so comfortable. She could recite short poems, tell innocent jokes, and would often be invited for tea or a cup of hot chocolate so that she could revive stale conversation between people who'd been in one another's company for too long.

At these gatherings, she had learnt the essential manners of being a lady in a way that no governess could teach. She'd learnt how to hold a false smile and how to deliver a quip with a sincere expression. How to file a criticism away for another day, and how to shift a conversation on behalf of another when words touched a delicate memory. Finishing school had given her manners. The Aster's dining room had taught her how to wield them as both a shield and a weapon.

The Aster fronted a wide boulevard opposite the sprawling parklands. In a flip on the general order of things, guests entered through a small, discreet foyer on a quiet side street, rather than through attention-seeking front doors. This way, Father said, he could more easily control things—keep the path free of mess and manure, tend to the trees so that they always looked healthy, ensure his own lighting was both warm and welcoming. Other places trumpeted their guests as an extension of the advertising. Aster made them feel like they were special, more like a family member returned home.

The dining room to the left of the entrance shone with mid-afternoon light from the arched windows which ran along the wall facing the main thoroughfare. Guests loitered in here, ordered a second pot of tea, or in the evenings, brandy. Lunches extended into the afternoon. They watched the world go by and made comment on those they could see from behind the refuge of ivy and roses which framed each window. This was a place where they could see and *not* be seen, unless they chose otherwise.

Rosanna moved to the arched entrance in front of the dining room, and patrons turned in her direction. Conversations shifted to whispers. A few people threw covert glances in her direction, then huddled into discussion. She had chosen her dress with care in the hopes of emanating the same image of status and fashionable elegance that she'd crafted since she'd entered society, but now she wavered in her decision. Perhaps the red velvet bows over black and white gingham were too much for the wife of a clerk, even one who was the daughter of a successful businessman. Perhaps she should have chosen something simpler and more in line with who she had become. But who had she become? And who was she going to be?

'Use it.'

Rosanna startled and shot a quick side glance at Phineas, who had sidled up beside her. 'Where did you get a waiter's uniform from? How did you find a waistcoat with the hotel crest—'

'Not important.' Dressed in the simple black and white uniform, his hair combed slick, and one hand crooked behind his back, almost everything about Phineas's stance and appearance mirrored that of a member of the Aster waitstaff. Only his eyes betrayed him as he scanned the room as if searching for something instead of merely observing.

'Someone will recognise you,' she whispered.

'No one in this room looks beyond the waistcoat.' Phineas gestured with a movement that could have formed part of a general conversation between an employee and their senior. 'The whispers, the rumours. They are curious about you. Use it to your advantage.' Phineas nodded at a table by the central window on the opposite side of the room. 'In Edinburgh, Mr Redgrave had a finger in every untoward contract that went bad. Men at clubs complain about him constantly, but those he targets lack both the courage and the funds to challenge him. The woman claiming to be Mrs Redgrave is having tea with Miss Summers, who is new to town. They are awaiting Mrs Vincent. What do you know about her?'

'Miss Summers? Nothing. But Mrs Vincent has been staying with us for years, although the Mr Vincent that she dines with each day is not her husband but his brother. Her husband passed away three years ago. The staff are always gossiping. They say they rarely make up his bed.'

Phineas nudged her with his elbow. 'They have secrets. Give them breathing space from the fear of making a slip. Your own circumstances will be a welcome distraction.'

'Miss Hempel? I mean, Mrs...'

Rosanna extended her hand towards the newcomer. 'Mrs Babbage. Good afternoon, Mrs Vincent.'

'It all happened so fast! We barely had time to catch the fortunate groom's name,' Mrs Vincent replied.

A twist of anxiety sparked in her stomach. Gossip. She had become fodder for gossip.

'*Use it*,' Phineas muttered.

Use her embarrassment? Her humiliation? The abrupt alteration in her life's trajectory? She wanted to growl at him like he did at her most mornings. But instead of his patronising scowl, she found him regarding her with a slight curve to his lips that could have been the beginning of a smile, with the hint of a dimple on his cheek. Could she turn the middling opinion of others to her advantage, like he seemed to think she could?

Rosanna turned to Mrs Vincent. 'Given that we live beside one another, once we decided, there was no reason to wait.'

'Not even for the banns to be read?'

'I'm sure you felt the same about your own dear husband, may he rest in peace.' Rosanna pinned her sweetest smile to her lips. 'You must miss him terribly. Is that why you've come to town? In memory of past pleasures?'

Mrs Vincent's stare narrowed, and she glanced at Rosanna's waistline, as if searching for some hint of a scandalous explanation. Her curiosity unsatisfied, she turned to the dining room. 'Would you join us for tea? We'd love to hear your story of impatient love.'

Rosanna looked at Phineas, bemused.

He winked. 'Allow me to seat you,' he said.

With a deceptive glint in his eye, Phineas led the way across the dining room to a circular table with room for six. It was currently hosting two ladies, one holding a champagne flute, the other sipping a cup of tea. Phineas pulled out the chair beside the woman who claimed to be Mrs Redgrave, and once Rosanna had settled, she leant back so that he could flick a serviette across her lap. Starch and soap, the familiar scent of the hotel laundry, invaded her next breath, along with the slightest tinge of his sweat and sternness. Leaving the seat beside her vacant, he moved to the next place and pulled out the chair for Mrs Vincent. Mrs Redgrave—or the dark-haired beauty claiming to be her—tapped at her glass, then sniggered. Phineas took a bottle of champagne from a stand and began to fill Mrs Redgrave's glass, but before he could finish, she swiped it from the table. A few drops spilled and slid down the stem to land on the cloth, unnoticed by Mrs Redgrave, who took an energetic sip.

'Do you know Miss Summers?' Mrs Redgrave asked in a coarse whisper. 'She's tremendous fun, although she doesn't look it.'

'You are telling stories again, Mrs Redgrave.' Miss Summers blushed and twisted her cup on its saucer. She glanced at Rosanna, her blue-grey eyes holding Rosanna's for the briefest moment before she looked back to her tea. 'We have not met, but I have heard of you. Congratulations on your nuptials. You must be so happy to be married.'

Mrs Redgrave leant back as Phineas poured her another glass. 'Tell us all about your new husband. How are you finding married life?'

Phineas attended to her champagne flute next. He tilted it to the perfect angle, then began to pour. His mouth twitched the smallest bit before settling back into a thin, expressionless line.

'My husband is so grumpy,' she said as she lifted her glass from the table. 'He cares entirely too much about small things like dirt from shoes or if I am using the same knife for jam and then marmalade. From day to day, I never quite know who he might be.'

He placed the bottle into the stand, gave an unacknowledged bow, and moved away. At the next table, he caught a napkin before it dropped to the floor. The guest thanked him, and he nodded in acknowledgement.

'We've lived beside one another for years, yet it seems that until recently, we didn't really know one another at all...' Rosanna's voice trailed off as she watched him work. All this time, she'd lived next to a man who carried out small, unacknowledged kindnesses like investing in Iris's business and helping Arley and Vivienne... even feeding the cat. All while grumping at and baiting her father. Rather than bland, he was a conundrum.

'I meant, what did you think about *it*?' Mrs Redgrave leant in close, her champagne-soaked breath rolling in a slurred whisper.

'It?' Rosanna asked.

'You know. *It*. The one-eyed snake. The shifty pirate.' Mrs Redgrave squinted one eye, wiggled her head a little, then sniggered before taking another gulp of champagne. 'His *appendage*. Did it horrify you? My mother hadn't told me what to expect, and I was completely bewildered when I dared to finally open my eyes in my marital bed.'

Rosanna fidgeted with discomfort at the memory of Phineas stripped to his waist, of the little stray droplet of water that caressed the lean lines of his chest. She had not been raised in an ignorant household—she was the eldest of ten children, after all. Her parents were pragmatic about such information, especially when it came to their daughters. But her knowledge of married life was exceedingly theoretical, consisting of anatomical descriptions and a lesson on the creation of babies. She understood what went where, and how a life began, but beyond that... What would the experience entail? Pleasure or horror? Would Phineas, all hard edges and rough skin, reveal all his secrets to her and treat her tenderly? Would he take care with an intimate education as he pressed his firm body against her? Or would he be rough and roguish and use her as it pleased him?

Heat crept along her neck. 'I... I... Uhm... He's very... and I was...'

Mrs Vincent laughed. 'Leave her be. Mrs Redgrave is too brash. Look at her, still in the flush of early marriage. She's likely still lying stiff, knees akimbo, counting down until it's over.'

'Counting?' Rosanna asked. No one had ever mentioned mathematics being involved.

'Try it.' Mrs Redgrave took up her flute and chuckled. 'I can't imagine intimacies with a clerk are overly inventive.'

'Should he be inventive, or should I be?' Her face burned hot, and warm needles ran along her back. All three of the ladies at the table laughed, loud and unabashed. This was worse than being scandalised. They *pitied* her.

'We all thought you were going to make an agreement with the Marquess of Hanley's son,' Mrs Redgrave said through the last of her laughter. 'Such a lovely young man. Here he is now. Lord Richard!' Mrs Vincent half stood and waved across the room. 'Join us.'

Thoughts of bodies, thoughts of married life, thoughts of anything else evaporated. Rosanna's next breath shuddered through her as Lord Richard exchanged the usual etiquette across the table, then occupied the vacant chair beside her. Pleasantries and small talk bounced and hummed through the air, and Mrs Redgrave downed the last of her champagne. Rosanna could only try to breathe.

'Mrs Babbage. It is Mrs Babbage now, isn't it? How pleasant to see you.' Lord Richard balanced his hat on his knee and twisted in his seat. He spoke with the same intimacy, the same comfort and companionship as he had the night when they'd walked through the park. When he had told her she was interesting and that he thought her family charming, when he had squeezed her fingers with one hand and reached into his pocket with the other. When her life had been dazzling and bright and her own.

Lord Richard placed a small white box tied with a pink ribbon onto the table before her. 'I was going to leave this for you at the desk. I suppose you should think of it as a wedding gift.'

Rosanna stared at the little box. What would it be? Another flower or an animal or something surprising, like a dragon or a gondola? A kitten or a pair of scissors? How she longed to pick it up. To tug the ribbon, remove the lid, and feel the delight of being a young woman with a future opening before her. To feel fresh and new and fawned over. As she reached for the box, her wedding band glinted, and her fingers trembled.

Those days had been a lie. He had not helped her when she'd needed him. Phineas had.

Rosanna tucked her hands into her lap. 'I am a married woman. I cannot wear jewellery gifted from a man who isn't my husband.'

'I hoped that maybe we might remain friends.' He leant in a little closer, and his hand brushed against her knee, then withdrew, like it was an accident. He lowered his voice. 'Or perhaps, something more? Despite the injury you made against me, I do think of you fondly.'

'Against you? You left me,' she accused. At the park, with him running, she'd been vulnerable and weak—what she hated most. Like some damsel who had to be rescued, and not by a prince but by the grumpy clerk next door. When she spoke, her voice cracked, and the sting of his rejection filtered through, bitter and too loud for polite society. 'You just *ran*. Everyone thought I had been compromised. I had no choice but to marry.'

'I tried to contact you. Did you not receive my letter?'

'I didn't want a letter. I wanted you to call on me!' All her indignation at being made a laughing stock, at having her dreams snatched away, cascaded through her. 'I needed help *then*. That man hit me, and Mrs Crofts and her society were all pointing at me.'

'Mrs Babbage. There's a message for you at the desk.'

Rosanna kept her stare straight ahead as she tried to tamp down her frustration and her fury. 'It can wait.'

Phineas maintained his blank expression, but fury blazed in his eyes. 'It's from your husband.'

Rosanna shook her head. 'I will collect it later.'

'The messenger was *most* insistent.' Phineas's jaw clenched. 'You absolutely must come to the desk and read it.'

Rosanna flung her serviette onto the table. 'Fine. Let me see this message.'

Once out of view of the dining room, Phineas grasped her arm and tugged her down the service hallway leading to the laundry and drying rooms. With an irritated shove, he pushed her into an alcove. Rosanna spun and pressed her back to the decorative glass panel. Phineas's normally stoic expression had turned dark with fury. 'What was that?'

'He blamed me for everything. Said I slighted him when he was the one who ran off! That no-good, lying—'

'What about Mrs Vincent? What did you learn?'

Rosanna stopped, horrified. Apart from their brief discussion on snakes and pirates, she hadn't spoken with the woman. She'd been too worried about herself.

Phineas swore under his breath. 'This is why I work alone. This is why I shouldn't even have tried to help you. I should have just left you—'

'Why didn't you?' she shot back, all her anger at Lord Richard still roiling in her blood. 'I didn't ask you to help me, I didn't—'

Phineas pushed her deeper into the alcove, pressing her hard against the wall, and covered her mouth with his palm. Rosanna squawked, but he held her firm, his tension and sternness stronger than her indignation. He hushed in her ear, then, low and coarse, muttered, 'Shut it, Hempel.'

Ire roared through her, but in the tense moment between Phineas removing his hand and Rosanna drawing a furious breath, a thump came from nearby. She turned to the glass through which the indistinct shape of dark suits and tall men moved fuzzily, their bodies stark against the light walls.

One man grunted, and another swore. Phineas squashed closer. His chest, his thighs, every part of him aligned with her, his body all tight with frustration and disappointment. Her heart lurched before her memory caught up. One voice belonged to Lord Richard, and she'd bet her monthly allowance that the other came from the man from the park. The angry man who had hit her.

'I'll get the money,' Lord Richard stammered. 'I swear it—'

'Mr Pennington don't like being lied to. He likes to be paid. You said the chit had your money.'

'Not *with* her,' Lord Richard snapped. 'Young ladies don't carry their dowry with them when they go courting. I needed to marry her, but she turns everyone down. I was about to create a scenario where she couldn't say no when you interrupted and botched it—'

'And then you said,' the man from the park's voice became louder, 'that you had her in the palm of your hand and that she'd be begging for an affair. That you'd convince her to sign some money over. But she doesn't seem swayed by your charms.'

He hadn't meant to propose—he'd meant to force her hand. That's why he had led her into the garden. Not for some romantic gesture but to create a scandal. The realisation burnt bitter in her throat. All her fretting and care, all her attempts to show she was worthy of being the wife of a lord—and more, worthy of love—had been unnecessary. The pounds that were rumoured to be attached to her name were all he saw. All any of them saw.

Phineas pressed closer. His cheek touched hers, and their shallow breaths bloomed across the glass. His body softened as if, instead of interrogating her, he might create a cocoon.

'Who's her husband?' the man from the park asked.

'No one. Some bank clerk who lives in the next townhouse. Landed in a goldmine just for walking through the park at the right time.'

'He smitten? If she was to go missing, would he pay to get her back or keep the money?'

'You've seen her,' Lord Richard said, his tone edged with innuendo.

Rosanna glanced at Phineas, but his expression remained impassive, his stare hard. As if he himself might pay the men to take her.

'New plan. You'll nab her one day when she's out and send him a note. Her money for her. You said she was too uppity and didn't care for rules. Won't take long. This is just a roundabout way of getting the same coin.'

'I am a gentleman. I cannot go about kidnapping young women—' Lord Richard's voice strangled, then squeaked.

'Do it, or it'll be *your* family getting the note about *you*.'

One last thump echoed through the hallway as the man from the park pushed Lord Richard against the wall, then left him to slide to the floor. His shadow shifted, a confident blur through the patterns in the glass. Lord Richard stumbled to his feet, bent in half, gave a strangled sob, and followed.

Rosanna clenched her teeth to tamp down tears. Her pride was still shattering into miniscule shards of foolishness.

'Don't leave the house unaccompanied,' Phineas growled. 'Take the groom when you go riding. Any other time you leave the house, it's with me or your brother.'

'Johannes wouldn't hurt anyone. He's strong because of his work, not because he's a brute.'

Phineas stepped back and straightened his waistcoat. 'Really, Hempel. I thought you above anyone would know that, in this city, appearances are all that matter.'

CHAPTER ELEVEN

'And I don't understand why he can't give him some space. What is it with men and their sons? After Johannes left in a huff—a quiet one, because, *Johannes*, I went down to the kitchen and then to the desk, and you won't *believe* what Pierre had to deal with from some uppity countess from up north...'

Once upon a time, Phineas's days had been spent in silence.

He'd eaten breakfast in silence.

He'd walked to the bank in silence.

He'd scribbled in ledgers, ruled columns, and discussed fiscal questions in hushed whispers. Even his conversations with Taylor about fraud and financial mismanagement had been carried out with a quiet temperance.

But now? There was nothing quiet, nor temperate, nor peaceful about his afternoon walks escorting Rosanna from the hotel back to Honeysuckle Street.

'And after that, well, Father came down, and he was livid—told Pierre that no one would speak to his staff that way. The pair of them settled their accounts and grumbled something like they preferred the Langham anyway, which is ridiculous because everyone knew it wasn't true. No one voluntarily leaves the Aster early.'

Ever since that afternoon when they'd overheard Pennington's man suggest that Lord Richard kidnap her, she'd started taking his elbow as they walked. She talked, incessantly. About staff and their grievances, arguments, problems with guests, her favourite colours, new boots she was thinking about purchasing, whether she had enough ink to finish all her correspondence... Anything that came to her mind almost immediately found voice on her lips. Around Trafalgar Square, she finally drew a breath. A little further along, by the river, another. And, as they moved into the dappled shadows beneath the cherry blossoms in the park near Honeysuckle Street, she paused for the third time.

'It is possible to walk without talking,' Phineas said, compacting his words so that they fit into the small wedge of quiet.

Rosanna tightened her hold on him. 'You hardly say a word. If I didn't talk, we'd be walking in silence.'

'What an incredible thought. Let's give it a try.'

She rolled her eyes and her lips, but perhaps sensing a competition, she held her tongue. For three glorious steps, the only sound between them was the rustle of her skirt and the crunch of his heels on the gravel path. For three glorious steps, there was nothing but the robins and the breeze and the grey clouds, nothing but the scent of roses and sunshine. Her delicate fingers pressing into his bicep. The brush of her body against his.

'I've made up my mind about something,' she announced.

'What dress to wear tomorrow?' Phineas drawled. 'Or that you need new gloves?'

'I want you to bed me.'

Phineas stumbled over an uneven edge of the path. 'You are not obligated to. This isn't a real marriage.'

'But everyone believes it is. The other day, Mrs Redgrave spoke about marital duties, and all the counting involved, and I felt like a fool because I was supposed to know what she meant, and I didn't. I was so flustered.' Rosanna stopped, and with a slight tug, pulled him to face her. 'If you aren't very good, I won't mind. It will give me something to complain about.'

'Books,' he declared. 'I have books on this subject in the library. You can look at them.'

'I've *read* books,' she said, exasperated. 'Those women will know I am fibbing if I keep stammering like I do now.' She threaded her fingers through his. Thus caught, he let her pull him a little closer. 'You really must be terrible.'

'I'm not terrible at it. I'm actually very good.'

'Prove it,' she said.

He tried to step back, but she held him firmly in place. Eye to eye, toe to toe, her spring green gaze met his, and her crisp confidence hovered like the beckoning point on an unattainable horizon. A fool, he was a damn fool. As he slid a hand around her waist and drew her close, he knew he was walking a tightrope. He tried to think of some throwaway line, some provocation, but in the quiet invitation of her gaze, he lost all comprehension of language. One kiss would show her he was not *terrible*. Then he would send her to the library to learn more.

He grazed her lips. Light. Soft. Just enough to feel the heat of her mouth and a wink of desire. A singular sigh of connection. A long, tilted moment of quiet yearning, and while he longed to press more, taste more, and feel more, he instead nipped her bottom lip and pulled back. But before he could mutter, *I told you I was not terrible*, Rosanna slapped her palms flat against his cheeks, fixed him in place, and planted her lips rudely against his. Luxurious, luscious softness. He considered fighting, but why? What a sweet relenting, what a delicious experience of *silence*. He chased her sweetness, then dared to seek out her tongue with his own. The lovely swell of her breasts pressed against his chest, and he hitched her closer so that he could kiss a little deeper. Beyond divine. She sought him, tentatively flicking her tongue against his own before she seemed to decide she liked the sensation and fully parted her lips. She was all acceleration, moving from modest to tempest in the time it took him to take a little gasp of air before surrendering to her again.

He could lose himself in her. He was losing himself. He was drowning. She sighed against him as she threaded her fingers through his hair.

Phineas dredged up his resolve, squeezed her hips, then pushed her away so hard she stumbled. She blinked fast, her brow knitting in confusion.

'That shouldn't have happened. I told you already—'

'You're not interested,' she snapped. 'I remember.'

He'd almost forgotten the throwaway line on their first night, spoken after too much whisky and not enough brooding. He'd searched for words of comfort and safety then, but instead blurted out a cross between an excuse and a jibe.

'I'll walk ahead,' Rosanna said, already on her way. 'You can follow. Then you can have your peace and quiet.'

Phineas retreated to one of the remaining uninhabited rooms on the fourth floor. He would have gone to the fifth, to put as much distance between himself and his wife as he could, but he didn't want to risk running into the lady's maid or the house mistress or whoever occupied the rooms at the opposite end of the corridor on the topmost level.

On the way, he met Felix on the stairs.

'Bit far from your quarters,' Phineas said.

Felix ground to a halt. 'I was... I was checking the linens. In the store cupboard.' He turned to point.

'And?'

'We have many types. At least three different blends. All lovely.' Felix crossed to the other end of the stair, then descended a few steps. 'Are you staying home instead of going to your club? I can send something up if you aren't dining with Mrs Babbage.'

'Yes. And whisky.'

'Problem, sir,' Felix replied. 'You tipped it all out. Remember?'

Blast it. 'Soda. With syrup. The one Viscountess Dalton sends over. And toast. With unspoilt jam.'

Phineas trudged the last few stairs to the landing before he clicked the lock on the door open. Once inside the fourth-floor front bedroom—the one with the coveted extra windows—he half closed the door and readied his key. Then he stopped. It was a ridiculous habit, keeping these rooms locked. It had seemed essential when he'd first moved into the townhouse, in a city where he knew not a soul and trusted even fewer people. That was before he'd hired Felix. He'd been caught in a flurry of sleepless anxiety, then. He'd spent his days wandering between the rooms in the front corner of the townhouse, peering through their windows into the park, watching out for a sign that he'd been followed, and waiting for Pennington and his men to find him. All the while he'd wracked his memory for some hint of what might have happened to Imogen. A desk in the corner, high with loose leaf, scraps of paper, and dust, was a pathetic relic to his failures. He'd promised to keep her safe. He'd failed.

He'd known he'd failed for so long, and yet he'd stayed. Stayed on this street with its mishmash of neighbours who fought and loved and asked each other for help. It had all started with damn Petunia Hartright, who'd convinced him to join her choir. Saying no would have been rude, and two sentences into his first conversation with her, he'd known she'd be a persistent woman. Part of his cover, he'd told himself, essential to blending in. He'd made every excuse to no one but himself, and like a fool, he'd believed his own lies. Helping Iris, helping Arley, feeding that cat... The mess of them had drawn him in, as if he might be able to line them up like numbers in a tally, wrest with the equations of their problems, and set them straight into a solution.

If he hadn't stumbled upon Rosanna, if he hadn't fashioned himself into her saviour, would he have left?

Or would he have skulked the street and found some other reason to stay, some other cause, as he had done so many times before? For seven ridiculous years.

Night chased his brooding. The park turned silver as the greens desaturated to grey. A light scratch sounded at the door. 'Phineas?'

'Mmm?' he hummed, forcing himself to stay focused on the world outside.

'Why won't you bed me?'

Because I don't deserve you. I will only taint you. I will darken your light. And I fear one breath of you, and you will become my oxygen.

Every sense, every nerve in his body, every fizzle of energy under his skin told him not to turn, but still, he did. He sat forwards in his old armchair, in its puddle of moonlight, to regard his wife. Framed by the doorway, she wore a dressing gown of practical, warm flannel, tied at the waist but still revealing a white triangle of nightgown. She held a flickering candle stub before her, and its light danced across her cheeks, her full rose lips. It placed a delicate glimmer in her eyes, eyes that had seen so little, that were so innocent and so warm, so ready to see the potency of the world, of life. The spoilt little rich girl who was selfish and self-flattering... Yet, somewhere amongst all that self-assuredness, she could also be kind and find joy in a raincloud and forever in a sunbeam.

'You know why,' he grumbled. 'This is not a real marriage.'

'I know you will leave.' She crossed the room with barely a huff of slipper on the carpet. She paid attention. Even through all that prattling, she listened. 'It will be years before I can marry, if ever. How can I trust any man? Might I be independent for a short time?'

'And fucking makes you independent?' He meant it to sound crass, a barb, and from the way she flinched, she took it as one. 'I won't leave you with a child.'

'There are other things, aren't there? That a man and a woman might do? I am not completely naïve. If you are to make me a widow or an abandoned wife, I'd like to not be a fool. And I would like to think that I was not so hideous to you as to be unbedable.'

'That's not a word,' he said.

'It is now.' She lifted a handful of gown and swung one leg over his thigh to straddle his lap. The candlelight jiggered with the movement before stilling. She settled against him, her knees resting on the chair seat until the inside of her thighs ran the length of the outside of his. The faintest hint of her scent—woman, roses, and sex—tinged the air.

Phineas breathed slowly, as if he could taste her fragrance on his tongue. 'You are too brash, Hempel. It will do you no favours. This is not a world that rewards confident women.' He ran a finger along the soft angle of her nape and stroked the dip at the base of her neck. 'You would be best served to be more demure. And less curious.' And he kissed the hollow, slow and measured and indulgent, like he had not been dreaming of the taste of her skin for days, like the thought had just occurred to him. She was sweetness and tang, like strawberries warmed by the sun.

She exhaled into him, her tension almost palpable as it rippled from her body into his, rolling through him and settling there before evaporating.

'Show me the candle,' he said as he leant back.

She frowned a little as she raised it into the space between them. Its amber luminescence made her skin shine. Her eyes glimmered almost black in the shadows, and her lips glowed copper, which meant they were blood red and ripe.

'Blow it out,' he said.

'You don't want to look at me?' she asked. Beneath all that bravado, how could she be so fragile?

'More than anything.' He trailed a finger along her bottom lip. 'If this were for me, I would turn up every lamp and light every flame, even burn the house down if it meant I could see you with perfect clarity. I would strip you and spread you and feast on you with my eyes and my mouth.' He kissed her shoulder, then nipped her gently with his teeth. 'But this isn't for me, it's for you. And I work better in the dark. So quit arguing with me and blow the damn candle out.'

Chapter Twelve

As she exhaled, he caught her breath. She heard it, felt it. It rippled the air.

The acrid whiff from the extinguished wick lingered before it dissolved. Grey smoke caught the moonlight before it, too, disintegrated.

Rosanna let her arms go limp by her sides. She dropped the candle holder. The carpet smothered its brassy echo as it landed.

For a moment, there was only breath, hers and his, hot and humid in the small space between them. The rough tickle of his stubble grazed her cheek, and his lips brushed her ear. One hand settled hard on her waist. His other began a gentle dance of fingertips over her nightgown, so light that, at times, he barely indented her skin. At others, only the faintest touch of fabric gave any indication of his presence. He pulled her closer, her thighs spreading wider as he settled her into his lap. At the same moment that he pressed a kiss into her ear, his thumb glanced her nipple. A shiver arced through her, and a small gasp escaped her lips.

'I liked that,' she breathed.

He laughed, softly. 'I know.'

Rosanna tried to calm herself, but his words sent an unexpected tension, a bite of apprehension through her. As Phineas scraped his teeth over her earlobe, her body pinched with an anxiety born from somewhere so deep inside, she'd forgotten she'd locked it away. Were they smaller, more delicate lovers he had known? More complaisant than her?

'How do you know?' she asked. 'Have you had many women? Do you have a routine?'

'Shh,' he whispered, and, placing both hands lightly on each cheek, he drew her close, kissed her forehead, her nose, her lips. 'I know because I listen. We reveal ourselves with more than words. Everyone speaks with their bodies, their eyes, and their breath. Relax, Rosanna. Let me hear what you have to say.'

He obviously had no use for anything she might say aloud, because before she could draw breath, he pressed his lips to hers. As languorous as a ray of summer sunlight, he tasted her, explored her; and when she half opened her mouth in invitation, he pushed harder, seeming to shift from delicate to ravenous. His hands on her thighs tensed and eased, his nails slightly scratching her skin with each movement. Perhaps listening. Waiting.

What did she want to say?

Your kisses destroy my logic.

I wish you'd touch me again.

Rosanna rested her arms on his shoulders, wrapped them around him, then pushed her fingers through his hair. So commonplace, the straight, compliant cut of the everyday London clerk. She tousled it, caught a handful in her fist, and released.

Phineas's touch held less teasing now. He negotiated the hem of her gown, grasped handfuls of her hips, pushed his body higher. What stories was *he* telling? The hardness beneath his trousers rubbing her thigh, the hunger in his eyes, the heaviness of his breath. His slow tug on her dressing gown cord, coupled with the rough way he shoved it from her shoulders, told a deceptively simple story.

He wanted her.

And then her nightgown was over her head, discarded somewhere on the floor. He had only unfastened a collar button, while she sat astride him completely naked, and the disparity felt dangerous and obscene. Phineas took her nipple in his mouth and flicked his tongue over the tip. Rosanna's entire body tensed with exquisite joy. It was like spring burst from her heart, like life curled its tendrils across every inch of her skin. Teeth scraped, and fingertips pinched, and she let out a strangled groan in a tenor she was certain she had never hit before.

'I cannot decide,' he said, his voice muffled against her body as he kissed his way over her collarbone, along the line of her neck, over her chin, then back to her lips, 'if I should show you the pleasure of my fingers or my mouth. And you give me no clue as to what you might prefer.'

'I've not known either,' she whispered. 'Except for my own hand. Surely, you know that?'

Phineas groaned hard against her. He rubbed his thumb across her breast, following the line in the centre of her chest, then travelling across the indented curve made by the stretch of skin between her hip bones, like he was mapping her body. Every sensation, every bump, every kiss, every touch felt reverential. 'You are too pure for me. I will treasure corrupting you.'

He held her tight, his body stiff. Rosanna shivered in anticipation of his decision. She did not know what she wanted from him, could not know what she might prefer, but she knew she wanted to be subsumed in his attentions, to disappear in his gaze, then let herself be devoured, over and again. She desired to become a slate as blank as he presented himself to the world, for him to write his passions across her body as he did now. He grasped her bottom and pinched the skin like he meant to pulverise her with his desire, then flexed his fingers and gently swept them across her thighs. He breathed into her neck, and she groaned into his attentions. She unfastened button after button of his shirt until she could press her palms against the lusty inhale and exhale of his chest, over the mark that concentrated his secrets with dozens of shameful blue dots, her body desperate with a capital D to draw his story from him. But not tonight. Not now, not in this moment of passion and pleasure and presence.

'Which do you like more?' she asked. 'Touching or tasting? I leave myself open to your preference.'

'Oh, you beautiful creature.' His fingertips scratched harshly over her thighs, then skittered upwards, her every sinew shivering with his lightness. One hand scrunched her hair and pulled her against his mouth to kiss her with that same, steady attention. 'Do you like my fingers in your cunt? Do you like it when I stroke your clit?'

He rubbed a little, then eased before he drew a long, slow line between her folds, a shallow swipe that set every nerve blazing and made her thrust as she tipped her head back to groan with abandon. He felt so delicious, so light and incongruous, his attentive touch at odds with the man who made her grit her teeth in frustration. He grabbed her hair so tight it bit her scalp, and yet his fingers teased at her, as soft as rain and as gentle as a petal. And like the dastardly, delightful, devilish thing that he was, he stole even her grunt of pleasure with his mouth. Then his fingers were inside her, not a little, but hard, his knuckle rubbing against her entrance, two, three digits, the sensation all-encompassing. He slid his fingers deep, then retreated with torturous control before thrusting inside her again. It felt so good it hurt, and her next moan was a mix of pleasure and pain.

Phineas eased. 'You are magnificent. I could destroy you. Come for me before I hurt you.'

'Come?' She rolled her hips, trying to feel more of him, wanting him deeper. With his fingers firm inside her, he rubbed her clit with his thumb and took her nipple in his mouth.

'Ride the good feeling until you burst. Don't hide it from me. Don't hide anything. Show me, darling.' He pressed his nose against her cheek, nipped her lobe, caught a kiss. 'Surrender.'

She didn't think she could kiss and breathe so much at once. Could exhale her wants and inhale his bliss, could expel the shadow of her old self and breathe in the possibility of Phineas.

Like everything in her life that flooded her with emotion in a heartbeat, her pleasure began slow and timid, then roared and rushed through her like water through a bursting dam. Her body, braced against his, thrust against his palm in total surrender, every little jerk part of an ever-escalating crescendo of furious bliss. She forced his face between her breasts, and he bit her hard as her body rattled and roared. Quivering, she tipped back and moaned her exhilaration at the ceiling.

They stayed locked together, tense and shivering through a protracted muteness. Rosanna could not form words, only the blurred shape of them as every firm edge seeped into the indistinctness of ecstasy.

Phineas's breath raced warm over her tingling skin. Not his usual steady, controlled inhalations, but heavy and out of sync. 'Touch me, please. Stroke my cock. Let me feel you as you feel me.' He unfastened his trousers, loosened them a little, then slipped his manhood free. 'Like this,' he murmured as he wrapped her hand around his shaft and covered it with his own. 'Follow my pace. You'll know soon enough. I'll show you.'

Her first few strokes were awkward, perched as she was across his lap, but with his help, she found his rhythm. Her own body hummed, fuzzy with fading light. Phineas leant against the chair, his eyes alternating between closed and intent on her. Soon, she recognised the momentum of the wave and stroked him a little faster, gripped him a little tighter.

'You are extraordinary.' He buried his face between her breasts and clasped her waist roughly, his hold both pinching and primal. A few short breaths and a grunt, and his cock throbbed. He covered both their hands and his body with a handkerchief before he exhaled the lightest moan and arched his back.

The moonlight kissed pockets of light under his eyes, which closed softly. As he released his pleasure, his rigid barriers fell away. And for all his common looks, his ridiculous ordinariness, in that second he took on a statuesque beauty. He had the longest eyelashes, which brushed little shadows over his cheeks. The smallest bracket hugged the edges of his lips as he almost smiled, and a hint of a crease whispered the possibility of that dimple.

He blinked a few times, then completely opened his eyes. The softness that had fallen on him evaporated, and every little intricacy retreated as he took on the demeanour of the man she had always known. Instead of sitting astride him completely naked, they might have been meeting one another outside their front doors.

'You have sufficient knowledge now to hold your head high?' he asked, tucked himself away, and fastened his trousers.

'I shall tell them they should all find a clerk to be their lovers. All that writing gives them dexterous fingers.'

He leant to the side to retrieve her nightgown before flicking it at her. 'I'm going downstairs to the library. I'll walk you to your room.'

The staircase was wide enough that they could have walked side by side, but Phineas hung back, following her as she descended the levels to her room on the first floor.

On the landing right before her door, she spun to face him, and he moved a little closer until his chest touched hers.

She could invite him in. Into her bed. Into her life.

He stood waiting, his arm resting on the doorframe. Then he reached behind her, fidgeted with something, and the door fell away. She squawked as she stumbled into her room.

He chuckled. 'Goodnight, Hempel,' he called, back turned, and already descending the stairs.

Chapter Thirteen

Thank heavens she knew so little about bedding.

Or she would know how extraordinarily spectacular last night had been.

And not even in a bed. Just hands and kisses. Simple. Astonishing.

He hadn't slept so deeply in years.

'Have you spoilt the raspberry jam?'

Rosanna startled, blushed, then frowned. 'I do not like raspberry jam. So no, I haven't.'

Act normal. And normal meant being particular about jam.

Phineas tried to focus on his broadsheet, folded into a more manageable half as he scanned the news. He only read the paper so that if he had the displeasure of engaging someone in small talk, he might find some common ground for conversation. He followed the lines of the columns, took in the headlines, then allowed his longing to draw his gaze over the top of the page, across the cloth, to the opposite side of the circular table.

To Rosanna.

She wore the same dress as she had that day she'd come to the bank, all light fabric and embroidered temptation.

A flurry of sordid yearnings contorted in his imagination. From unfastening the pins and combs in her hair and letting her dark curls spill over one shoulder, to tasting her from the arch of her foot to the crease of skin at the top of her thigh, to swiping the table and upending every condiment onto the floor and spreading her before him and feasting on her body until she cried out again and again... Desire pulverised his senses. Last night in the darkness, he'd licked the traces of her taste from his fingers as he'd walked the lonely path to the library, and now, the sweetness and tang of her was all he could think of. He'd woken hungry, famished almost, as if nothing but her would satiate his appetite.

Phineas crunched into his toast.

Morning sun lit the neat braids in her hair and drew a line of light across the table where it streamed in between the rose-patterned curtains she'd had hung up last week. Both of her elbows rested on the table, and she cupped her chin in her palms. She leafed through one of her catalogues, then looked up, her eyes darting across the walls and examining the architraves around the doors and windows.

'Don't even think about it,' he drawled.

She paused in her observations, only her gaze shifting to him. 'This room would be so much brighter with a floral print. Or even something simpler, like this geometric style with gold leaf. Or even paint. Any colour but limewash—'

'You have your rooms.' He turned over the paper. 'Leave me mine.'

She grumbled and flicked the next page in her catalogue. Narrowed her eyes as she scanned the page. Smiled, possibly planning some future conspiracy with Johannes to do whatever it was she wanted to do.

Licked her lips.

Sweet mercy. Those lips.

'I mean it. Leave my rooms be.' Phineas shook his paper to its full width and slunk behind the print. She'd already taken too much, inched her way into too much of his life, into his mind, his dreams.

His walls would stay as they were.

The butler, Hugh, entered the room. Past the rim of his paper, Phineas watched as he placed a flat package wrapped in brown paper and tied with a sensible string bow before Rosanna. She tapped it, thanked him, then broke off an end of croissant and dunked it in her coffee. Her tongue caught a drip before it fell. Phineas buttressed himself behind his newspaper and waited.

He turned a page.

Read an article.

Turned another page.

Phineas peered around the side of his broadsheet. 'You never wait to open a delivery. What is it?'

She placed a protective hand over the package. 'You won't be interested.'

Phineas folded his paper and laid it aside. 'Try me.'

A piercing glance across the top of her coffee cup stilled him. A curl of heat unfolded beneath his skin, like a frond tendril unfurling, and for an excruciating moment, only one image saturated his every thought, his every breath.

Rosanna naked. Splayed across his lap. Groaning. Soft. Tensing against his fingers.

Her eyes creased at the corners, and although her mouth was obscured, he knew she was smiling. 'As long as I don't bore you with it.' She cast a look at the door. 'That is all, Hugh. Thank you.'

As the butler left the room, Rosanna pulled the string. Phineas rose from his seat and slipped around the curve of the table. Her slim fingers stroked the long length of thick brown paper as she folded it aside, first one half, then the other.

'It seemed prudent to order a set,' she said, her hand sweeping over the stack of light cream paper. 'I am so particular about these things, and I thought it might be noticed if I didn't. And if I had married you in sincerity, one of the first things I would have done is order new stationery.'

From the pen of Rosanna Babbage. It seemed so false, so heavy, especially considering Babbage had only been his name for such a short while. And yet, the intertwined *R* and *B* dented the paper so elegantly and purposefully with their calligraphic swirls and thick letters with flowing curls. Like they were always meant to be.

'Who will you write to?' he asked. She'd had no callers to the home apart from her family and Elise, as far as he was aware. He rubbed at a tightness in his chest. That was likely because of him. Mrs Babbage did not receive calls the way Lady Richard would have done.

But then, Lady Richard would have been locked in a marriage where her usefulness expired as soon as the ink had dried on a bank transfer.

'It's only for appearances.' She folded the paper over. 'But the monogram is pretty, isn't it?'

'The R and B look nice together,' he said. The clock in the hall gonged. 'Come, Hempel. We have business to attend to.' Phineas buttoned his coat and made for the door.

'Are we going spying?' Rosanna scrabbled to her feet. 'Have you found new information? Do you need me to meet with the ladies at the hotel again?'

He waited for her at the top of the stairs. They walked down to the entrance side by side. Phineas took Rosanna's coat from Letitia and held it out. She slipped her arms into the sleeves and shrugged it over her shoulders.

'It's Tuesday. We have a Spencer and Co. board meeting.'

'Is that all? I hardly need my coat to cross the road.' She tucked her hand around his elbow, and they set off across the street at an angle, making for Number 4. 'You are going to take me spying again, aren't you? Unless you want to be married to me forever. We need to do something other than wait for me to be kidnapped.'

'We could, I suppose.'

'Go spying?'

'Wait for you to be kidnapped. I might get some peace until I rescued you.'

'Provided you *can* rescue me.' Rosanna laughed, light and carefree, before her joviality became weighted with realisation. Even the birds seemed to quiet their chirping as silence tensed between them. 'I didn't intend to sound so mean,' Rosanna said as she loosened her hold on his arm. 'We'll find Imogen. I just know it.'

He couldn't rouse anger or even a grunt. Instead, he shrugged her off and stepped up the kerb and onto the path.

Who was he to think he could save her—save anyone? He'd positioned himself as some knight for a bright young woman with the world before her, but what if he dragged her down, too? Intentions couldn't fix the past, nor could they secure the future. What if, with his rashness, he'd made her life worse?

They climbed the stairs. Rosanna clapped the knocker, its brassy thump low and hollow against the wood. She stepped into place beside him.

'I won't let that happen to you,' he said as he forced himself to keep his focus on the swirls and splinters in the wood grain. In his periphery, he caught the turn of her head. 'I'll look out for you and keep you safe. Whatever it takes.'

Her delighted laugh banished the tension, and she snuck her hand through the crook of his elbow. Her shoulder rubbed his. She really was exactly his height.

'Do you really believe I would allow anyone to kidnap me? I would like to see him try.'

The door swung open. The smile on his lips died. Instead of being greeted by the theatrical jubilance of Mason, the Abberton's butler, they were faced with the grey shadow of Albert, Iris's father.

He wore a dressing gown over trousers and a white shirt with braces and was wrapping a bright blue scarf about his neck with great concentration. 'Are you joining us for the opera?' he asked. 'I never miss opening night.'

'Sir!' Mason clattered into the entrance at a slight jog before skidding to a halt. 'Iris will take you for a walk after the meeting. Come rest in your sitting room. I'll help you.' Mason wrapped an arm around Albert's shoulders, then directed him to the stairs behind the entrance hall. 'They're in the front room. Can you two find your way?'

Proper manners dictated they turn away, move out of sight, or at least stop staring. Yet Phineas found himself unable to lift the weight in his heart that anchored him in place. The pair of them stayed outside the door, watching as Mason led his employer away.

'It's so unfair.' Rosanna's voice cracked. 'He was such a good man.'

'He still is a good man,' Phineas said. 'Just because he's forgotten, doesn't mean we do. Goodness like his doesn't end.'

Rosanna pulled at the ribbon beneath her chin. 'Have you seen that before? A man forgetting himself?'

'In the army. I saw men who became lost in their memories. To the fighting and such.'

'Did any of them get better?'

Phineas closed his eyes against the silent agony of all those faces, the lost stares, the mouths that could not form words. He shook his head. 'I don't remember anyone ever recovering.'

Grief, shared and palpable, hung between them. Rosanna wrapped her hand around his arm again and leant in, forging a half embrace, whether for her own comfort or for his, he wasn't sure. He absorbed her affection and squeezed her fingers in return. Mason and Albert disappeared around a corner at the top of the landing.

'Enough of that, you two!' Hamish caught the side of the doorframe and leant into the entry. 'We're all in here, waiting. You pair have made the meeting start late.'

Phineas coughed into his hand. Rosanna set her bonnet onto the side table. Hamish winked, then withdrew from sight again.

'We should...' Phineas gestured down the hall. 'After you, Mrs Babbage.'

Iris, at least, seemed a little brighter than she had at their last meeting. She sat at the head of the table with a low stack of folders and papers before her. Hamish took the seat beside her as Phineas settled in his usual space. Rosanna paused. Her eyes flicked between her regular place opposite him and the vacant seat at his side.

He couldn't say why his breath corkscrewed in his chest—she must be missing her family and her friend, and it was natural she'd long for the familiarity of the seat between Elise and her father. They were the stalwarts of her life, both past and future. And they weren't married. Not really.

'Miss Delaney is an apology.' Iris gestured at the vacant seat normally occupied by the soprano. 'She wouldn't mind.'

Rosanna scooped her dress beneath her bottom and took her place beside him.

'Before we start, we really need to speak about the unexpected events that have occurred since last meeting,' Iris continued in her warm, yet business-like tone.

Hamish coughed and spluttered into his tea. 'Unexpected? All the ways you could describe these two getting married, and you're going with unexpect—'

'All this time,' Iris raised her voice to smother her husband's, 'we had no idea that the two of you were...' She flicked a look at Lawrence, who crossed his arms and leant back in his chair with a scowl. Iris bent her head and tapped at the papers before her. 'Possibly best not to dwell on the details. But sometimes, that's how it goes.' She flashed a conspiratorial look and a sly smile at Hamish, then slid a manilla folder tied with a bright red ribbon across the table. 'A belated wedding gift. From all of us.'

Rosanna pulled the bow apart, flipped the folder open, and gasped. Phineas leant across. His fingers brushed her dress beneath the table, resting against the strength of her thigh. Listening. When she didn't flinch, he let his hand settle.

Rosanna held up a folded map of the world. On a white card, pinned to the front and written in Iris's smooth hand, was a simple message.

Together, a new dream.

'You two haven't had a proper honeymoon. Nor have Hamish and I, but that doesn't mean you can't go abroad. Anywhere in the world you'd like to visit, just name it. Elise will arrange everything.'

The world... What a lacklustre impression it had made on him. Scurvy and seasickness, iron bars and gallows. Daily life dictated by incompetent, pompous, pen-wielding administrators, by spare heirs too stupid for government and too cowardly for command who settled into bureaucracy with all the enthusiasm of a prison guard.

'I cannot imagine where we might go.' Rosanna spoke before his cynicism found form, her voice thick with the wonder of possibility. She twirled the ribbon around her finger, then uncurled it. 'I've always dreamt of seeing Italy or Egypt or even beyond. Thank you. We are so excited by the prospect.'

'We'd best get started.' Iris flipped open the top folder. 'Item Number 1. Profit and loss for the quarter...'

Rosanna rested her hand over his. And there he was, sandwiched between the small parts of her, the loving parts, the desirable parts. He flexed his fingers, considered withdrawing his hand, then didn't. She tucked her fingertips into a gap and inched into his palm.

She isn't yours. You can't stay. She'll do better when you cut her free.

Phineas slid his hand from her grasp, withdrew his pen from his pocket, unscrewed the lid, and leant over the papers.

Rosanna cleared her throat and shuffled her notes with both hands.

The meeting followed the regular pattern. Phineas sifted through the words as Iris, and occasionally Elise, reported on the standard agenda. Profits. Losses. Opportunities. Failures. When the meeting ended, Phineas stood and swiped his notes from the table. He needed to get across town, to the bank. Taylor could only make excuses for him for so long.

Rosanna followed, but at the door, she turned back. 'Excuse me, Iris.' She moved to the table where Iris and Elise were gathering up their papers and the company books. 'I'd like to learn more about ledgers and bookkeeping. I've seen the ones we keep at the hotel and for Spencer and Co., but I'd like to see something different that's not related to travel. Do you have the latest report to shareholders for Abberton & Co.?'

'It's the Argonauts Trading Company now,' Iris said, her tone sharp with bitterness. 'They renamed the company last year. Erased Papa in less than a month.'

'But you remained shareholders, didn't you?' Rosanna asked.

'I sold our interests back to them before they launched to the public. I held them for a while, naïvely hoping that after I'd married, they might think differently and reinstate us on the board. But after a time, I couldn't bear it.' Iris tidied her papers and tapped them against the table to level their edges, then tucked them into a folder. 'Watching reports come in, wondering what they were doing, and why... It became too much. If profits were up, was it because they were exploiting the workers? If they were down, were they making rash decisions? And Papa no longer knows what he created. Once they collected all the paperwork, I saw nothing but a short report again. Mr Sanders keeps the books to his own liking now.'

'He doesn't keep the books.' Phineas sidled closer, trying to follow the thread that his wife had picked up. 'They send them to Empire Savings and Loans. A senior clerk looks them over before they come into the office.'

'That is unfortunate,' Iris replied.

'Why?' Rosanna asked. 'I thought such a tedious task would be the first thing one would want to be rid of.'

Iris shook her head. 'Ignoring tedium is a certain way to disaster. That's what Papa always said. I mean, really...' She gestured at the perfectly maintained opulence of the dining room that had been converted into a board room. 'Do you think we lacked the funds to pay a clerk to tally the books? Papa always insisted on knowing his own numbers. That's how he taught me how to run a company. It's the only way to understand what is happening—really happening—in a business. The ledgers are a company's heartbeat. If the workers are being paid too little and become careless or if the warehouse is lax on security, you'll see it in the columns. Even here, now, for Spencer and Co.' Iris tugged a heavy volume from Elise's arms, thumped it onto the table, and flipped the cover open. 'Everyone loves chocolate. Why not a week with a Belgian chocolatier? Our first tour sold out within a week. Tour two almost as fast. Yet our third is selling poorly. No one has complained, so when the guests return to London, they feel happy. But when they have time to think, they are not recommending us. Is it the hotel? The guide? The chef? You must coax the truth from the ledgers, but it's always there.' Iris's eyes narrowed as she scanned the columns. 'The world is full of fraudsters, but the ledgers never lie.'

Rosanna held her skirt aloft in one hand as she half skipped down the stairs. Outside, on the pavement, Phineas made to cross back to Number 1 to fetch his umbrella. Rosanna tugged at his arm and pulled him back. 'Where are you going? I thought you'd want to investigate.'

'Investigate what? The chocolatier? The problem is obvious. It's summer. The chocolate melts, then resets. It tastes horrible once they are home, so they don't tell their friends out of embarrassment.'

'Not the chocolate. The ledger. You said it was too perfect, didn't you?' Rosanna waited, her eyes bright with discovery. He shrugged. 'It's *obvious*. The ledger at your bank is a lie. There must be a duplicate. We need to find it. If we can find the original, we'll learn everything.'

CHAPTER FOURTEEN

'It's been a while. I'll get it.'

Rosanna shoved Phineas's arm. 'Will you just let me try?'

With a reluctant sigh, he passed the thin steel lock-pick up to her. Rosanna scrunched the grey tartan skirt of her walking dress around her knees and crouched beside him.

'Skirts are so awkward. I should have ignored you and dressed in trousers.'

'Rule number one,' he repeated his words from the house with a sullen frown. 'Blend in.'

Rosanna angled the pick until the mechanism inside the lock clicked. With an easy twist, the door to the upstairs office of the Argonauts Trading Company swung open.

She handed his kit back to him. 'Rule number two. Don't allow important skills to atrophy.'

'That is not rule number two.' He folded the tools into a cloth and tucked them into his coat pocket. 'How'd you learn?'

'Father taught me when I was little. He taught Johannes, too. He said it was prudent to learn, in case there was a problem with keys at the hotel, but I sometimes wonder if he was struggling to adjust to a life on the straight and narrow, and passing on some wayward skills to his children made it easier to change his ways.'

Phineas nearly always kept the same impassive face, even when she deliberately provoked him, but as she said the words *his children*, he looked away, head bowed. As if he were studying the floor for clues.

It wasn't a surprise that he knew her secret. How her mother had found herself abandoned, unemployed and with child, and Lawrence had helped her and claimed Rosanna as his own. Phineas seemed to know everything.

'Save your discomfort,' she snapped. 'Maybe not by blood, but he's my father in every other way. He's never treated me any different from the others.'

'He saved you from a terrible life. My mother was unwed when I was born. We lived in a poorhouse for a time. He's a good man.'

'If you think he's such a good man, why are you always so horrible to him? He'd make friends with anyone on the street. He loves that place.'

'Friendship brings hesitation. It's easier to act when you don't have to think of others.' With a determined turn of his back, Phineas pushed the door open and slipped into the office. 'Let's find these ledgers.'

Rosanna steadied herself against the doorframe as her eyesight adjusted to the dark. A childhood in a poorhouse was a piece of his puzzle that she'd never imagined. While she had never known the deprivations her parents had shared, she had grown up in a household weighted by their experiences of limitations and thrift. An odd, off-kilter clash of irritation and tenderness collided in her, and she had to press her fingers into the cut of the doorframe to centre herself. A life that could have been her own *had* been his. Poverty beyond imagination, every day tainted with a stamp of unworthiness. Being labelled a bastard. So many parts of herself that ran counter to what the world valued were ingrained in him, too. Both of them hiding—her behind her confidence and bravado, while Phineas... Phineas just hid.

'Are you waiting for an invitation, Hempel?' he growled.

'Are you extending one?' she shot back.

He grunted, then continued to explore the room. Rosanna stepped inside the front office of the Argonauts Trading Company.

The moon painted a thin curve in the sky, so even though it was a clear night, shadows slanted at odd angles across the desk, and a faint shimmer reflected off the glass-fronted cabinets and bookcases. Phineas made for a tall filing cabinet tucked into a corner. Rosanna blinked a few times until she could follow the shapes of the wooden furniture, the frames on the wall and chairs set on either side of a desk. A hallway led away from the room, possibly to individual offices. Wood squeaked on wood as Phineas opened a drawer.

'We have a book. At the hotel. Only at the main one, and only for us. We list important information about guest habits, little changes and observations. If we try something new on the menu, do guests spend more on wine? Is French brandy more popular in summer or winter? Hardly scandalous—Father has no interest in the guests' secrets—but the sort of thing that would be useful for competitors. Not something you want just any member of staff to have access to, in case they take a position elsewhere and pass that information on. And we keep ours...'

Rosanna scanned the cabinets behind the desk and the heavy leather chair. In the hotel office, ledgers, accounts, and records were kept in easy reach to make daily work easier, in a side drawer or behind the desk. But something important that wasn't needed every day would be too conspicuous in a drawer and only be a bother. Something important but not regularly referenced was better kept in sight, in a steady line of vision, to give some comfort that it was safe. Rosanna paced before the cabinet on the opposite side of the room. A sheen reflected off the glass, and foil and gold leaf gleamed and dulled as her shadow followed the curve of each book spine. She opened the centre cabinet and crouched, her skirts fluttering as air rushed from beneath them. A crystal decanter half full of amber spirits sat on the centre shelf, but beneath that, the ledge and panelling didn't sit flush with the rest of the woodwork. The ends didn't quite line up. Rosanna stripped a glove and ran her fingers over the woodgrain. A small, uneven notch had been carved into the edge, possibly by an unsteady hand with a penknife. Just large enough for a man's finger to hook over to tug a drawer open...

'What have you found?' Phineas crossed the room just as she hauled the heavy book from the drawer.

She thrust it into his arms. 'This.'

Phineas grasped the leather-bound ledger in both arms. It must have been two foot high, and he thumped it onto the desk and flipped it open. He struck a match and lit a candle stump, and the flame danced a mix of amber and shadows across his skin. His brow furrowed in concentration, but behind the sternness, a spark shone in his eyes.

Something came alive in Phineas when he focused on numbers, ledgers, and calculations. She understood columns and tallies and could make a tidy sum, but his comprehension was so different, so much deeper than her own. Like he saw beyond the numbers into an entirely new world. He ran a finger down a margin, turned the page, then traced another, all the while muttering to himself in low tones.

Rosanna leant over. She followed the staggered sums, the rough workings and notes to the bottom column. 'What is it? I can't see in this light.'

Phineas drew a breath, as if he was about to start one of his explanations, then paused. With a nod at the book, he stepped to one side. The light he'd been blocking spilled over the desk. 'See if you can figure it out.'

In the orange candlelight, the pale blue ledger paper took on a green tinge. The first few columns were names, addresses, and occupations. The next few columns were all numbers—finances. Rosanna raised the candle so that its glow cast a wider circle and found the familiar symbols that tallied up pounds, shillings, and pence.

'The date. The share price. The number purchased. Dividends, and when they were credited. It's a record of investment returns.'

Rosanna turned a page. Yet, it wasn't quite the same as how they ran the books at the hotel. They had extra columns for expenses and wages, and additional books to record the details of costs in the kitchens or the laundry. Rosanna flipped to the front of the book. Here, Father kept a table of wages and set costs for easy reference, but this book didn't have one of those. She flipped to the back. Just more columns and lists, and a swathe of empty pages.

'There are no expenses recorded. Do you think there's another book? Why would they pay dividends before they've taken out the costs? Abberton & Co. were a trading company. There should be figures for imports and exports, or even warehousing. They *are* still trading, aren't they? Surely it must cost something to run—' Rosanna bit her lip and flipped a few more pages. 'There. Mr Collins. His payout is a far greater percentile than the five per cent paid to Miss Jennifer Lancaster or to Mr George Jones or to any of these smaller investors. And Mr Vincent is receiving a substantial amount, too. They're drawing off thousands of pounds.' And with a turn of the page, all the disparate pieces fluttered into place. 'They're using new investments to pay out the dividends. They're not paying their expenses. The entire operation is a shambles.'

A grunt and a smile from Phineas—likely the only acknowledgement she would ever receive from him. Rosanna muffled the perverse burst of pride in her chest that sparked with his small compliment. Phineas pointed at the page. 'See this column? Since the additional shares were made available, almost everyone has reinvested their supposed earnings. Investors think they're making money, but it's only on paper. None of it is real. That's why they need new investors to contribute cash to fund the next round of payments. If one or two of them sell their shares, they get paid out of the money coming in, as the board has drawn most holdings off and into their own accounts. There's no collateral or reserves. If everyone sells at once, the company will collapse.'

'Why would anyone invest in a business like this instead of something more stable?' she asked.

Phineas placed his hand over the names, almost protectively. 'They would take their money elsewhere if they knew. Companies can choose what information they provide to investors. The law does not force them to tell shareholders everything, or even anything. And when men like your Lord Richard become involved, many less affluent people see the shine of the aristocracy and follow with their savings. Look at these addresses. Not the slums, but hardly Mayfair. His involvement is like a stamp of approval in a sea of swindlers and schemes.'

'Stop calling him *my* Lord Richard. He's not mine. I don't want him.' She knew she spoke too bitterly and with too much anger. For once, Phineas didn't deserve her ire. He spoke so casually with an ignorant tap of his finger at the amount Lord Richard had invested. For once, Phineas didn't know everything.

His investment matched her dowry to the pound.

The amount he likely owed Pennington.

He'd spent her worth before he'd even begged her hand.

The building creaked. With the sharp fizz of light extinguished, Phineas snuffed out the candle with his fingers. *Hush*. The word was barely a breath, as quiet as the wick's hiss.

Rosanna forced calm into her body, through her chest, all the way to her feet in her boots, which still longed to stamp and rage at the ledgers. Her anger coiled in on itself, and its bitter bite turned to sadness. She reached for Phineas—just to find the anchor of some kindness in the dark. He wrapped his arms around her.

'Apologies, Hempel. In the future, I'll mind my tongue.' He spoke with a low rumble, barely a whisper, the shape of his words caressing her cheek. His stubble, prickly and unwelcoming, scratched her skin.

'Am I worth nothing more than an entry in a column? A tally of pounds and pence?'

Phineas's shoulders tensed. They always did when she interrupted his thoughts or talked too much. They'd done so last night, when he'd still been arguing with her about bedding, and then again right before he took her nipple in his mouth. His arms—strong and bracing—tightened around her as he drew her closer, his hands resting against her back with the same protective splay that he'd shown the names in the ledgers. On her next breath, she inhaled his stiff resolve, his practical soap and clean linen.

'What's rule number one?' he asked.

'Blend in,' she replied.

'And rule number two?'

'What does that matter?'

'Just think on it.' He pressed his forehead against hers. 'It's more important than the first, although comes after it. What could be more essential than blending in?'

Intense, cold, indifferent. Rosanna searched the unemotional angles of Phineas's expression as the question turned in her mind. Blend in, he always said to her. She'd always craved the opposite, but how much of Phineas's demeanour was about blending in, and what had he shown her that was different? How much was a facade to keep others at a distance? His closeness compressed her skirts, and she held his level stare in the low light, hands touching but not holding, just humming living energy into the small shard of space between them.

What did the efficient bank clerk obscure?

He let Spencer drink milk from his table every morning.

His sharp tongue was one edge to a perceptive mind.

He didn't have to help her when Mrs Crofts accosted her in the park.

He listened to her body until she was both screaming and speechless.

'Never be what they expect you are,' she said.

His mouth twisted into a slight smirk of acknowledgement. 'And beneath all the prattle and gowns, you are nothing like I expected.' And he eased into her just a little more, so that his cheekbone pressed firm against her tingling skin. His lips skimmed the shell of her ear. A meandering hunger, a tingle of want tentatively fizzed and flickered through her. 'We shouldn't,' he whispered.

Rosanna hooked a finger around his. 'No, we shouldn't.'

Phineas turned his cheek, and the bristle on his chin scuffed her lips. Stiff, unmoving, he retreated into himself, even though they remained pressed together. 'Just the pipes,' he said, then shook her free. 'We have what we need.'

Rosanna slid the ledger back into the drawer. Phineas cast his gaze across the desk, and slightly adjusted the placement of the candle and a blotter. She waited for him by the door. Her heart beat out of sync in an odd patter, and she rubbed at her breastbone to try and quell its unease. When he ushered her out of the office and hunched to work at the lock, she lingered in the finesse of his fingers as they twisted and adjusted his tools. The thin wisps of hair behind his ears needed a trim, but he'd probably have Felix eradicate them in the morning. Her heart stuttered again. She inhaled until it steadied.

Phineas stood and returned his tools to his coat pocket. Rosanna slid her hand into the crook of his arm. They walked in silence for some time. Argonauts had maintained the offices of Abberton Trading, which were a convenient walk away, and after a few blocks, they reached the far end of Honeysuckle Street. The lamps threw small circles of yellow onto the path, and their shadows merged and bunched as they shifted from light to dark.

'That number upset you.' Phineas said. The words were a statement, not a question. 'Lord Richard's investment.'

'It was the same amount as my dowry, to the pound. Seeing it there, so stark, reminded me how foolish I was. I detest feeling like that.'

'Why did you want to marry a lord? Of all the people in this world, why a noble? And why marry at all? Why not—'

'Live my life on my own terms? Become my father's protégé? Why not shun a life of domesticity for business?' Rosanna tapped out the pithy arguments she'd heard before from women like Elise and Petunia or her own sister, Beatrice. 'Why must I choose? I didn't want to marry a lord, I wanted to be loved. I want a family. And I wanted to keep working with *my* family, to continue to be a part of what I've helped to build at Aster. I wanted both those things. No one would ever ask Johannes to choose. Lord Richard said all the right things, had a good name, bought beautiful gifts. I was stupid enough to believe him.'

He patted the back of her hand, then flexed his palm to resting. He stroked the contour of her gloves, and when he burrowed his fingers beneath hers, she couldn't tell if he was giving her solace or seeking a place to hide. They crossed the street before Number 8 and walked by the Hartrights and their bright pink door. Then past Mrs Crofts's home, the only door in the row that was still painted in its original black.

'Mama told me during my first season that some nobles wouldn't see past our name,' she continued. 'Not even the name, because it was fresher than a rosebud. I thought I understood, but I didn't. I learnt fast, though. At my first ball, a viscount's heir from a very old family tore my hem as he tried to compromise me in the bushes, and later that same evening, I received a declaration of eternal love from a man before we'd finished a cup of tea together. There were so many more after them. They weren't even eager or rash. Just desperate. I was nothing more to them than a full purse. I still held hope that things might be different for me. That someone might love me. And I figured that the sort of man who might do so was one who did not need my money. Is that so terrible? To want love?'

'That's not how love works.' Phineas kept his head bowed as he spoke. 'Love is painful. It's sacrifice.'

'You are an expert, I suppose.'

'Not at all. I don't think I've ever...' He looked up and met her eyes as his sentence trailed off. Dark and fathomless, she lost herself in their sparkle for too long until he focused on the path again. 'I have no right to claim expertise on matters of the heart. But think what you've seen, just on this street.' He kicked at a stone, and it rolled along the path before tipping into the gutter. 'Your father puts his family above everything. Arley didn't cut ties because it made his life easier. Iris and Hamish could commit Albert in a moment and retire to the Dalton estate, and no one would judge them. All of them have much simpler choices available. Yet they tread harder paths. And for what?'

Again her heart kicked and spluttered to that unfamiliar beat. Her skin felt so warm it almost itched, prickling despite the late summer breeze that met them at the edge of the park and greeted them as they reached the end of Honeysuckle Street.

'Given that we're both so terrible at matters of the heart, we should practice. Do you know how you could show the world you are an affectionate husband?'

Phineas slowed his step. 'I do try, Rosanna. For appearances. I try to be kind and considerate of you. What more could I do?' As soft as a kiss, a tender hesitancy caressed his confession. Her heart seemed to pause, suspended, before galloping in her chest. When they stopped in front of the stairs to Number 1, she drew him to face her, eyes level.

'Let me paint the entryway. I was thinking bright yellow. And maybe hang some prints. It would be so much more welcoming to step into a room like that at the end of the day.'

Phineas grumbled, threw his hands in the air, and stomped ahead, shaking his head and muttering to himself as he trudged up the stairs. Spencer leapt from the bushes onto the landing, and Phineas shooed him away. Spencer flicked an ear. Rosanna chuckled to herself. She'd always thought him emotionless, but now she could read the discomfort that sat so close beneath his skin, and the agitation that circled him like the cat winding around his legs until Phineas ushered him over the threshold. He kept everyone at a distance, yet she'd been the one to see past his stiffness to raise his hackles and make him laugh. A flick of memory teased her mind, and with a shudder, she relished the thought of his fingers working at her, of the burning he'd both stoked and quenched.

Her heart thumped hard, just once, then turned, like a cog shifting and falling into place with a dull clunk.

'Oh no.' Rosanna covered her mouth with her hand to smother the realisation, even though there was no one close by to witness her unravelling. And the cog creaked, wound tight, then rolled into motion, as unstoppable as an engine.

This was bad.

This was very, very bad.

The worst thing imaginable had happened.

She was falling in love with her husband.

Chapter Fifteen

Fat drops thwacked against the stretched skin of the umbrella. Phineas skirted a puddle. Ahead of him, the tall wall of his home came into view, and against the gloom, the windows which faced the park glowed warm with yellow light. He took his next few steps a little faster. He'd stayed back later than he'd intended to help Taylor with some paperwork, and rain had settled in sometime between his arrival and departure at the end of the half-workday Saturday.

Provided she hadn't decided to decorate another room, Rosanna would likely be discussing the week's menu with Jean or maybe visiting Elise or her family. She would be busy, and the house would be quiet, and he would be able to think through the problem of Argonauts Trading and Lord Richard and just how much Pennington had to do with it all. If he reported it to senior management, they might pull back from selling shares, but that didn't change what Lord Richard owed, and it didn't change life for Rosanna. He'd promised her a clean break and a future on her own terms. He couldn't fail. Not again.

Those two wheel ruts in the snow... The memory of them was seared into his eyelids, taunting him whenever he closed his eyes to sleep. Over the years, he had returned to the bridge at random times to try to conjure up some spark that might lead to a clue, but he visited the place every day in his memory. Christmas had never been much of a happy time, but ever since that day, the richness of it was infused with his failure. The stone, normally grey blue, blackened with moisture and glistening stark against the crystals of snow. The smell of pine and woodsmoke, harmonious choruses; the cleanness of cold air... All of them screamed, *Where were you. She trusted you. You failed.*

Phineas paused at the bottom of his front steps. The cat sat on the landing before the door, his tail flicking lazily back and forth.

'Evening, Spencer,' he said, as if the cat might give him a response.

Spencer licked a paw. He sniffed the air, then leapt off the landing and scampered into the bushes.

A slight light, wider than it should have been, painted a line around the edge of the door.

His front door stood ajar.

Phineas took the steps in two swift strides. Shouts, cries, and hollering came from inside, and cold fear ran through him. Had Lord Richard come for Rosanna? He'd imagined his home, full of staff, even in their bumbling ways, a safe place for her. Had the lord been desperate enough to break in? Phineas threw a silent prayer to the god he didn't believe in that she was giving them the better of the fighting.

He listened hard, then nudged the door open. He closed his umbrella and scanned the entrance for a more suitable weapon, but amongst all the knick-knacks and things stuffed onto the side table, there was nothing more menacing. He twisted the umbrella handle between his palms. Anything was better than nothing.

'Raah!'

Phineas tensed and swung—but stopped when a person half his height and wearing a homemade wolf mask leapt into the doorway. The creature clawed at the air.

'I am a huntsman,' someone further down the hall bellowed. Not *someone*... Was that Hugh, the butler? 'I will get you, wolf.' The wolf squealed and scampered out of sight. Hugh's broad frame flashed across the entrance to the hallway, so fast that Phineas only knew who it was from his voice.

Phineas lowered his umbrella. Pandemonium echoed through his house. Laughter bounced off the walls, colliding in the landing of the stairwell and the hall. The lights cast odd angles, and the air weighed heavy with the smell of sweat and sugar and hot food.

It was not the chaos of a home invasion.

It was far, far worse.

Hempels. Hundreds of them. Perhaps not actual hundreds, but far more than the one he was accustomed to, and she was problematic enough. One clapped down the stairs, screaming, while another followed, growling like a bear. One shrieked, another cried out, then giggled, and feet tramped and ran and pounded from all directions. One of the small ones leapt into the entrance, turned in a lopsided pirouette with her hands raised above her head, and tiptoed away.

'Felix!' Phineas shouted. 'Are you here?'

A head poked around the corner. Not Felix. 'Evening, Mr Babbage. How was your morning?' Nanny Abigail scooped a child up and onto her hip. This one was smaller than the princess one, with blonde curls and green eyes the same shade as Rosanna's.

'Productive. Confusing.' Phineas looked past her, still searching for Felix or any member of his staff, even the one that was always singing. 'Why are you in my house? You should be next door.' He patted the dividing wall in demonstration. 'Through there. Where you all live. And I can't hear you.'

The child on her hip squeezed a cheek, and Nanny Abigail jerked her face out of reach, brushing a curl aside with a tender hand. 'Little baby Hazel had a fever these past two nights and half of today. It seems like she's come through the worst of it, but poor mistress is terribly tired but still so worried she can't sleep. I don't think she's closed her eyes since the babe first felt warm. Mr Hempel is with her. He promised to watch the baby so she might relax a little and hopefully get some rest.'

'Where is Rosanna?'

Nanny Abigail bounced the child in her arms. 'She's gone to the Aster with Johannes. There's a big crowd in tonight, and Grandpa Robert, he's good with a menu but not much good in a crush. And Mr Hempel doesn't trust anyone but Rosie at these things anyway.'

Phineas pinched the bridge of his nose. 'But why are all these small people *here*?'

'I was lining them up to take them to see the ducks, but the weather turned dark before we'd crossed the street, and we don't need any more sniffly noses than we already have. Rosie—I mean, your wife, Mrs Babbage—said to bring them over. I can take them home if it's a problem, although heaven knows how I'll keep the noise down. They've been as worried as poor mistress, although they don't show it in the same way. You don't mind, do you?'

He did mind. He liked quiet. And peace. He had been staring at columns all day, and right now, he needed to think about transport and shipping routes to chase his hunch about Argonauts into proof or obsolescence. Phineas shoved his umbrella into the stand. 'Do you need anything?'

Nanny Abigail shook her head. 'Felix has been ever so helpful. He's brilliant, isn't he? He has the children in the dining room having a picnic. He really loves his work.'

'Sir!' Felix, bounding down the hallway, pulled to a stop before the entry. He wore a hat folded from newspaper, and as he twisted direction, it slipped to one side. 'Can I take your coat? This afternoon, we moved your hook and made a cloak room. It was Letitia's idea. Look!' He swung open the door into the room behind the entrance. Phineas peeked around the corner. A row of red coats and scarves lined the wall. Felix slung Phineas's black coat onto a hanger and hung it on the rail. 'We are having tea in the dining room. Hugh and I rolled out blankets because the table is too small, and we are pretending to dine *en plain air*, so that everyone has space to sit and eat. Would you like to join us?'

Before Phineas could reply, Felix, hollering as a small troop of children dragged him out of sight, was swept from view.

Phineas leant into the lobby. Raucous laughter and calls echoed down the hall. He shuffled along a little further.

'Are you going to join them?' Nanny Abigail asked.

'No.'

'Not even for tea? Jean has made shortcake and sandwiches.'

'Especially not. I will be in the library.'

'Suit yourself. I've been run ragged all day, and I am itching for some food. I'll tell Felix to send something in, shall I?'

Nanny Abigail left, but Phineas was not alone. A small boy, his height in between the tiny dancing one and an adult, stared up at him. He had dark hair like Lawrence, freckles like Rosanna, and a sombre expression. He thrust his right hand at Phineas, then swapped it for his left, before deciding on his right again. 'Good afternoon. I am Amadeus. I'm ten.'

'Congratulations.' Phineas stepped out of the lobby and into the hall, away from the commotion at the back of the house and towards the sacredness of his library.

'That's not how it goes.' The child, indignant, trotted behind him. 'After I introduce myself, you introduce yourself.'

'Phineas Babbage,' he called over his shoulder. 'We are not strangers. We've lived beside each other for seven years.'

'We have, but we've never been formally introduced.'
The boy scooted around, jostling him to the side, then
pulled up short, squarely in Phineas's way and obscuring
his path. He offered his hand again. Phineas took it and
gave it one swift shake. 'Pleased to meet you, Phineas
Babbage,' the child said. 'Your house is very noisy.'

'Why don't you tell them to be quiet?' Phineas flicked
his fingers. 'Go on. Shoo.'

He sidestepped the medium Hempel and finally crossed
over the threshold to his library. But as he turned to shut
the door, the child popped up in the centre of the room.
How did he move so fast?

'Uncle Phin...'

Phineas glowered down. 'I am not your uncle.'

'Who are you, then?'

'I am your brother-in-law. Of sorts. I suppose.'

'Oh,' Amadeus said, his voice thick with
disappointment.

Phineas spun to the bookshelf and investigated the
presented spines. Railways... the Midlands... handbooks...
guides... where were his maps? He tapped through the
books and scanned the embossed titles. Then he stopped
to look down at the child. 'What do you mean, "Oh?"'

'Nothing.' The boy flopped to the floor and crossed his
legs. 'It's just, I've already got so many brothers, but no
uncles. I always thought it might be nice to have one of
those. Someone to take me to the park and show me how
to shoot, like in a boy's own adventure.'

'People don't shoot in the park.'

'Oh,' Amadeus said, even more disappointed than he had been before. 'I suppose it doesn't matter that I don't have an uncle.' He plucked at the rug, then scuffed his heel against the edge.

Phineas turned back to the bookcase. 'What number are you?' he asked, half over his shoulder.

'My name is Amadeus. I have no number,' the boy replied, frowning.

'Of course you have a number. Somewhere, we're all a number. In your family, are you seventh? Eighth?'

'Number six!' Amadeus shouted with a half jump. 'Garnett was above me. But he's gone now. So, when people look at us all lined up, I'm number five, but Mama and Father say, and we all know that I'm number six.'

Garnett. That was the boy they'd lost. Done a sight better than many a family—especially the families in the poorhouse where he'd grown up—in only losing one. And those they'd kept seemed healthy and whole. One tragedy amidst so much life would have been considered a blessing.

But even a little loss marked a person.

And a battlefield of loss?

It scorched a person's soul.

'I miss him,' Amadeus said.

'You weren't even born when he died,' Phineas said, then regretted the words, not only for their brutishness but for their simplicity.

'I know,' the boy said, either not noticing or choosing to ignore the harsh angle of his tone. 'Doesn't mean I don't miss him.'

Phineas walked his fingers along the book spines. There. *The Railways of Great Britain and Ireland, Practically Described and Illustrated*. Phineas took the book, pulled out his reading glasses, and settled into his chair.

'Uncle Phin.' Amadeus climbed over Phineas's knee and settled into the small space on the cushion.

Phineas shifted aside with a huff. 'We discussed this. I'm not your uncle.'

'Will you read to me?' The boy slid, stiff with bony angles, against the chair arm.

'The Railways of Great Britain and Ireland? You want me to read it to you?'

The boy pressed the back of his hand against his mouth as he yawned. 'Is it exciting? Are there pirates with swords, or magic?'

Phineas opened the book to the title page. 'Not exactly. This book is full of something better. *Answers*. Have you ever been on a train?'

Amadeus shook his head. 'I see them, but we walk everywhere. Nanny says it helps us sleep. Or helps her sleep. I forget.'

The spine cracked as Phineas opened to the first chapter. 'If I am going to read to you about trains, you must act like people do on a long train journey. Everyone on a train is very quiet, because they are too busy looking out the window and enjoying the view. Can you be quiet like that?'

'I'll be quiet, Uncle Phin,' Amadeus said in a loud whisper, and made a motion like he was buttoning his lips.

'Very good. Now. Let us begin. *The Permanent Way Railway is laid to the English standard gauge, viz, four feet and eight and a half inches. Although the land taken is wide enough for a double way, being about seventeen yards, there is, at present...*'

After a few pages, Amadeus's chest slowed its rhythm. He rubbed his wrist against his nose, then fell back against Phineas's shoulder and snored softly.

Phineas turned the page slowly, keeping his torso still and only moving his hands. He arched a little into his chair, and when Amadeus mumbled, Phineas froze until the boy settled back into his sleepy silence.

Children were uncomfortable.

And when they were asleep, they made all sorts of noises. They snuffled. Snorted. Grunted. Even giggled.

They were also warm. And heavy.

Very heavy.

Phineas turned another page. The letters grew fuzzy, and words lost their familiar shapes. He turned into his shoulder and yawned.

Amadeus jerked, and his elbow dug into Phineas's hip. Phineas stifled a yelp.

Children were also painful.

Ten years old... Had he ever been like this child? Phineas counted through the years, the places on the road, and the hovels of his childhood. Could he even remember ten? He tried to place a city or even a country, but through the blur of memories, one outpost was so very like another. Ten was certainly after his mother had married the corporal, a man much older than her, but one with a steady income and who appreciated the regimen they'd learnt to live by in the poorhouse. Ten might have been when Phineas had learnt how to play the bugle. It was after his stepfather had taught him how to read, but before he'd learnt how to dodge a hand angry with too much rum. Where had those days even been spent? Nova Scotia? Port Arthur? Or further afield, in the tropics? Maybe ten had been those days when the sea had stretched into the sky, and buzzing insects had carried his mother away, not on their wings, but with disease.

The book dropped from his hands and landed on the rug with a thump.

His memories grizzled and pawed at the edge of a dream. So much of his life since she'd left him had been turned backs and closed doors. The prison cell slamming shut after he was found in a tavern instead of at his post. The quiet hush as his stepfather turned his back and left the court once he'd heard the reduced sentence. He'd been spared the coffin closing, and for that, Phineas was grateful, because if faced with the steady tap of nails entrusting a man like the corporal to the afterlife, he wouldn't have known what to feel. Gratitude? Remorse? Shame? Anger?

As it was, he had the option of feeling nothing.

Feeling nothing was for the best.

His memory settled into a monotonous monotone, one of those simple sleeping constructions that meant nothing in the land of sleep or waking. A deep breath, and the shapes fragmented, and swirled away. Amadeus grunted, then snorted. Phineas patted the boy's back until he calmed.

A different dream of the world right outside his door bit his thoughts. Of the world he tried to keep his distance from and remain an observer of but was forever finding himself dragged into. For all their sullenness, his Christmases with Arley had been something of a comfort. The two of them had found one another one evening when Arley had escaped his own house after Abberton took it over for a party and some mother had tracked the duke to his office and insisted he meet her daughter. And then there was that other afternoon, not even two years ago, when Phineas had been walking home, and Hamish's manservant had demanded he come to Number 4 to hear some business proposition. By that time, he'd already sniffed out Iris's scandal, but Irving had said he could make things better. His undoing, over and again, was in trying to help.

The front door clicked. Phineas blinked his eyes open. He listened from the edge of his thoughts, absorbing the familiar step on the floorboards, her boots probably spreading dirt everywhere. The worry around his heart loosened a little. She was home.

Outside the library door, Rosanna paused and had a whispered conversation with her sister Beatrice. Johannes flashed in, then out of view, and through slitted, heavy eyelids, the slow procession of older children carrying younger children paraded by. The second boy, Elliot, carried the small girl who always sang. Beatrice clasped the other small girl around her hip. Nanny, small yet strong, balanced the toddler she was always chasing against her chest.

'Ammie?' Rosanna called, her voice soft, yet edged with worry.

'In here.'

Rosanna stopped in the doorway. Johannes bumped against her.

'I'm too scared to move. Everything hurts,' Phineas croaked, as loud as he dared. 'Help.'

Johannes chuckled, his deep baritone like a gong in the settled silence. 'Ammie sleeps like a brick. You could have pushed him onto the floor, and he wouldn't have woken.' Johannes caught his brother beneath the armpits and scooped him into his arms. Amadeus snuffled, his head lolling backwards. Rosanna laughed softly, pecked his forehead, and arranged him into a more comfortable position.

The front door closed. The familiar tap and tread of the staff as they moved down or upstairs faded away to silence. Phineas stretched into the firm leather of the chair, and his back cracked with relief.

Rosanna slipped his glasses from his nose, folded the arms, then placed them on the table. She smoothed his hair. 'Do you need to be carried off to bed, too?'

Her touch brought back all his senses, and his memories collided. The bright burst of terror that had rushed over him when he'd thought someone had come for her lit in him like a furnace once more. 'I was so worried about you.'

'Johannes was with me, just as you told me. I was only at the hotel. Lord Richard was there, dining with Mr Vincent and skulking about, but he didn't come near me—'

Half asleep, half twisted with anxiety, all of him flooding with relief, Phineas grasped her skirts with both fists and yanked her closer. He had no right to claim her softness with a husband's assertion, but his body yearned for her physicality, ached for the certainty that she was well and whole and *here*. She yielded to his tug and slid onto his lap with a giggle. Before she could say anything, he sought out her lips as a balm to his anxiety.

She returned his kiss lightly, then deeper in intensity, like a whirlpool drawing him to a precipice where he floated, dreamlike, knowing he should stop but so unwilling to even try.

'What is this?' she sighed against his lips, their familiar softness nipping his. 'Between us. Is it becoming more?'

Phineas crawled her skirts into his palms as he grasped her tighter. Could he imagine a world where he would give her the life she wanted, the freshness and freedom she needed? More of what? Family? Laughter? Light? Which of those things could he give her? They could not become more because he had nothing more to give.

'Nothing,' he said, his voice gravelly and harsh. 'This is nothing. I forgot myself. You shouldn't do that.' He shoved her from his knee until she stood, and with a mumbled goodnight, he stumbled from the room.

CHAPTER SIXTEEN

Ammie, his eyes concealed by Mama's hands, his smile somewhere between caution and expectation, reached into the space before him. Framed by the ornate arch of the entrance to the hotel's dining room, the two of them seemed so small. Ammie almost matched Mama's height already. Neither of the Hempel parents were tall; in fact, they were probably lucky to have reached the five foot they had after growing up in an orphanage. Mama pulled her hands away, and Ammie took in the expanse of the room. Bright red and white crepe rosettes hung in every corner, long twists of ribbon cascaded from the ceiling to the floor, and on the table in the centre of the room sat a three-layer cake. Family, friends, and a few neighbours filled the room. Ammie's anticipation turned to wonder as he flung himself around Mama's neck and hugged her tight, shouting, 'It's perfect!' He raced across the room to where the other children were gathered, presents in hand.

Elliot pushed to the front and shoved a wooden crate at Ammie. 'I made you firecrackers. Whizzes and bangers. Father said we can let them off outside the hotel, as long as we're quick and scarper if the coppers come.'

Rosanna neatened the bow on her gift—a set of coloured pastels. It was wrong to have favourites when it came to siblings, especially in a family as big as hers. No matter how warm their hearths or how attentive their parents, everyone had trouble getting a smidgeon of attention. But in moments like this, she couldn't deny it—Ammie was special. Almost three years after the loss of Garnett, her mother had quietly announced over breakfast that another baby Hempel was on the way. The following months had been slow and shadowed, laced with worry and anchored in unease. But for all his reserve now, Ammie had come into the world screaming with health and gusto, and from early smiles to floor-slapping crawling, he'd brought a new vitality to their home. He was the baby who did not know the pain or the heartache of before, but who must have felt them regardless as they infiltrated everything in the Hempel household. With every rosy-cheeked laugh, flat palm against her cheek, or tug of her long hair, he'd brought a peace to their lives. Not a forgetting, for that was impossible. More of a settling. As grief turned to memory and agony to acceptance, the family had moulded itself into a different type of happiness, and he had unknowingly been at the centre of it.

Ammie had that effect on people. Even on her aloof, impenetrable husband.

When she'd returned home the night before last, she hadn't been worried until she'd clambered out of the hackney cab, followed by Johannes, the pair of them wrung out with conversation and decisions. Only then had she questioned what she might find inside Number 1. Chaos? Anger? When she'd climbed the steps, slid her key into the lock, and entered a house of happy humming and contentment, she'd felt something completely unexpected. She'd come *home*. The fullness of the feeling had been swiftly pursued by a wave of dread. The little red coats lining the cloak room. Phineas's hung up beside them. In the dining room they'd found scattered crumbs while the air had been rich with the smell of the simple food children liked. The sense of completion and gnawing terror vied for dominance until the final blow—discovering her husband, stiff and uncomfortable, with little Ammie nestled beside him. The affection stirring inside her had turned into an avalanche.

And later, when they were alone, his possessive fisting of her skirt, his determination to feel her... As if he were reconciling her like a number in a column, checking her tally and finding her sums correct. Then he'd underlined it with a kiss...

Those moments where she'd niggled and nudged him to frustration or low chuckles, when she eased around his defences and drawn out a different man, had become too treasured. She'd dared to ask... *what is this*? Three simple words that created a tangle of complexity.

Nothing, he'd replied, his dismissal like a blade across her traitorous heart, but also the absolute truth. He was fast becoming her everything, but she mustn't allow that to happen. It had to be, had to remain *nothing*.

He wanted to leave. He wanted to escape the monotony of their lives. He wanted to start over and leave everything behind.

And always, the ache of Imogen hung in the room. Rosanna refused to take second place to anyone, even a memory. If she didn't contain her ridiculous heart, that's what she would be. The runner-up. The first loser.

Such certainty did not stop the little pang in her chest, nor the altering of her heart's rhythm as her husband entered through the double doors, nodded at the staff behind the counter, and paused to survey the room. It didn't stop the light flitter of anticipation when his gaze found her and he crossed the room in a direct line.

'You are early,' she said.

'Bank holiday,' he replied. 'Some anniversary. We closed early, although the rest of the world keeps moving.' From his dry tone, she couldn't tell if he was happy with the half day's leave or annoyed by the break in his week's rhythm. He frowned across the hubbub of the dining room. 'What's all this?'

'It's Ammie's birthday. He's eleven.'

Phineas's brow furrowed deeper. He picked up a rosette off the table and spun it between his fingers. 'Quite a fuss for eleven.'

'It's our family tradition to celebrate double numbers at the hotel. If we had a big celebration for everyone each year, it would be never-ending parties and planning. But Papa takes any chance he can to ignore society's rules, so he doesn't like to focus on sixteen or twenty-one. He decided that double numbers like 11 or 22, even 33, were special.

We still have cake and songs at home for other birthdays, but double numbers we celebrate here.'

'Master numbers,' Phineas said confidently, and when she frowned, he added, 'Angel numbers. Some people believe that those numbers carry meaning. Those who follow the occult and such.'

'I didn't think you'd be one for the spiritual sciences,' she teased, enjoying the return to familiar terrain. This she could manage. She would keep herself in check.

'I'm not. It's ridiculous. Numbers are just that. Numbers.' He pulled out his pocket watch. 'How long will all this take?' he asked.

'Maybe a couple of hours. Mama is putting on a brave face, but she's still tired. I can't imagine she'll let things drag.'

'I'll return before then.'

'You can stay—' she began, then stopped. He had already spun on his heel, crossed the hall, and left. Petals from one of the bushes beside the entrance skimmed across the mosaic tiles, flipped over one another, and scattered across the path.

'That doesn't bode well for the happy couple.'

'Shut it, Johannes.' Rosanna crossed her arms as she turned away from her husband's absence to look up at her younger, although considerably taller, brother. 'He's busy, is all.'

'I think slow, Rosie, but that doesn't make me a fool. There's more to this than being compromised in the park.'

'You didn't hear Mrs Crofts...'

'You expect me to believe that Father would let Mrs Crofts even whisper about us, especially you? Out with it.'

Rosanna looked across the room and picked out the handful of staff. Pierre, Nolan—both people they knew and trusted. If anyone overheard, they'd likely not gossip. She lowered her voice to a conspiratorial whisper. 'You can't tell *anyone*. Not even Elliot.'

Johannes nodded, then took her by the wrist and led her into a corner of the dining room. They knew from their childhood days that this spot was both in the open, and yet the acoustics wouldn't carry quiet voices.

At first, the words came out confident and indignant as she told him about the scene in the park and the man who had hit her. She trained her voice into steadiness as she spoke about the way Lord Richard had run off and how Phineas had intervened, how he had thwarted Mrs Crofts's accusations with a stoic declaration. She spoke of the kidnapping plot to ransom her for her dowry. Only at the mention of the mysterious Imogen on the mantlepiece did her voice catch.

Johannes was always the epitome of a calm, cloudless day, but a hint of ire crept into his tone. 'What will happen to you when this is over? How is divorce or annulment any better for your reputation?'

'It's better than if Lord Richard had compromised me and forced my hand. There's paperwork, so much paperwork to protect me. Phineas promises I'll have a clean break, and I'll be able to start over. He says I'll have a free life.'

Her brother watched her, his blue eyes penetrating and unsettling. He saw too much, thought too deeply, and who knew what lines and connections he was pulling together in his mind. 'We should get back to the party,' she said, but as she turned towards the family, Phineas crossed the threshold once more.

He clasped a small rectangular package wrapped in brown paper in one hand. With a nod at the doorman, he made direct for the dining room. He wove a path between tables and guests towards Ammie, who sat at the table beside Nova, the pair of them wolfing down cake. Johannes made as if to speak, but Rosanna shushed him and inched forwards, her ears straining to hear over the hubbub of the room.

Phineas tapped Ammie on the shoulder, then thrust the parcel onto the table. Ammie sat back in surprise, looked up, and, grinning broadly, scrabbled at the wrapping. The paper fluttered to the floor, and Ammie raised a book to eye level so he could scan the cover.

'It's a book about trains,' Phineas said. 'So now you can read on your own. Without me.'

Ammie's expression softened into a slight sadness. 'You don't want to read with me?' he asked.

'I do, but if I'm busy, and you... you know. Want to read about trains.' Phineas tapped the cover. 'You won't have to wait for me. You can do so whenever you wish.'

Ammie stood on his chair. He leapt at Phineas and clasped him around the neck. 'I love it, Uncle Phin!' He hung there for a moment, legs dangling, before Phineas patted his back, caught him about the sides, and lowered him to the ground.

'Chairs are for sitting, not standing. You'll get dirt on the seat.'

And there it was again. That sliver of kindness, that shielded moment of connection, appearing and disappearing with a blink.

Never be what they think you are.

If only he'd kept it all hidden from her.

'Oh Rosie,' Johannes muttered. 'You haven't fallen for him, have you?'

Rosanna bowed her head, refusing to look at her brother. 'Only a little. I didn't plan it.' She drew a circle on the inside of her palm, trying to ignore her brother's disbelieving stare. 'A lot. I like him a lot. I don't know what to do.'

'Father wants me to go to Brighton to look at possible hotel locations. You know what the guests like better than me. Tell me a date. I'll book a ticket. We'll get away, and you can have some space.'

'We're so close to figuring everything out.'

Johannes took her by the shoulders and turned her to face him. 'You're one of the strongest people I know, but you can't bottle up your emotions. It's not in you. If you mean it, that he's going to leave, you need to step away first. And soon.'

'I can't leave before all this is done.'

'And when it *is* done?'

Rosanna looked at the floor and shrugged.

'This might be a silly question...' Johannes bumped his elbow into her side. 'But did you ever think about asking him to stay?'

Chapter Seventeen

'You any closer to sorting all this out?' A few inches shorter than himself but formidable nonetheless, Lawrence Hempel pulled up beside Phineas, hands in his pockets.

'Closer every day,' Phineas replied, keeping his stare determinedly ahead. 'I can feel it.'

'You said Rosie would be with you for weeks. It's been that.'

Phineas grappled for some cutting remark, but none sprung to mind. For years he'd antagonised his neighbour for the simple reason that he did not think a friend would be an asset to him. Now, he stood beside him as a failure.

Lawrence adjusted his shirt cuff. 'No one fucks with my family, Babbage. I trust you because the duke did, and because Iris does. Not because you've earned it from me. I've heard of Pennington. I'm not a fool. You said you'd keep Rosie safe, and you have, but she also needs to be free. She's got a bright life ahead of her, even after all this. I'd hate to see her bogged down and constantly looking over her shoulder, weighed down by a man who can't figure things out.'

'I don't want that either. She's determined. She's strong. She's—'

'Solve it your way soon, or I'll solve it mine.' And Lawrence set off across the room to Amadeus. The boy excitedly showed his father the book and some other toy before pointing to the box of firecrackers. With a mischievous grin, Lawrence hoisted the crate onto his hip. He shot a sly look over his shoulder in the direction of his wife, who was occupied with the baby as she spoke with Iris and Odette. Then he hurried a few of the children out a side door. Their shadows danced across the curtains as they ran the perimeter of the building before each line of grey conspiracy faded into London.

He'd known he lived beside a family. Their constant red-dotted parade past his windows and the occasional thump and rattle through the walls were regular reminders. But a family... He'd never considered one for his own life. What an odd beast a family was. Fighting and compromises, gentleness and antagonism—a family was composed of so many shifting components. Had he, the corporal, and his mother been a family? Perhaps, in the lines of regiment, in the perfectly ordered camp with lessons and bugle practise, they had been, in their own way. An awkward thrumming, a type of nostalgic tick wedged a part of himself open, and a bizarre confluence of affection and discomfort trickled through him. This was his place, but only temporarily, and yet, it felt nice to belong to something bigger than oneself. Something that wasn't about duty or work. Something that simply *was*.

Phineas scanned the room, his gaze flicking from chair to chair until he found the anchor he craved. Rosanna. Heavens, another new dress, this one emerald green. It hugged her breasts and skimmed over her decadent body until it disappeared beneath the table. He rolled his tongue against his palette, for a moment cherishing the memory of her nipple, hard and taut, in his mouth. And in that moment of depravity, she looked up, half rose in her seat with a smile like sunshine, and beckoned to him. And he, completely lacking in restraint, trotted over. She kissed his cheek, and he kissed hers. She tasted like... like *happiness*.

'You got Ammie a gift.' She squeezed his arm, then settled back into her chair. 'He loved it. Although it *is* Ammie, and he loves everything. But he's taken a shine to you.'

Phineas shrugged through the burgeoning warmth in his chest. He unbuttoned his coat and took a seat at the table. 'It seemed the proper thing to do.'

A waiter set a plate of cake onto the table before Rosanna. Outside, a piercing whistle was followed by a fizz of light flashing through the gaps in the curtains. Energy and gunpowder crinkled and cracked. Sparks of yellow light edged the windows before a muffled shout of, 'Run, kids! Through the lane and into the kitchens,' echoed. Wilhelmina rose and looked across the room with a frown. Rosanna stifled a laugh against the back of her hand.

'As usual, the worst behaved child is Papa. I suppose this is all a little crazy for a steady bank man like yourself. I suppose I am all sorts of crazy in your life.' She separated a small piece of cake off with her fork but didn't raise it to her mouth. Just twisted it on the prongs and divided it into increasingly smaller pieces until the entire wedge was a collection of crumbs.

'I *like* order. I can manage its alternative.' He inched his fingers across the table and stole a morsel of sponge from her plate.

'Do you mind!' she scolded, then smiled and pushed the cake across to him. 'Perhaps, but we both know that before my arrival, your house was so ordered. And I've seen the bank. It's all so tightly managed. We are completely capricious, and the hotel is far worse. Each day is a flip of the coin, sometimes several. Your world is so different. So predictable.'

Phineas was raising a triangle of sponge to his mouth but halted mid-air. 'You think I'm boring.'

'No!' Rosanna ran a fingernail along a crease in the tablecloth. A pink tinge inched along her neck and cheeks. For weeks, all she had done was unsettle him. How marvellous to have finally made *her* uncomfortable. 'If all of this is too much for you, and you'd like to go home to eat, we can. That's all I'm saying.'

Phineas chuckled. For all its unfamiliarity, the sound settled against his chest, a familiar tune when it came to Rosanna. 'I'm just teasing, Hempel. But do you really think finance is like that? Predictable quiet and columns?'

'*You* are all quiet and columns. All blank walls and black waistcoats. Why would I imagine that world any different?' She pulled her plate back across the table, stole his fork, and deftly snuck a wedge into her mouth. A tight crumb adhered to her lip, and with a quick flick of her tongue, she knocked it free. An ache, a need, a hunger rippled along his spine, and while he chewed the cake he tasted her, that delicious lingering of her essence that had clung to his fingers after she'd come to him on the upper floors and demanded her pleasure.

'I am not all quiet and columns.' His voice came out husky and raw, scratching his throat. Rosanna rolled her lips like she was trying not to laugh, a light glimmer in her eyes as she shot him a conciliatory smile. 'I'm not! And I will show you.' He studied her dress. Subtle folds gathered to cinch her waist. His breath snagged in his chest. 'Very pretty, but you cannot wear that.'

'What's wrong with my dress?' she asked, slightly flaring the skirt as she stood.

'It won't help where we're going. Does the hotel have a stash of things guests leave behind?'

He led her by the hand for the first few blocks as they took backstreets and alleys away from the hotel. Her silken skin felt warm against his palm, as smooth as his own, worn to luxury after years of ledgers and pens. As they approached the high street, he released her, but before she stepped into the thoroughfare before Capel Court, he gripped her shoulder and pulled her back.

'Let me check you. One last time.'

He was a cad, a scoundrel. A damned lusty schoolboy with an infatuation, and as she adjusted herself into a stiff, formal pose, he tried to feel guilt, but appreciation—no, damn himself, nothing so ordered, it was simply lust—smothered it all. Tight trousers which hugged her behind, a tucked-in white shirt, and a waistcoat that skimmed her curves. A too-loose coat concealed her breasts, and with much effort, they'd tucked her hair into a bowler hat. If she could hold her tongue and they stayed in shadows, she might blend in enough.

'Do I look like a clerk?'

'You'll do. Head down. Hat on, preferably low over your face. And if you hear the words *fourteen hundred*, I want you to run for the exit. Don't wait for me, and don't look back. The words are code, used when someone has spotted an imposter. It's one thing to be sprung without a membership, but I've never known a *woman* to be caught in here.'

'What do they do when they spot an imposter?' she asked.

'If it's a man, they'll rough him up. Knock his hat, tear his clothes, manhandle him all the way to the doors. Are you ready?'

Rosanna checked the buttons on her coat, then bit her lip to hide a smile. She craved testing boundaries as much as he sought their comfort. Only small tells, like her fidgeting with her coat sleeves or worrying her bottom lip, hinted that her stiff confidence and stomping forthright walk was a lie.

They ascended the short stairs and passed between the tall columns to cross the portico, blood thrumming loud in his ears. As they walked through the heavy wooden doors, Phineas had to tap at the back of Rosanna's hat in a silent reminder to keep her head down because she craned her neck to look up, taking in everything.

Once they had made their way beneath the royal crest of the lion and unicorn with the words *Dieu et mon droit* carved into the stone—*God and my right*—he ushered her between the strips of shadow and light along the outer corridor. There he found a space where they could stand, inconspicuous and obscured by heavy sandstone blocks and tall columns. Rosanna steadied herself against him as she peered between the arches to take in the cacophony of the trading floor.

The London Stock Exchange. A chaotic, bleating, bleeding morass of fortune, misfortune, and chance. In so many ways, the stock exchange was gambling elevated to the status of respectability, of a profession. In these walls, debt became an asset, interest an opportunity, and fortunes were built and demolished in an instant. Here, men made deals worth thousands of pounds, shook hands like gentlemen, then stole hats and chalked each other's backs like naughty schoolboys. Shouts of trade and business were coupled with teasing and pranks. A bowler hat tipped and flew across the room, and when it landed, the men in its vicinity kicked it amongst themselves like it was a football—until one man sent it sailing through the air again with an extra energetic kick, pursued by its hapless owner. Rosanna clutched the lip of her own bowler. Phineas tapped her hand and shook his head. 'They'll spot you if you look nervous. Be confident, like you belong.'

Phineas leant into Rosanna, as close as he dared without looking too intimate. 'The bank might be all order and quiet, but this is real finance. It's chaotic. Unpredictable.

Ruthless and unforgiving. A man might have a crowd of admirers one day and be abandoned the next. Here, there are no connections, no loyalty. Only money.'

'Does money matter so much to you?' She pulled at her coat collar as she searched his face. 'I hadn't realised. I thought you only liked numbers.'

'Everyone *likes* money, especially those who grew up without it. When I was free of the army, I swore I would take charge of my own life, and that meant not merely earning money, but understanding it. I swore I would never again be dependent on the whims of employers who might be fair or mean, or officers who'd bought their commissions and didn't understand what a day's march felt like, but who ordered men to take them, regardless. When I started as a clerk, I learnt fast. When I had enough savings, I made my own investments and built my own stability.'

A loud thump and the cracking whack of a mallet against the wooden wainscot reverberated through the room. Phineas pinched Rosanna's coat by the elbow and led her to the side, partially for greater obscurity, but also so that she might have a better view of the ritual that was about to unfold. Another thump filled the air. Then the third beat finally cracked the raucousness of the chamber, and the shouts and talk faded away into mutterings. Almost everyone turned towards a liveried man who stood atop a small plinth. He raised a speaking trumpet to his mouth.

'Mr Reginald Ronald Billings is hereby barred from undertaking business at the London Stock Exchange.'

Across the room, another man scratched out the offending name on a chalk board. Normally after this ceremony, a few men shouted or swore, and the room returned to the hefty noise of trade. But today, a different kind of energy raced through the gathering, and the shouts turned accusatory and bitter, much louder than they had been before.

'Oh dear. He was not expecting to be called out. Poor fellow, he's here.' Phineas pointed at the thickening of the crowd. Rosanna pushed herself onto tiptoes, catching his arm to steady her balance. Instantly, that delicious shiver she created in him rippled through his skin.

'What has he done?' she asked.

Phineas swallowed his distraction and clutched at words of explanation. He pressed his nose to her ear. 'He's defaulted on his debts. The committee has declared him a lame duck, as is the term. It means he's bankrupt, unreliable, and no longer welcome in the world of finance. Most men avoid the ceremony if they are aware its coming. He had no idea.'

A group of men swarmed around the unfortunate Mr Billings. An elbow raised, perhaps to deliver a blow, or maybe just to knock the man's hat from his head—Phineas could not tell. They circled around him, calling and shouting, and the occasional cry or plea for mercy leaked out between the insults. The group of traders shoved and passed Mr Billings, one to the other, and he staggered between them.

'It's like being tied in the stocks,' Rosanna observed the rough shoving and shouts until the group ejected Mr

Billings, not hatless but with a torn coat and only one shoe, from the chambers. 'It's humiliating.'

'It's meant to be. Finance is not pretty. Far from it.' Phineas glanced up over the tall arches, to where the echoes from the floor swirled and butted against the ceiling before they bounced back down. 'Although it looks different from a distance.'

Phineas grabbed her hand. In a room full of men who eyed one another, keen for a way to wring a pound from their flesh, it was a rash thing to do. Her bare palm against his ran soft as cotton, and she gasped in exhilaration as they clapped up the stairs. On the first floor, he dodged between the columns and the makeshift offices built out over decades of haphazard renovations until they leant over the mezzanine balustrade that ran along the edge of the room. Here, he released her, and rested both elbows against the rail. She copied him, her fine fingers clasped before his in a mimicry of his pose, and they looked down through the cavity, to the spectacle of the trading floor below.

'In the bank, we take all of this.' He swept a hand across the concentrated activity of the arguing and madness, the negotiations and confusion, the handshakes and blows. 'And we make order out of chaos. We create a world of calm and understanding. But it's more than that. It's about security. Some people want riches but don't want to work. Others, like Pennington, seem to enjoy breaking the rules. There is never enough for men like that. They cheat and swindle and exploit every bit of trust to amass fortunes. But those types are the exceptions. Most people in the ledger we found the other night are honest people, hoping to make their lives a little more predictable and comfortable. They are so easily taken in by smooth talkers and charlatans, not because of greed, but because they have hope. I understand this. I can help them avoid the pitfalls, or at least stomp out the fraudsters before they get too confident.'

Raw energy thrummed through the exchange. Rosanna, her eyes darting across it all, flashed him a coy smile, and his entire body set aflame with a glance. She understood what it meant. She understood *him*.

'It's both crazier and more magnificent than I imagined. It's the world ticking over, isn't it? From small wishes to grand schemes.' She rubbed at a freckle on the back of her hand, as if trying to erase the evidence of too much time in the sun. 'Does Lord Richard invest in stocks like this? Is this what he wanted my dowry for? To gamble on the world's fortunes?'

Bitterness clung to her voice as she almost spat the word *dowry* into the void. So much more than a tidy sum of cash to ensure her well-being after marriage. *Dowry* meant her body, her freedom, her associations, her future of either poverty or comfort, even the presence of tolerance or love. A simple number attached to the life of a woman. Was it any wonder that, when her doting father had given her the momentous freedom of making her own decision, she had agonised and drawn the men of the city into columns of possible cads and possible beaux? She elucidated her thoughts by saying she wanted to be loved, and that was part of it. But more than that, like almost everyone in the columns, she wanted to be safe.

'He didn't deserve you.' The ruckus from the trading floor threatened to smother his confession, so he leant in closer and took her hand, squeezing his fingers into her palm. 'And he deserves to be hung from a lamppost for making you think so little of yourself.'

He'd stolen too many kisses from her already. As he leant close, a part of him felt the pinch of guilt even while his impulse stomped over his resolve. But another part of him reasoned that of all his crimes, one more did not matter so much. He moved mere inches, but when she turned to meet him, her lips ready and accepting, he capsized and crowded her space with his desires.

Both innocent and eager, Rosanna's kisses splintered and cracked his barricades, and with each little sigh as she tipped her head, as the brims of their hats bumped together, he felt himself slipping dangerously close to her sunshine. Without dresses, boning, petticoats, and whatever else she normally layered herself with, the heat of her body met his hungry touch, and he ran his palm along her torso, over each fantastic curve, over the bold, healthy undulation of her hips, her waist, her arse. Only a thin layer of fabric separated him from all her delectable places.

'We shouldn't,' he whispered. Yet he still drew the edge of her earlobe into his mouth.

'Why not?' Her breath warmed the space behind his ear, and dear heavens, she licked him—a light kiss of her tongue in the shallow of his collarbone.

'Because... Because...'

Rosanna silenced his stammering with her mouth, kissing him with her fervour, her abundance, her everything. 'When I came to your room and you touched me, did you enjoy yourself?'

He couldn't even find a *yes*. Only a groan.

'You asked me if I would like your fingers or your mouth. I've looked in your books and not seen anything about oral intimacies. Will you show me what you meant?'

His fingers curled in on themselves and gouged the decadent curve of her hips. She had mastered how to circumnavigate his defences, how to slit her blade through the small exposures in his armour. And now, surrounded by noise and with so little between them—just a thin cotton shirt and his ever-eroding restraint—he inhaled the sweetness of surrender, of roses and sunshine. He'd carry the memory of her forever, so why not give himself a little more fodder for the impending days of empty loneliness? He slipped the button on her waistband, inched his hand across her soft stomach, then teased his finger through her coarse hair and stroked until he found the top of her slit. He crept a little lower. Just enough to feel the heat of her most intimate parts, to coat his fingertip with her wetness. Then he withdrew and sucked the pad of his fingertip.

'Delicious. Delectable. Divine.' He stroked her again, and she loosened, collapsing a little with a moan.

'We can't stay out here,' she said, her breath racing over his ear as he kissed her nape. 'Can we?'

'We need to go somewhere else, so that you can be loud.' Reluctantly, he withdrew from her trousers, catching her hand and tugging her towards the hallway. 'I know the perfect place.'

Phineas tried handle after door handle until he found an unlocked and abandoned office at the far end of the corridor. The steady tap and whirl of hole punches and machines from the room next door hummed, pattering and discordant, through the walls. He slammed the door shut and pushed Rosanna against the wood, hungrily finding her mouth again.

'What's that noise?' she asked with a pant.

'It's the tickertape machine. It prints out prices of stocks from all the other markets. Does it bother you?'

'No, but... do you *like* the sound?'

He chuckled. 'Not in *that* way. But I like that it's loud. Because when I make you scream, no one will hear you but me.' Possessive and brutal, he gripped her chin and kissed her, hard. As with everything Rosanna, she met his firmness with her own strength before softening and yielding. And for a moment, he imagined a world where she cried out his name every night, not that of some other man—one worthier than him who would one day fill his place in her life as a proper husband. One who could give her the status and stability that she deserved.

Phineas banished the torturous image as he grappled with her shirt buttons. Now, here, she was his, and this memory would belong to no other man. She demanded his mouth, and that's what she'd get, but he'd take his own time and make his own decisions about where and when and for how long. He plucked at her loose stays, mouthing the gorgeous swell of her breast until he nudged a nipple free. Drawing it into his mouth, he grunted. Nothing in the world tasted as good as his wife, and he swirled his tongue until her point hardened.

Working back to her mouth, he dragged his tongue across every fortification, winding around her battlements, searching for her weakness, feeling for what she wanted but did not say aloud. Listening to her body, listening to her air like it was his only oxygen. She moved and trembled without pause, a cacophony of emotion that he had to shut his eyes to just feel. Strung tight, she trembled with fear and anxious desire.

'So scared.' He eased, kissed her neck, pressed his lips behind her ear. He unfastened another button, knocked her hat from her head. 'Why?'

Bright afternoon light squeezed through the edges of the curtains, and thin strips fell in stark lines across her face. She pinched her eyes tight and shook her head. 'I'm not scared of anything,' she said, her voice deep and raspy. And before he could counter, she jumped and wrapped herself around him, her arms around his shoulders, her legs around his waist. The slight tug of her leap against him nearly sent them both toppling, and her acceleration and momentum were intoxicating. Staggering and giddy, he cast about the room for space. Rosanna tightened her legs around him, far too trusting that he would lead the way. At last, with a bump and a giggle, he found steadiness against a desk. He knocked away a dry inkpot and a few scraps of paper to perch her on its edge.

Phineas tugged at her trousers, not wanting to stop kissing her for a breath. Damn buttons, damn ties, even the few small barriers were too much. Rosanna fumbled, her fingers flicking his out of the way, deftly unfastening her trousers so that he could tug them down. A proper gentleman would take the time to remove her boots, but he wasn't one, and instead the clothing gathered at her ankles. He wrestled the offending garments from her body, then dropped to his knees and pushed her thighs wide.

When donning her disguise, she'd kept her own stockings and her own boots. Phineas pinched the end of the pink ribbon above her knee, slipped it loose, then drew the silk down to expose her soft skin. He nipped the indentation of her thigh and drew a languid pattern with his tongue over her flesh. He should take his time. He should torture her with his mouth until she knew no other word but his name. He should punish her with pleasure.

With a light grunt, almost a squeak of discovery, Rosanna tucked one leg over his shoulder. 'Do you want me like this?' she asked. 'Is that how it's done?'

Phineas sucked air between his teeth, forcing himself to find control. Everything about her subsumed him. From the tantalising scent of her sex to the decadent curves of her soft skin, Rosanna suffocated him with her eagerness, her desire, her neediness. He laid a trail of kisses along her thighs. Her muscles tensed, and in the same instance, she arched her back and moaned.

Control. Time. No need to rush.

Rosanna placed her other leg over his shoulder. The back of her boot pressed into his lower back. Her thighs rested against his cheeks, her body wrapped around his, and Phineas gripped at her, pulled at her stocking like it was a rope dangling in salvation and he stood teetering on a precipice. Like everything in his life, he had turned fucking into another examination of order and mastery. Yet, without realising it, Rosanna gently undermined his stability even here. Eager and uncertain, innocent and shameless—how could one person contain so many contradictions, so many thoughts and feelings? She carried her complexity with such lightness. And when she shuffled her arse a little further forwards, when she spread herself a little wider, Phineas released every restraint and let himself fall. Still, before his eyes rolled back in concession, he forced himself to maintain a modicum of order to steal a look, a look to last him a lifetime.

Truly disordered, everything about her disobedient, Rosanna sat perched above him like a wanton goddess. From her open shirt, her skewed stays that half concealed one breast while the other sat free, to the loose curl draped over her shoulder and her half open mouth... Everything about her radiated lust and energy and life. When he caught her gaze, reason slipped from his fingers. And when their eyes locked, an instant stretched into eternity.

Tender expectation, longing, trust, and anticipation—all carried in a look. She splayed her fingers through his hair and drew him closer, directing him to her damp cunt. Electricity rippled through him, and he bowed to her, subservient.

'You would like the pleasure of my mouth?' Phineas breathed the words across her thigh, to the decadent line where leg joined hip, where earth met heaven. He stroked her slit and parted the coarse curls to reveal her softness.

He flicked his tongue against her soft bud. Sweetness and tang. Phineas circled and licked as he explored her taste, so much better than from his fingers where it was tainted by his own skin. This was pure Rosanna.

Rosanna moaned. 'No one will hear me?'

Phineas kept his mouth on her sex as he shook his head, then pushed firmer, drawing her clitoris into his mouth before releasing. Rosanna groaned, deep and degenerate, her entire body vibrating with the effort.

'This is so much better with someone else,' she gasped. 'Don't stop, oh sweet heavens and mercy, don't ever stop.'

So slick and wet, opening just for him. He slipped his fingers inside her and stroked. 'How often do you touch yourself?' he rasped.

'Much more often since I came to live with you.' Rosanna grasped him and manoeuvred him like a helpless, licentious puppet, forcing his face back to her core. How many nights had she been lying in her bed, pleasuring herself while he stroked himself in the room above with her image in his mind? The thought was more than he could manage. He scrabbled at his trouser buttons, shoved down his smalls, and took himself in hand.

Rosanna moaned again, a long rattling sound. Her back arched as she presented herself, and he licked and laved, circled her tenderness, sucked hard on her clitoris, dipped his tongue into her body, and teased at the length of her slit. With every shift in his attention, she writhed and jerked against the desk. Palm tight around his shaft, Phineas pumped harder, lost and abandoned to her essence. She seemed to clamber over him, opening wider, ankles crossed against his back, ensnaring him and making him captive to her desires. She sang her bliss, her words like an orchestra to his ego. Over and over, she said his name. *Yes, Phineas, I like that, Phineas, I love your mouth, do that again, Phineas*. And when her words lost form and became nothing but whimpering, he tightened his grasp on himself with one hand and slipped a finger inside her with the other. Rosanna bucked and pushed his face into her cunt so hard that he thought he might suffocate, but no other heaven even mattered. She quietened to tiny pants and whispered whimpers, *don't stop, don't stop*, until her quiet became a roar, and the most magnificent rumble of exhilaration spilled from her lips. She pulsed against him, and he greedily drank and lapped at all of her. Slackening, she collapsed over him like a cocoon of intimacy as she panted into the background hum.

Then she pushed him from her body with a gentle nudge. 'Are you touching yourself?'

He grunted, still driving himself forwards, his eyes on her wetness, on her gorgeous sex, swollen and glistening from his mouth and her orgasm.

'I want to watch you,' she said. 'Stand up.'

Phineas obeyed mutely, his hand still working and stroking at himself. She gripped his chin and kissed him, light and tenuous, then pulled back to hold his gaze. 'Don't you look away,' she ordered as she slid her hand beside his, into the restraint of his clothing, cupped him, stroked him, inexperienced and experimental. Each little touch and flutter as she caressed his body swallowed his senses, and still, barely blinking, she watched him. And when he panted harder, heavier, when he grunted, she continued to hold him in place with her grip and her eyes. Her eyes bored into him, deep and relentless, and while his years of solitude and silence railed against the intrusion, something more debased, more vulnerable, revelled in the intimacy. With all his forced composure, he held her stare until, with a moan of her name, he found his release. He spent against her thigh and tumbled, both lost and found, adrift and anchored, into the mired agony of uncontrolled bliss.

Every part of his body hummed and buzzed, frenetic. He tucked himself away, broke her stare, and retrieved a fresh kerchief from his pocket to wipe at her thigh.

With her palm against his cheek, Rosanna drew his attention back to herself. 'Don't be embarrassed. I like seeing you like that.'

'Watching me? As I—'

'Uncontrolled,' she said. 'I like seeing you lose yourself.'

'I shouldn't. I don't like to lose myself.'

'Shh...' She stroked his cheek, then leant forwards and kissed him.

There was nothing extraordinary about it. It was a kiss of satiation, of endings, of consumed desires. A kiss of embers. Yet unlike every other moment with Rosanna, it did not career headlong into chaos. She remained gentle, supporting him, firm and steadfast. And in her kiss, all the restlessness in him settled. She held back, for him. She saw him; she understood the confusion, and she reached out. Even as she broke their connection, she held him until he could retreat and close himself back into his safety, his quiet familiarity.

Yet not familiar. Something within him felt off kilter. His heart did not sit as it should, like it had completely detached. Instead it dragged itself across the dusty floor, flopping, pedantic, ticking like an over-wound watch. And as he felt its rhythm, as he looked to the sublime panting of his wife, to her scarlet red lips and her chest puffing with exhilaration, to the endless comfort of her eyes, he knew his heart would never again feel comfortable inside his own chest.

Because it no longer belonged to him.

The realisation stabbed him, like he was a wounded spectre dissolving into oblivion. There was nothing else for it. His heart was now hers. From the slight curl of her index finger in the centre of his palm, to the laughter that spilled from her crimson lips, to the pink of her cheeks, to the pull of her buttons... When faced with all her decadence and innocence and obstinance and compassion, he was her slave. The yearning comprehension in his chest filled him with terror, but mostly, relief. He could love. He was not ice and stone. For all its danger, the realisation of his love freed him.

He would never, ever tell her. He couldn't burden her with his own longings, create obligation when he had promised he would not.

But nor could he keep her.

It was time to let her go.

CHAPTER EIGHTEEN

Maybe she should change into the ivory dress, the one with the embroidered flowers, instead of the mint green. When she wore that dress, he always looked up and stared a little longer than at other times. But the green was bright and fresh and a contrast to high summer. Green spoke of new beginnings.

'And my white bonnet, please, Letitia. The one that sits back from my face.'

Letitia removed the white cotton and lace from the box. Rosanna steadied the fluttering in her stomach. It was only one tiny sentence. Simple, especially for her, who always had a word for the silence.

I want you to be my real husband. I want to live here, even after everything is sorted. I don't want a lord or an heir or anyone else. I want you.

Oh, the agony. It wasn't something she could blurt out over breakfast or tuck into a conversation over the headlines. How could she find the right moment to spill the secrets of her heart?

What if he said no?

On the walk home from the exchange the night before, her arm linked in his, her every step and breath heavy with incandescence and exhilaration, the words had hummed on her lips. But when she looked to him, he looked away. When she eased into him, he pulled back. He had seemed to fold in on himself, lost. The man who had been so transparent and giving had shuttered himself more rigidly than ever before. But after sharing so much, feeling so much, and touching so much, she couldn't be imagining the spark. There had to be the possibility of more.

'There you go, milady. Pretty as can be.' Letitia straightened a curl into obedience. 'Is there anything more? Are you going riding today?'

'I'm hoping to spend the morning with my husband,' she replied.

Rosanna rose from her seat before the dresser and checked herself in the mirror. Smooth dress, cinched waist, neat hair... Perfect. Her slippers hushed along the hallway, and as she walked, she trailed her fingers over the fabric wallpaper that she had chosen, which Felix and Hugh had hung the week before. As her fingertips rubbed each ridge between the joins, her body felt a little more grounded, like the walls welcomed her, like she might belong in this house. At the top of the stairs, she paused to settle the fear and hope in her chest.

Just three words, Rosie. Of all the millions you've spoken in your life, it's only three words.

The wood pressed firm through her slippers as she swept down the stairs. Maybe over breakfast she'd suggest that she could join him on his morning walk to the bank. Or he could take her to the hotel. Or she could...

A scuff and a knock came from the entrance. In the lobby at the base of the stairs, Rosanna turned away from the hall that led to the dining room and the smell of their small mornings. She inched around the corner.

'Have you already broken your fast?' she asked, her voice catching.

Phineas barely flicked a glance at her, staring at the paper in his hands. 'I am heading to the bank early. We have a new client. He is very particular about his margins.'

'No, you aren't.' Rosanna stepped fully into the entrance hall. The sun streaming through the arched window over the door had turned the air stifling, and it clogged her next breath. 'You don't have your umbrella. You never walk to the bank without your umbrella. You've carried it all summer, like every bank clerk.' She sidled around the room to stand between him and the door. 'Where are you really going?'

'To the bank,' he repeated. He opened his coat, but before he could shove the note into his pocket, she strode forwards and ripped it from his grasp.

'That's my mail!' he growled, and lunged to snatch it back. But Rosanna was too fast. If she could sneak the last biscuit from a plate before the other Hempel children, she could out-swipe Phineas. She shook the piece of paper out and scanned the typeset of black and red ink.

'Argonauts Trading have a warehouse by the docks? I'll get my coat.'

'No!' Phineas snapped. 'It's too dangerous! If Lord Richard sees you there, he might try to hurt you. And you... You'll only make a mess of it. You will cause problems, like you always do.'

'Make a mess of things? I help you,' she protested. 'I picked the lock. I figured out the duplicate ledgers, and I—'

'Beginner's luck, Hempel,' he said, his tone flat and dry. 'I don't need to rely on it. This is too important. I've had enough of this city and of you. It's time this finished. We both need to move on.'

The bitterness of his words hung in the architraves longer than their echo. Silence lingered until it ached, and her heart, that pathetic lump in her chest, seemed to stop beating with the harsh whipping of his words. He snatched the paper from her grasp and kept his head bowed as he folded it into an uneven mass, halved over and again too many times, then shoved it into his coat pocket.

'But—' her voice scratched. She needed three words. Three little words.

'Pack your things,' he said, each syllable hard and splitting. 'You'll be home before nightfall. I hope so, anyway.'

'You *hope* so?' Anger, frustration, and damn it, embarrassment clashed and collided in her chest. 'You hope I will be gone? *You* started this.' She stabbed an accusatory finger at him. 'You brought me here. You insisted we do things according to *your* plan—'

'And you forced yourself into my work, and you made everything complicated! You filled my house with people and noise and mess—'

'With life!' Damn the pleading in her voice. 'I thought you liked it. I thought you might—'

Love me. I thought you might, one day.

A knock came at the door, a brassy beat that echoed into the emptiness.

'Out of the way, Hempel. I have work to do.'

Rosanna held her ground. If he went, he might get hurt. If he went, he might solve the mystery without her.

If he went, he might not come back.

The thump at the door came again, more insistent. Hugh stepped into the entrance, humming to himself as he forged an oblivious path between them.

'I am not taking callers,' Rosanna said as she sidled out of the way. 'I am about to go out.'

'Like hell you are,' Phineas growled.

Hugh paused for a long moment, his unsure gaze flicking between the two of them. The knock came again, and before Hugh could dither further, the door opened. A hand slapped against the wood, and Iris, her cheeks flushed as red as her hair, stamped into the entrance.

'No one came.' She clutched a roughly typed sheet of thin, blue copy paper in one hand and shook it at the two of them. 'We have our meetings every Tuesday morning. We have held meetings on a Tuesday for more than a year. I plan and I organise and I compromise. People sleep through them. People avoid them. People pick fights and create issues, and still I try. But I shouldn't bother because no one cares, because no one came!'

Cold guilt shot through Rosanna's rage. She had completely forgotten, and to judge by the way Phineas adjusted his collar and bit his lip, he had, too.

'I am needed at the bank,' Phineas said softly, his tone weighted with apology. 'Why don't you discuss it with Rosanna? She is staying home this morning. Hugh, sort tea for the ladies.'

'I am not staying home,' Rosanna snapped. 'I don't give a damn what you say, I am going with you, and Iris should come too!' Rosanna kept her eyes locked on Phineas as she pointed, rudely, at Iris. 'No one knows Collins, Vincent, and Sanders like her. She can help.'

'I cannot put the future countess in danger,' Phineas said, with a glance over Iris's shoulder to where Lord Dalton was just stepping off the road. He ascended the stairs, taking them two at a time.

'Danger? Who's in danger?' Hamish reached the doorway and stopped beside his wife. 'Are we going on an adventure?'

Phineas slapped his hand onto the entrance table, its thump resounding and silencing all discussion. '*We* are not going anywhere.' He gritted the words out between clenched teeth, his nostrils flaring. 'There is no adventure. *I* am going to undertake some work for the bank. Like normal.'

Iris barked a laugh. 'Normal? For heaven's sake, Phineas, we all know you have some secret double life.'

Phineas's mouth contorted through silent objections and questions. How delightful to see him not purposefully quiet, but utterly lost for words.

'We do?' Hamish said, looking between Iris and Phineas.

Iris rolled her eyes. 'I've travelled the world and met many people. And yes, many people from banks. I may not know the specifics of what you do, but you are obviously more than a clerk. Now, what's this about Mr Sanders? Has he been acting *inappropriately*?' Iris, normally so calm and kind, bristled with ire. 'Hamish, call Mr Rogers to prepare the carriage. And will you sit with Papa until we return?'

'No.' Hamish may have been a future earl, but he could still stamp his foot like a petulant child. 'I am not staying behind while everyone has another adventure without me.'

'But...' Iris stalled as she looked to her husband. A narrow, discordant gaze settled between them. Worry creased Iris's brow.

'Mason will manage,' he said. 'Or send for Jonah to sit with him.' Hamish took Iris's hand and kissed her knuckles. 'You are my everything. You know that. But we need more than memories. We need fresh adventures.'

Outside of her own parents, Rosanna couldn't remember seeing such a moment of normalcy, of marital misalignment, of two souls so perfectly suited butting heads. Of humble perfection.

A small grin tugged at Iris's lips. 'It has been a while, hasn't it?' She lunged at her husband and planted a kiss on his cheek. 'Come on Lord La-di-dah. Fetch the cavalry. I'll tell Gena.' Iris rounded on her and Phineas. 'I could spot a swindle from Scotland. You will not leave without me.'

'But—' Phineas stammered.

'From Scotland!' she repeated, and with a swish and a cackling laugh of excitement, Iris and Hamish rushed down the stairs and crossed to Number 4.

Phineas waved a hand in surrender as they left. Rosanna murmured to Hugh and gave him his leave. She leant against the wall while Phineas paced the length of the entrance, grumpy and agitated. With each frustrated turn, her heart tore a little more, the rip primitive and pained. This was it. Like Iris and Hamish, they were setting off on an adventure, but theirs would cast their lives into disparate directions instead of forging a new bond.

Phineas reached for his umbrella, then hesitated. Rosanna took a slow breath of confusion and maddening panic. The jagged edges of loving without receiving love in return grated, visceral and raw. She would help to free him from this life that he wanted to escape. She would cast him into the horizons of possibility by planting both feet firmly here, in the street of all her life. And at the end, she would let him go.

Inside the carriage, Iris settled beside Phineas. 'Tell me everything,' she said.

Hamish leant back in his seat, shook his head, and chuckled. 'This street.'

The horses took each corner, travelled each street both too fast and too slow. Every pause jumbled Rosanna's breath, and she stared out the window, only holding the world inside the carriage at the fringes of her awareness. Buildings, people, life jumbled and blurred as they passed.

Eventually, Iris ran out of questions and reached across the carriage to hold her husband's hand.

Phineas bunched his fingers into a fist and propped his chin against them as he studied the line of traffic outside. The carriage slowed, then stopped. Tall brick warehouses flanked each window, and in the distance, the Thames slapped against ships' hulls. The clang of industry hummed through the air, a mix of engines huffing, whistles screaming, and the mournful bellow of a steamer. Phineas tapped her knee. 'We're here,' he whispered, then flung the door open. 'Ready for one last escapade, Mrs Babbage?'

'After you,' she said.

But he had already gone.

Chapter Nineteen

Phineas didn't cast a look behind him once he hit the path. He couldn't—one glimpse of Rosanna and the life about to be lost to him, and his resolve would flee. He was going to lose the shape of breakfast in a sunlit room and walls that changed their pattern every other week and plump lips and indulgent smiles. He ground his teeth in commitment.

He would set that free. Set *her* free. Maybe make amends for every other failure in his life, too.

'Are you certain you have the right address? This place looks as if it was abandoned decades ago.' Rosanna tipped her chin upwards. A dot of light pinched her lovely upturned nose.

Phineas turned with the rest of them to look up at the old warehouse.

Paint peeled from the front door in thick slivers. The pintucked mortice between the red bricks, crisp and purposeful, spoke of past pride in construction. Dirt and soot caked over small rectangular panes on large windows with brick lintels, and a sunbeam snagged on a jagged corner of freshly broken glass. Slashes in the iron veranda over their heads let in strips of morning, and while the holes and loose nails suggested desertion, the solid beams and decorative cornices spoke of care, an artistic eye, and purpose. Once, this place had mattered to someone.

Phineas jumped to bash the steel sign over the door, then took a few short steps back to avoid the shower of dust and soot that scattered over the path. Hamish, who was taller than him, took a handkerchief from his pocket to wipe at the bottom edges.

'A. Is that a B? And another B... Iris... Did your father have a warehouse here?'

Hamish continued cleaning the sign until he had swept the bottom half of it and only a thin film of dust coated the top half. The gold had lost its sheen and mellowed, but the word itself was unmistakable. The building had once belonged to Iris's father and had proudly displayed the name *Abberton—Merchant and Trader*.

'Papa used to talk about this place. Before he... well, before. I think this was his first warehouse, from when he started importing tiles from Italy. He said it was near the river and the bigger traders. He used to watch them. At times, he'd go down and talk to the foremen and the workers, to try and understand how he might become a little better than everyone else. As he grew, he leased space rather than purchase bigger warehouses. I didn't realise he had kept this one. Although maybe he didn't either.'

Hamish wrapped his arm around his wife's shoulders. Iris took a slow breath and gave him a weak smile as she patted his arm.

'What's the plan?' Hamish asked.

'There is no plan because none of you should be here. Especially not you.' Phineas glared at Rosanna. How could he keep her safe if she was so determined to put herself in harm's way?

'This whole mess directly concerns me. I absolutely should be here,' she replied with a huff.

'For once, could you not argue with me? Could you perhaps—'

'Shh!' Iris tapped his shoulder. 'There are people inside. I can hear them.'

The four of them gathered beneath a window which stood slightly ajar. Phineas and Hamish crouched down, while the ladies in full skirts flanked either side of the glass. Rosanna tilted her body towards the sound, looking anywhere but at him. Good. Her anger would make today easier. If he baited and goaded her, as he'd done so often with others, would she voluntarily cast him aside? Everyone had left him—his mother, his stepfather, Imogen, Arley... Why not Rosanna, too?

Phineas tipped his ear towards the open window. A mélange of yelling and frustration teased the air, but nothing distinct enough to be understood. He pulled himself up. Four vague shapes were moving behind the soot-streaked glass, disappearing and reappearing in blurs. Phineas lifted the window frame a half inch. Shouts and criticisms squeezed through the small gap. The four of them leant closer in unison.

'...ridiculous... gone too far.'

'We agreed this... what we would do!'

'People might get hurt.'

'—said profits were up, that you... managing the business better... Abberton and his daughter. If we'd known...'

'Money does not last forever! I thought you wanted a little extra, not to buy another townhouse for a new mistress!'

Rosanna grasped her skirts, hoisted them up, and crouched between him and Hamish. Iris joined them. They crowded over one another, elbows and knees jostling for space until the four of them slotted together and watched through the gap.

The four men of Argonauts Trading—Mr Collins, the horse-racing enthusiast; Mr Vincent, the philanderer; Mr Sanders, the fastidious bookkeeper; and Lord Richard, the failed investor of the exchange—circled one another like angry street cats vying over a discarded bone. Wooden pallets and crates formed a wall behind them. The boxes looked as if they'd been sitting idle for an age, dappled with grey dust and with faded black stamps along the woodgrain.

Hamish peeked up over the sill. 'What's in all those boxes? Is it stock for the department store?'

Rosanna shook her head. 'That stamp is for Thornfield and Co. They went out of business ten years ago. And women may do ridiculous things for fashion, but no woman is going to wear a dress that needs a crinoline any longer. Who do they think they are going to sell these things to?'

'I don't think it's for selling,' Phineas said. 'I think it's for kindling.'

Still arguing with one another, the men of Argonauts Trading clustered around the boxes. Mr Sanders dropped a heavy ledger, maybe the one Rosanna had found in their offices, onto one. Lord Richard flipped the book open and ripped a large page from the binding. He scrunched it into a ball and stuffed the mass between a gap.

Rosanna rested her elbow on Phineas's knee to steady herself. Then, curse her, she stayed. Reliant on him. Needing him.

He leant in as close as he dared, hoping to avoid her scent, but he still inhaled her freshness, the lingering aroma of roses and sunshine. 'Why would they burn it all?' he asked. 'They'll have nothing to sell for their big share push, and the company's expansion—'

'But maybe that was the plan all along,' Rosanna finished for him. Phineas held her gaze as realisation lit between the two of them, then fizzed and burned as they solved the riddle in the same instance. 'That's how they're going to keep everyone's money,' she continued. 'They'll say they lost all their stock in the fire, then claim bankruptcy.'

'It was one thing to take the company from us, but I will not let them destroy it. This is not how Papa's dream ends.' Iris stood and marched past the rows of grimy windows to heave the door open. 'Gents!' she bellowed into the cavern. 'Might I have a word?'

'I am not missing this.' Hamish scarpered after his wife.

Rosanna rested a hand on the window ledge, as if she was about to push herself up to follow, but paused. Instead, she turned to face Phineas. She brushed at the dust that had settled on his shoulders. 'I'm sorry for ruining everything. And for making your life intolerable. It's likely little consolation, but I... I will always be grateful for your help.'

'I didn't mean what I said, about you ruining everything.' A little of the dirt from the windows had smudged its way onto her cheek, and he wiped it away with his thumb. 'I work best alone, is all.'

'Have you always worked alone?' Rosanna asked.

'Of course,' he replied.

'Then how do you know that's your best?'

Always one for the off-hand questions with complex answers. The simplicity of it crunched, like an unexpected punch. He didn't know—but oh, how he yearned to find out. He ached to take her hand and confess as much, but he shoved the urge down. He was a former convict, a bank clerk with a name that wasn't even his. She'd do better without him. He couldn't give her even a sliver of the life she deserved.

'Do you want to watch from here or follow?' he asked.

'Follow,' she said, and gave him her most spectacular and mischievous of grins. Sunlight in her eyes, energy and anticipation in her step, brimming with life and vitality, she skipped past him. 'As if I'm going to watch Lord Richard's downfall from a distance.'

Phineas followed her into the warehouse.

There, the four men of Argonauts stood frozen with their mouths hanging agape, like a line of well-dressed fish. They were all staring at Iris. Hatless, gloveless, stiff with rage, she glowered back at them, even as they shuffled their feet with guilt. Iris crossed the distance to the boxes and the ledgers at a steady pace. Lord Richard took a menacing step towards her, only for Hamish to pull himself up to his full height. Lord Richard promptly faltered, then moved back into line.

Iris possessed one of the keenest minds Phineas had ever known, not just for numbers but for pounds and pence. She tallied columns, read annotations, and, like him, she understood the stories hidden in the margins. Methodically, she scanned each page of the heavy book, then turned to the next, her brow furrowing deeper. Lips set thin, she turned to Mr Sanders.

'It wasn't meant to be like this,' Mr Sanders stammered. 'At first, it was just one little advance. It seemed so harmless. Then half a per cent increase in the dividends. Things became a little worrisome, so we thought a new board member to replace Abberton might help. Lord Richard seemed to know so much about shares. But he lost as much as Mr Collins at the races. It all happened so fast.'

'You took over one of the healthiest companies in London. It's gone.' Iris slammed the ledger closed. 'You must refund the shareholders. You have to tell them it was a lie. Or I will. I will take it to the papers.'

'No!' Mr Sanders cried. 'If this becomes public, the investors will come to the office, demanding answers. Crowds like that grow angry, sometimes violent. If you make it public, all those people will lose everything—'

'They don't *have* anything,' Iris countered.

'But they think they do!' Mr Sanders pressed his palm against his forehead, his eyes widening with panic. 'They have bits of paper that are their fortunes. If you tell them the truth, you'll destroy them. Terrible things happen when companies fail. Remember Tipperary!' Sanders pleaded. His hectic gaze darted between all of them, settling on Phineas.

'Tipperary? In Ireland?' Hamish asked.

'Not Tipperary the place, the Tipperary Bank,' Phineas said. 'The owner lost all the money, everyone's money, in bad investments on the stock market. He took out loans from other banks, stole customer's bonds, embezzled the family fortune. When he couldn't find a way out of the debt, he shot himself. But when the bank's failure became public... Let's just say he wasn't the only one to suffer a terrible fate. People will do things you can't imagine for money.'

They would pretend to love. Pretend to hate. They would destroy other people. They would shatter a world.

The only thing more malicious than greed was revenge.

What would Iris do?

'How much debt?' Iris asked. 'Show me.'

'It looks worse than it is. It just—'

'Show me!' Iris roared. Mr Sanders startled, then turned a few pages before pointing at a column. Iris raised a shaking hand to cover her mouth. Her shoulders sagged, and she pinched her eyes closed, drawing a deep breath. When she opened them again, she turned to Mr Sanders. She pulled out her purse and unclasped the fastening. 'You are going to sell the company to me. The entire company. Every building, every share, every piece of old merchandise. I will make you an exceedingly generous offer. I will pay one pound to you...' Iris laid a coin on the table. 'One for Mr Vincent.' She placed another beside it, then two more. 'One for Mr Collins. And one for Lord Richard. I will manage everything from here. If you try to launch another company, my associate Mr Babbage will have you all denounced at the Exchange, and you won't even be able to open a bank account or get a line of credit at the grocers. Do you understand?'

Mr Sanders slid the coin from the table into his palm. Still not meeting her gaze, Mr Collins and Mr Vincent nodded.

'That's not enough,' Lord Richard protested. 'I need more than a pound. I need—' He looked straight at Rosanna. 'You.'

Desperation drove some men to violence and depravity, but in others, it brought on intense stupidity. Lord Richard, a man of panache, flair, and smooth words, was clearly one of the latter. His foolishness made him fast, and with a lunge and a cry, he grabbed Rosanna and wrapped his elbow around her neck. 'Don't think I won't hurt her!' he shouted. 'I will. Give me her money. All of it.'

Fear lit Rosanna's expression for a sharp second before she found Phineas and he held her steady gaze until the nip of terror dissolved. With an eye roll and a smirk, Rosanna brought her heel down hard on Lord Richard's boot. When he yelped, she slid from his hold, but instead of running like Phineas had taught her, she turned and shoved Lord Richard in the chest. He staggered, but before he could fall, Phineas strode forward, caught him by the collar, and dragged him away. He hauled the lord across the dusty floorboards, then shoved him against the wall. Lord Richard winced as his head collided with the bricks.

'No one touches my wife!' Phineas spat. Fury engulfed every inch of him, more than the coward deserved, but when it came to Rosanna, everything engulfed him. 'Where is Pennington? Why is he in London?'

'I never met him, only his men,' Lord Richard spluttered. 'He swears he'll hurt my family if I don't pay. I have a sister. She's so little... Please. I never meant to hurt anyone. I don't know what to do.'

Phineas tightened his hold on the lord's collar. He tried to draw upon cold indifference. To let the man be the victim of his own stupidity. What was it to him if Pennington went after Lord Richard's family or the man himself? Phineas would be so far away by the time the news reached the papers, he'd never even know.

His grip slackened. He reached into his pocket and pulled out his cheque book and a pen. Then he scrawled Rosanna's worth across the bill of exchange. 'You no longer owe Pennington.' Phineas tucked the note into the man's pocket. 'You owe me, and you will repay me by staying away from my wife. One step wrong, I will call in my debt. I'm not a monster like him. I'm a far simpler man. I won't come for your family. I will come for you. Understood?'

Lord Richard coughed as Phineas twisted his collar. 'Understood,' he scratched out. 'I'll settle with him, then go abroad. I swear it.'

Phineas let go and turned away. Behind him, Lord Richard crumpled to the floor. Before him, Rosanna splayed a hand across her chest. He tried to read the look in her eyes, the grimness in her expression, but he ached, his body too wrung out and depleted to decipher any of it.

'It's done,' he said to her, his voice echoing hollow in his chest. 'You're free.'

CHAPTER TWENTY

Rosanna hauled herself into the carriage. Free. She was free. Free of Lord Richard's bungling, free of their arrangement. Except maybe what Phineas meant was that he, himself, was free of her. The liberation tasted bitter as she forced herself to swallow.

Free.

Iris and Hamish climbed into the carriage, and Phineas clambered in after them. Like pins on a map, all four of them fastened themselves into the corners. Iris held a fist to her mouth while Hamish crossed his arms over his chest. Phineas spun his hat. The vehicle pulled away, streaming past the warehouses and away from the river. Silence, brittle and angry, buzzed between them.

'Two companies?' Hamish shot at Iris. 'How are we to manage two companies? And the estate? The earl is not getting any younger. Neither are we.'

'I'm not going to run the company.' Iris kept her steady focus on the street. 'Not even a miracle could save it. I saw the numbers.'

Rosanna turned to Phineas, who nodded sagely. 'The ledgers don't lie,' he said.

Iris gasped her next breath, then tried to choke down a sob. Tears welled in her eyes, and with a blink, they spilled down her cheeks. Hamish slid across the seat and gathered her into his arms. Iris, strong, stubborn, and intelligent, collapsed against her husband's chest and snuffled into his coat with a wail.

Rosanna moved a little closer to Phineas. 'What will happen?' she asked.

'To settle the debts and refund the shareholders, any assets will have to be sold.' He kept his voice low. 'Property, stock. Invoices called in and payments squared. Some of the accounts have not been addressed in more than a year, and the board drew off heavy profits. Some traders, especially smaller ones, won't be able to find the money they owe. You could force their hand, but for what? To create more misery? Most will seek terms. Some will ignore the demands.'

'Everything he built. What we built. Gone.' Iris rocked with the sway of the carriage.

'What about the workers?' Hamish asked.

Iris wiped her cheeks. 'We'll give them notice of what's coming. Pay what they're owed, which is more than they would have received if the company had failed. They'll have time to find new employment. If there's one thing London always needs, it's willing hands and strong backs.'

'And those that can't find work?' Hamish asked.

'We'll find a way.' Iris sniffled. 'We always find a way.'

'Phineas.' Rosanna leant close. 'You can't let Iris sell off the company alone. It will break her.'

Phineas flicked her a scowl, then tucked his hands tight against his chest.

'Can't you help her?'

'I couldn't ask it,' Iris interjected. 'You two are newly married. You need time away to settle into one another. You need—'

'We aren't married.' Phineas announced. 'It was a front to stop Mrs Crofts from gossiping while we worked out what business Lord Richard was involved in. Everything will be annulled. And after this, no man would be stupid enough to think he can fool Rosanna Hempel into a loveless marriage for her money again.'

'You seemed so...' Hamish frowned. 'So happy. Not so much you, Rosanna, you're always happy. But I've never known Phineas to smile so much. Truth be told, I didn't even know you *could* smile.'

The carriage slowed to a stop, right at the point in the row of townhouses where Numbers 1 and 3 met. Phineas climbed out first, and on the pavement, he held out his hand. Rosanna steadied herself against him as she descended the few thin steps. After she had alighted and the carriage had rolled away, he kept hold of her.

'You don't have to leave tonight if you don't want to,' Phineas said. 'You can take a few days to get your things packed and moved. For appearances' sake, it probably shouldn't be too long though.' He squeezed her fingertips. 'Will you come inside?'

'I'd like to speak with my parents.' She withdrew from his hold. 'I'd like to tell them what happened myself.'

They walked in parallel up the stairs to each door, taking each step at almost the same pace. Phineas paused on the landing. Rosanna tapped at the door to her family home. Light spilled onto her feet, and laughter and family filled the brief incandescence.

'I'll be home soon,' she called across the gap.

The door to Number 1 snapped off her words.

Some hours later, Rosanna walked down the stairs of her family home, took the few short steps across the pavement, then ascended to the house where she had felt herself grow, where she'd learnt to feel love and passion. To the place where she had transformed from a girl into a woman. Into becoming all the things she'd been so certain she would have to flee home to experience, to fly dozens of bunched miles to understand. Yet, all along, she hadn't needed distance or forced bravado. Only belief.

Belief in herself. Belief in her worth. And to find a different way of understanding her value—not as a darling or a diamond, but as Rosanna. She fumbled at the key in her pocket, drew it out, and twisted it in the lock. The door clicked open. Once inside, she secured the entrance again. She untied her bonnet and laid it on the table.

From deep within, she tried to find the resolve to condense her feelings into a few sentences, into a plea for acceptance, and into a hope for something new. To mould her words into the argument she'd been so intent on making that morning. But her heart beat weakly. Her hope had shattered when she'd seen how viciously Phineas had questioned Lord Richard, how desperate he'd been to find Pennington.

All he wanted was the woman on the mantlepiece.

The clink of glass on wood filtered through from the library. A fresh bottle of whisky sat on the table between the two chairs, the amber liquor still inching into the neck.

With a smooth gulp, Phineas emptied his glass. 'I had Hugh go out so we could celebrate. I poured you a drink.' He clinked his empty glass against her half-full one, then let it drop. His head fell back against the leather. His breaths came heavy, his chest rising and falling with a slight snore.

Rosanna curled into the space beside his knee. He shifted with a slight *hmph*, making room for her in the chair, and she rested her cheek against his chest. His breath settled back into a steady rhythm. Just as she felt herself drifting into sleep, he trailed a finger lightly over her cheek.

Tomorrow, she would tell him what she'd learnt. About Imogen.

Tonight, he was still hers.

Chapter
Twenty-one

'I don't like surprises.' Phineas looked across at Rosanna, who sat opposite him in the cab they'd taken from Chelmsford station.

She smiled, but not with her eyes. 'You'll like this one,' she said. 'Trust me.'

Perhaps she was tired. Or maybe it was relief that this chapter of her life had closed. He knew from each transition of his own that sometimes, instead of elation, one only felt depleted. The small joy, the adjustment, perhaps even feelings of celebration would come later, but today, the gnawing emptiness and looming question of *what next* created a void.

And what next, indeed? His original plan remained within his grasp. He could still take the train south, then a boat, then another boat—and after that, he hadn't decided if he'd take another boat or a train. He would be completely lost to the system by then and would reinvent himself with a new name on a passport. He would forge it himself using the skills he'd learnt in Newgate, as he'd done before.

Outside, green strips of farms and long rows of stone walls and thick hedgerows sped by. Arley's estate had been close to this district, and with a mix of guilt and contentment, he thought of the duchess, Arley's mother. She must also be grappling with a life upended, still searching for the next in line to claim the title. Was his former drinking friend and companion in sullen Christmases happy? Had love been worth the sacrifice?

Rosanna steadied herself as the carriage leant into a slightly rougher dip in the road, and the next thump of Phineas's heart hurt a little more than any beat he'd felt before. Because the emptiness that gaped before him had nothing to do with resolution. It lay in knowing that Rosanna was free to return to her life. To petition for the separation and annulment that he and Lawrence had agreed on and that he wouldn't contest.

But what if he did? What if he made his case, not to a court demanding the vows they made be upheld, but now, to her?

His wife on the opposite side of the carriage. So distant, even though their knees brushed as the carriage swayed. If he stretched, he could take her hand. He wouldn't have to raise his voice. If he could find the words...

I know I'm not the life you wanted, but please... Could we be more? Maybe? Could we try?

Phineas jerked forwards as the vehicle pulled to a stop, then jolted back against the seat. Rosanna smiled again, that same stretched smile with only her lips. She looked out of the window. Phineas followed her gaze.

A rough wooden fence ran alongside the road. Behind it, a small stretch of lazy grass, clover, and wildflowers rippled with the breeze. A cow, ready for milking, lowered her head and ripped off a mouthful of pasture, then looked up to them, chewing methodically, as if in deep contemplation.

A woman in a pretty, practical floral dress and a white apron stepped out of a grey stone cottage. She paused, placed one hand on the doorframe, and used the other to shield her eyes from the light. A little older. A little thinner. But unmistakably—

'How did you find her?' he asked, his heart flooded with relief and fear.

'Rookeries have their own whispers. Father made some quiet enquiries and passed around a few coins. Country cousins and friends who've moved to the city don't talk readily to strangers, but they do trust one of their own. Eventually, he gathered enough information to piece together something worth chasing. He sent one of his friends, Seamus, who he's known forever and trusts completely. She looks almost the same as the photo on the mantlepiece, save for the colour of her hair.'

'No one else knows she's here? She's safe?'

'As safe as a woman in Essex can be.'

Phineas swung the door open, then turned back. 'I want to talk about what happens next. With us.'

'We have plenty of time for talking,' Rosanna replied as she fidgeted with her fingers, sliding one over the other. Then, catching herself, she stilled them in her skirts.

Again, that same painful thump beat against his ribs, but now it left a trace of hope. 'You swear it?'

'Go,' she said. 'Imogen has quite the tale for you.'

Phineas climbed down from the hack. As he approached the fence, he removed his bowler and spun it uselessly by the brim. Imogen moved to the edge of the shadows on the awning. 'Charlie?'

His name, the one he'd had before London, rang foreign in his ears. 'It's Phineas now,' he called.

She laughed. 'I should have known. It suits you better.' She crossed the yard. Chickens scuttled out of her path, then circled back behind her like small, feathered bodyguards. She swung the gate open. 'I go by Mabel now. Would you like a cup of tea? Ale? Something to eat?'

He followed as though caught in a dream, his feet touching the ground but no sensation registering. All this time, Imogen had been living a simple life not far from London. All this time, she had been safe.

Once inside her cottage, she gestured for him to take a seat at the small wooden table. He lowered himself onto the bench.

'What happened to you?' he asked. 'I waited by the bridge. I waited until morning. I thought he'd hurt you.'

'You didn't get my note?' Imogen—no, Mabel now—set a heavy copper kettle on the stove. 'I wrote to you, about three months after I ran. A card with no message except for my initial, to let you know I was safe. I didn't dare try before then.' She fed a few sticks into the flaming round belly of the fire. 'You needn't have worried. He wouldn't let me go, but he also wouldn't bother to chase me. He'd lost all my money. I was no use to him.'

Three months... By then he'd cut ties in Edinburgh and hopped from village to village with his new identity to piece together a string of new memories, both his own and in the minds of others. He'd changed his dress from tweeds to black, swapped his hat from a cap to bowler, and had found a position in the clerks' office at Empire Savings and Loans.

'I went to London to look for you. I've been looking for you for years.' Anger, resentment, and a hefty dash of self-pity collided in his chest. So many damn feelings. Part of him wanted to rage, but after the past few weeks, he lacked the will. 'Why run alone? Why didn't you meet me on the bridge?'

She set a mug of tea before him, then settled into the seat opposite. 'You wanted to save me, save anybody who came your way. I knew if I tried to explain that I wanted to move on alone, you wouldn't listen, and I'd lose my resolve. I'd been reliant on one man since I said I do. I would have just been trading him for another, as well-meaning as you were. I had to save myself.'

Phineas twisted the gold band on his left hand. Imogen—no, not Imogen, Mabel—nodded at it. 'She's quite something, your wife.'

'It's not real. She was in trouble and I—' He coughed over the words as they caught in his throat. 'I wanted to help her. And I did.' He slid the ring over his knuckle, not quite able to summon the willpower to take it off, even though there was no need for it anymore.

'And because she doesn't need saving anymore, it's over? Is that it?' she asked. 'There's a look on your face that I never saw when you were with me. And it's a look I recognise from the farmer across the lane who keeps bringing me flowers. I don't need his flowers, my garden is full of them. But still, he brings them.'

'I was going to ask her to stay,' he confessed. 'I can't find the right words.'

She took his mug to the sink along with her own and tipped out the dregs. Glanced at the clock, then out the window. 'You had better find those words, and fast. Or you're going to spend a good deal of time thinking about her leaving, and I think her memory will haunt you for longer than mine.'

His mouth went dry as he swung himself over the bench and pushed back from the table. He leant over the sink to peer out the window to where he'd left Rosanna in the cab. The view beyond opened to the small garden, the fence, and the road and paddocks beyond.

No cab.

No Rosanna.

Phineas grasped Imogen's shoulders, kissed each cheek, and dragged her against his chest as she laughed. 'Good luck with... With everything. I'll send you papers so you can marry that farmer. If you want to.'

He burst from the cottage. For the first time since that day he'd walked away from his post and deserted, he was completely without a plan. Panic and terror gripped him, but underneath it all lay a groundswell of joy. He had something, *someone* to worry about. Someone to fight for. Someone to beg, to chase, to risk everything for. He didn't bother with the gate, only gripped the rail and swung his legs over it to land firmly on the road. Little mounds of sticky mud gathered against two wide strips, where the departing cab had dug long lines into the mud. London wasn't even a smudge on the horizon.

He'd better move fast.

Chapter Twenty-two

It was better this way.

Rosanna rested her forehead against the glass. Thin fingers of cold leeched into her skin. In the courtyard below, rain dotted uneven puddles amongst the pavers. Thunder rumbled low in the distance before building to groan and grumble against the windows and walls.

London wept the tears she would not cry.

The pain of watching Phineas climb out of the cab and make his hesitant hello to the woman he'd lost felt more at home in a rainy city. Occasionally, regret burst in her stomach, and she had to blink through the haze until it quietened. While she knew she'd never be happy if she hadn't found Imogen, part of her scolded her stubborn self. Something had been growing between them, in an awkward and slightly haphazard way. But if she hadn't told him the truth, she'd always have known that she'd been his second choice. And she hated being second to anyone.

Either way, she was bound to lose.

Rosanna picked up the travel book she'd taken from the library downstairs and thumbed through it until she found an entry for Brighton. They could expect warm, clear days, the odd drizzle, sometimes a slight sea breeze.

Three light blouses, two jackets, just as many skirts, and one formal dinner dress should be sufficient.

Johannes would keep her busy looking at possible buildings to renovate, and hopefully he'd be too occupied with having a project of his own to make her talk about any of it.

Maybe the salt air would ease the ache in her chest.

This had always been the plan, and Phineas had kept his promise to see it through. Now he could start over with the woman he'd lost. He'd take on a new name, build a new life, and find some peace. He'd be happy. She wanted him to be happy.

As for herself and her plans—Father would process the paperwork, and the marriage would be annulled. She would move home and continue working at the Aster. And no matter what her stationery said, she'd be Mrs Babbage, possibly for the rest of her days. How could she imagine a future with someone else when she'd lost her stubborn heart to him?

Rosanna shook out a blouse, folded it, and placed it in her trunk. Thunder cracked again, so loud now that its vibrations filtered through her slippers. As it faded, a new chorus echoed against the incessant rain on the windows and the wind butting the sash. Thumping feet and shouts, high and panicked, reverberated through the house.

'Rosanna! Where are you?' Rain pelted the glass, and the wind screeched as it tried to pry through the gaps. 'Rosanna! Mrs Babbage! Are you here?'

Dear Lord, he had returned. An anxious tremor rattled her bones, more potent than the grumble of the thunder.

He hadn't brought Imogen here, had he? Would he force her to leave to make room for his beloved in this house? She couldn't stand the shame.

The door banged open, its crack against the wall accompanied by a flash of lightning that lit the walls with white clarity. Phineas stumbled into the room. Mist clung to the crests and points of his dishevelled hair, and he wiped a hand across his thin-set mouth to flick little droplets of water onto the floor. A splattered trail of mud ran from his hems to his thighs. Rosanna stared, transfixed by his disorder, her mind whirling with questions while his gaze jerked around the room, from her cupboard to her clothes spread across the bed, and on to the open trunk before finally landing on her.

'Where is Felix? Letitia and Hugh? And the other one, the singing one?' He pointed at the trunk. 'Where are you going?'

'Johannes and I are heading to Brighton tomorrow. A scouting trip to find a new location for another hotel.' She dumped the blouse into the trunk. 'I may be a spoiled shrew, but I can pack my own things. I gave the staff a half day. I needed some quiet.'

'I looked out the window, and you had just gone. I was—'

'Worried? As you can see, I am perfectly well. And with Lord Richard's debts settled and the company with Iris, there is no reason for anyone to come after me.' Rosanna crossed to the cupboard. She would not be sad in his presence. If she could not have his love, she would not settle for his pity. 'Where is Imogen?'

'At her cottage. Her home.'

'When are you going back there?' Rosanna flipped through her hangers in the closet. Maybe three jackets and another two skirts. That's what she needed. More changes of clothes. More things to pluck from hangers and fold into rectangles and place in the trunk to keep her eyes and her hands busy.

'I'm not returning. Imogen has built a new life. A neighbouring farmer brings her flowers. She's happy.' He pulled at his coat-sleeve, reached out, then curled his fingers into his palm. 'Thank you for finding her.'

Rosanna willed her hands to keep sliding between the hangers, but her stupid fingers refused to cooperate. Her blue blouse, she should pack her blue...

Only his breath, still harsh and uneven, gave any indication that he had moved and was standing behind her. That and his scent, the familiar starch and fresh linen mingled with damp wool and wet hair, which collided with the lavender and cedar of her closet. A cocoon of familiarity, of comfort, of *home* surrounded her.

The lightest touch—not even a touch, just an indentation of fabric—sent a shiver over her skin. A sigh betrayed her, and no sooner had it made its traitorous escape from her lips than Phineas rested his hands on her waist, firm, anchoring, and possessive. Another soft breath of yearning, and he moved closer. Pressed a cheek to her ear. Rested his forehead against her neck. Flexed his palm and dared to pull her into him.

Rosanna forced a shallow breath. She would not lose herself. She would not lose.

'If you think I will stay your wife because she is unavailable, you are wrong,' she rasped, every syllable grating her throat as she willed her pride into silence. Still, even now she failed. 'I will not be the woman any man settles for.'

A confident creeping, a sneaking embrace... and with a stolen kiss to the pocket behind her ear, in the secret place only he had discovered, he'd ensnared her in his arms.

'My darling, when did I say I loved Imogen? I worried about her. I thought I had failed her. And when I was young, she was someone I could care about. Someone I could save. I loved the idea of her, of being needed, but it wasn't love. I know it wasn't because I have never in my life felt the way I feel for you.'

Rosanna clutched ineffectually at her blouse as it slipped from her grasp. Phineas captured her hand and interleaved her fingers with his own.

'I want you to stay. Stay here, stay as Mrs Babbage. It's a cruel ask, I know, as it's a name that means nothing, that I pulled from a newspaper on a whim, but if you will have it, it's yours. I want you to make this house our home. I want you to leave your dirty boots on the floor. I want you to stomp through the house and change the wallpaper every other week. I want to come home to a table covered in magazines and swatches. I want your family to invade as often as they need to, I want new crockery and a dozen different types of linens I can't tell apart, and I don't care about any of it as long as I come home to you. Not this house, not this street. You are my home. You.'

With a commanding tug and a twist, Phineas spun her to face him, and fool that she was, she let him. She could not lift her face to his, lest she read too much in his features and found him untrue. Drops of water had collected on the surface of a button. She tried to rub it clean but only smeared it onto his shirt. Phineas clasped her hand and kissed her knuckles.

'I want to climb into your bed every night you'll have me,' he whispered. 'I want to come down to breakfast and find you've spoilt the jam. I want a house full of noise and staff that sing and croissants for breakfast. I want a wife who bullies me into walks and picnics and things that I cannot control.' Phineas raised her chin, forcing their eyes to meet. 'Say something. Or are you going to make me blabber all afternoon?'

Normally so stoic, so unmovable, Phineas looked at her with his brow furrowed in fear, a hesitant smile, a whisper of worry in his eyes—and, like a struggling blossom at the end of a branch, a bud of bright, fresh love in that dimple that only showed on one cheek. So many emotions. They all sat so uneasily on him.

She smoothed his cheek with her thumb, then kissed the dimple. 'You are a liar, Phineas Babbage. You don't mean that about the jam.'

'I don't, I really don't. *Please* stop mixing up the jam.' He smiled properly, completely, all sunshine and hope. 'But every other word is true. Please, be my wife. Forever.'

She clasped his cheeks, pressing her lips firmly against his in reply, and he held her so tight he squeezed the breath from her lungs. His edges eased as he drew her close, and their bodies, so perfectly symmetrical in where knees bumped, hips rubbed, and chests pressed together, melded and buzzed with electricity, with the warm connection of belonging. She nodded, and through small bubbles of laughter, managed to squeeze out, 'Be my husband. Be mine,' until he banished her words with his kisses.

Rain lashed the windows, and the wind careened around corners. In the quiet, the scrunch of fabric in his palms and his little sighs and grunts quavered against her skin. Like a brewing storm, he stoked heat in the pockets of air between her clothes and filled each inhalation with expectation. He showered kisses over her with total abandon, and Rosanna greedily took all of them.

'I love the taste of you,' he murmured as he trailed his lips down her neck and plucked at her collar buttons. Those deft fingers, so meticulous and proficient, never fumbling, slipped each little fastening open and travelled down her blouse. 'I'm going to kiss every part of you. Every little dip, every delicious, silken stretch of your body, every glorious inch. Thank heavens you sent everyone out. Can I take you to bed, my wife? Let me take you to bed. Let me have all of you.'

Something about the growl in his voice, about his hunger, threw the disparity between them into sharp relief. A chasm opened. For all her audacity, it weighed in her chest and stiffened her limbs. His wife. She would be *his*.

Phineas spun her by the hips so that she faced away from him. Tantalising and gentle, he skimmed the small bumps that rippled her exposed skin, and Rosanna sighed with longing. She bowed her head with the turbulent realisation of how lost she now was. Patient and delicate, Phineas wiggled the combs from her hair, slid out her clips and pins, and discarded them on the floor. Once they were free, he tickled his fingers through her curls, stroking her lengths until each disobedient ringlet draped smooth and easy down her back. Languorously, teasingly, he drew patterns between her shoulder blades and circled each bump of her spine. The whoosh of the cord as he untied her corset merged with another crack of thunder, and by the time the angry vibrations had finished sending their tremors through the house, he had loosened the ties. Rosanna raised her arms, and Phineas slipped her corset over her head. He unbuttoned her skirt, tugged her petticoat ribbons loose, and with a puff of fabric and layers, it all crumpled to the floor.

'Why are you scared?' he asked as he planted a line of kisses along her neck. She tilted instinctively to make space for him.

'I'm not scared,' she countered.

He flicked his tongue, as if tasting her temperament. 'Uncertain?'

'I've never been more certain in my life.'

The room flashed luminescent with lightning. Phineas spun her to face him. He took both her hands in his own and held them to his chest, looking at her with his firm stare. 'What's wrong?'

'You will have all the power. In everything.'

'I will? Rosanna, Rosanna...' He crooned her name against her skin, and with each soft brush of his lips, with each rough graze of his stubble, she weakened, losing herself even more. 'I just ran three miles along rough country roads to the train station. Then I rode in the luggage van after bribing the ticket master because there were no seats. And at Paddington, in the rain, I had to fight off a country gent to get a cab. Then I paid the driver triple the fare to get me home faster than was legal. I was so scared I would arrive home to find you'd come to your senses and gone.' Inching, teasing, he gathered her chemise into his palms. As soon as he'd drawn it over her head and discarded it, he splayed his hands over her nakedness, as if the small cover they provided might shield and conceal her. The chill air, the heavy rain, her dry mouth, his warm hands, the mingling of sweat and sweetness... all of them raged through her with increasing intensity.

'I will sign any sheet of paper you place before me if it makes you feel secure. Better yet, I will write a promise here on your body so you can keep it.' Starting on her left shoulder, he circled a fingertip, tapping and skating across the breadth of her back. 'I, Phineas Babbage, aka Charlie Moffatt, aka Robert Callahan, and many other names that aren't worth remembering, swear that I will never treat Rosanna as anything other than my equal.' His body pressed warm while his fingertips glanced cold, like he was made of fire and ice. She shuddered as he stroked along her hips and over her ribs before circling her nipple with the lightest touch.

Rosanna tipped her head back, and a throaty groan of longing escaped her lips. 'You swear it?'

He squiggled a line on her lower back, like he was signing his promise. 'I am a shell without you. You send me insane, then fill me with terror. You make me grit my teeth, then laugh. I feel everything with you. Since you invaded my home, all I have done is *feel*.' He twisted her to face him again and ran his thumb across her lower lip. 'Rosanna, my beautiful Rosanna, my annoying, frustrating, and ever so intoxicating wife. The world may disagree, but I am in the palm of your hand.'

'No wonder you never talk.' Rosanna took a bold breath and unfastened his top button. 'You become ridiculously sentimental.'

His low laugh cut through the next clap of thunder, and they settled into one another, a duel of hard-headedness, witty rhetoric, and sniping transforming to care, patience, and space. Men had so many fastenings, so many pieces holding them in place, and she searched for them with her eyes and fingertips, finding them down his shirt, at his waist, where they trailed into the long line of his underclothes. Phineas tilted his head to one side, his gaze flicking and dancing over her. He removed his coat, but when he reached for his shirt cuffs, she placed a hand over his.

'I want to do this. All of it. I want to unstitch you.' She unfastened his buttons, loosened his cuffs, and pushed his shirt from his shoulders. 'Unravel and expose you.' She kissed the line where his neck met his jaw, and on his next inhale, his breath rattled. 'You will not hide from me again.'

'You are torturing me. Fully naked while you take your time to undress me. Aren't you cold?' He caressed her inner thigh.

'A little,' she said, her confession devolving into a groan as he slid his finger inside her in one deliberate, penetrating stroke, then withdrew.

'I shall have to be an attentive husband and warm you up. I do not ever want a cold wife.' And he stroked her length, opening her delicateness and awakening each little nerve, every tiny bud of energy, of desire, of need. Finally, she'd untied all of him and tugged his shirt from him. His fingertips circled and teased, and with a growl he threw her against the mattress, its springs squeaking as she landed. He wrestled his trousers down, discarded his underclothes, and launched himself onto the bed beside her. He crawled her length and poised himself above her, palms pressed into the mattress on either side. Then he lowered himself to kiss and scrape her soft belly, tasting a trail between her ribs, and drawing a nipple into his mouth. Tongue flicking against the point, he grumbled, and the small reverberations ordered every follicle to attention. Through the veil of bliss and longing, Rosanna widened her thighs. Her core, pulsing with delicate want, grew wet, and she thrummed, needy and hungry for his touch—delivered by his mouth or his hands, she did not care. With a nip at her breast, he pushed two fingers into her.

Rosanna arched against the mattress, her moan drowning out the slap of rain on the glass. Phineas withdrew, then plunged his fingers inside her again.

'Break for me.' Phineas raised himself so that he was perched over her, their mouths seeking and meeting. With his free hand, the one that was not tapping and circling her clitoris before entering her again, he placed her palm on his cock. She tightened around him, his need familiar, his hunger for her written in every hard curve of his body. Rosanna drank in the sight of him—from his lean torso to his tense pectorals which rippled as he moved further and further from control—even as she thrust against his palm, her body demanding he conquer her.

Heavy breaths and searching lips. She chased the deep and primal need until an indelicate yearning coursed through every vein, surged into her belly, and pulsed hard at the tips of his fingers.

'More, my darling. Let me taste your crisis.' He moved so dexterously, without even upsetting the indentations of the mattress, and like a blur, Phineas settled his head between her splayed thighs just as the next vivid explosion of thunder and lightning hit almost simultaneously. Before the rumble had finished shaking the house, he'd drawn a slick line and buried his tongue inside her.

Her body forgot everything except the scrunched linen that she bunched into her palms, the heavenly play of his fingers as they moved faster, so unrelenting, and his mouth, kissing hard as if her body was his breath. And when she grunted, moaned, and struggled to inhale, the frenetic crescendo rumbled through her, loud with lust and release. Her cries wound through the melody of the rain. As the delicious spasms eased a little, Phineas lowered himself atop her. His cock pressed into her wetness, which was still pulsing with release, still craving more.

'Yes?'

Barely a question, one word full of so many possibilities, and all of them stormed in his eyes, slate grey and full of love and longing. It was an infinite question about tomorrows, about family, about the possibility of children, *his* children. A question about her life spent beside him and his introspection, his quiet and his particularity. A man of so few words, and yet this one held an eternity. They'd spoken about the life they were holding one another back from, but in his question, he was abandoning himself to her and asking her to do the same. There were no secrets or unexpected sacrifices. Only tomorrow.

'Yes,' she whispered. 'Forever and forever. I want all of it. I want to take every next step with you.'

Slow and gentle, Phineas entered her. He held himself tight, balancing on his forearms, but even with his delicate thrust, she cried out as pain bit low in her body. The centre of herself that still echoed with the perfection of his touch tore and split with agony. How could such an exquisite moment turn so brutal?

'I'm sorry,' Phineas panted. 'Dear heavens, you feel so beautiful.'

Rosanna wrapped her arms around his neck and pulled him closer. His weight pressed into her, his body tight with anticipation, yet waiting. With her next inhalation, she let her body loosen. He moved deeper inside her, and now he stung a little less.

When he thrust again, tender and restrained, a whimper escaped his lips. He pushed his fingers through her hair as he sought her mouth, and all of her felt opened and exposed, weighed by his body. He moved inside her hesitantly, and she rose to meet him, searching for harmony. Every touch turned into an invitation, and like each moment of reckless passion they'd shared, he listened not for her words, but for her body to sing.

'Do you still hurt?' He withdrew, snatched a kiss, then moved inside her again with that same aching restraint.

She shook her head. 'You feel nice. It feels... complete.'

'My wife will feel more than nice in her bed.' A slightly wicked glint twisted his mouth into a wry smile, and Phineas, his cock still inside her, his grasp possessive, leant back onto his haunches. As he moved, he hitched her body onto his thighs. Rosanna pushed the hair from her eyes and stifled a nervous laugh. 'Spread a little more for me,' he commanded. Rosanna stretched her thighs, and with his next thrust into her, he grasped her arse and pulled her higher.

A groan burst from her lips, high and surprised at the unexpected exhilaration. He bent his head and stared at the meeting of their bodies, lasciviousness drawing dark lines across his face, and when he caught her watching him watching them, he didn't hide, he merely licked his lips. 'Rosanna,' he said, his tone strangled elation. 'Look at me.'

Rosanna forced her eyes to remain open through the cacophony of perfection and the pounding that tensed her body, all of her moving to his rhythm. He held her gaze, his own demanding and fierce, and when she tried to close her eyes to surrender to the sensations raging through her, he grasped her chin and held her firm.

'Me. You and me.'

His eyes fluttered as his thrusts slowed, but he did not break his determined gaze. She caught his cheek in her hand. He leant into her and planted a kiss in her palm. He spoke so softly that she only heard the indistinct shape of his confession, but she felt his love like a brand on her skin as he whispered what he might never say aloud.

I love you.

Rosanna reached for him, and he collapsed against her chest. She pulled him tight against her like she might absorb him, the two of them an incredible catastrophe of writhing, quaking ecstasy. If only she could dissolve into the mattress, meld into its comfort and his compression.... She would disappear into his strength, his vulnerability and his heaving breaths, and lose herself in every way. Lost and found, weary and rested. Still her own, but now also his.

Rosanna drew him against her. They settled in together, sharing her pillow, snug under his grey and black blankets.

'Don't ever leave me,' Phineas whispered. 'Promise.'

'Where would I go?' she asked. 'I am already home.'

CHAPTER
TWENTY-THREE

Growing up, the time of the year when the sun only set for what felt like minutes, when evening became just a grey extension of day—it had all seemed normal. In the North, summer days had felt unending while winter days, drowned out by the monotony of the workhouse workday, were as short as an inch. It was only when he'd descended into the hull of a ship and traversed the seas, when he'd re-emerged on the other side of the world, that Phineas had come to comprehend days as a detail belonging to a place instead of an absolute thing. At the centre of the earth, days held some general, mirrored sense throughout the year. In the far north or south, days could last days, many days, and in winter, the night could stretch into eternity.

And in the first-floor bedroom of Number 1, Honeysuckle Street, in his wife's bed, with his wife tucked into his side, he could not decide if the small summer night had proved inadequate. In the ashen hues of dusk, he had adored the feeling of her cheek on his chest as he too drifted off to sleep. When the moon dawdled across the window, he had nudged her awake and rolled her onto her back to make love to her again, without pain. Her little breaths and moans, pattering in harmony with the rain on the window, had rung harmoniously in his ears. But now, as the first sunbeams elongated across the floor, it was the most magnificent thing imaginable to watch the room fill with faint light so that he could count the freckles on her nose.

His wife.

Her husband.

Would he haul his few things down into this room? Or would she want to be placed higher in the house? He knew one thing—this two-bedroom nonsense would not be for him. Lying in his room above, knowing she was resting below and feeling the agony of separation had been hard enough before. To endure it now when he had finally been able to articulate his yearning and she had confessed to feeling the same—he wouldn't be able to stand it. Maybe she could show him some of those catalogues and they could pick something to paper his room with, together. She would probably hate anything he suggested, just to be obstinate.

A lifetime of petty disagreements, of light snarking, of her refusal to be overruled, opened before him. He kissed the top of her head.

He could not wait.

A murmur and a movement answered him. Rosanna twisted against the sheets. She blinked a few times, cut off a yawn, and before he could draw her against his chest, she repositioned herself and sat upright, her arse against his hips, facing him. Even in waking she wasn't slow or gradual. She tucked her legs beneath her like a nymph lounging by a stream or a mermaid luring boats to their demise, then flicked her hair over her shoulders. Her tresses formed a frame around her body, showcasing her glorious curves, the dark thatch between her legs and her areola, the delectable roundness stark against her pale skin. His wife. His own.

'Good morning, Mrs Babbage,' he said, scarcely believing the words.

She tugged at the coverlet so that it gathered around her waist. 'I cannot believe of all the names in the world you could have chosen, you decided on Babbage.'

Phineas tucked a hand behind his head and propped himself against the bedstead. 'I did not plan on having it for so long. Most certainly not forever. I might have thought about it more if I'd known. I suppose I am stuck with it now.'

Rosanna traced the D stamped on his side. 'I was going to demand you tell me all your secrets, but I don't think I need to know them all. Only some. How old are you?'

'I don't exactly know. I think thirty-four. Maybe thirty-five?'

'How could you not know?' she asked.

'Not many parties in the workhouse or in the army. Keeping track never seemed important.'

She sat straighter and shook out her hair. 'You must have a birthday. I demand you choose one.'

'Why?'

'Because I said you must. I think you should be thirty-two. Then I can organise a party at the hotel when you turn thirty-three. Otherwise, I will have to wait until you are forty-four, and that is such a long time. I will arrange cake and songs and decorations. I shall invite everyone in the street.'

Noise. Attention. People. Small talk. The whole thing sounded awful. He would hate all of it. He would grump about it, and the people around him would laugh and sing and bring presents.

'February twenty-ninth. You will have to wait until next leap year.'

'You cannot!' she chided, then slapped at his chest.

Phineas caught her hand and lifted it to his lips. He nipped at her softness and planted a kiss on her wrist. More than roses and sunshine, she smelt like sweat and debauchery and bliss and contentment. How could one woman be so many things? How could she contain so many components in one body, in a form the same height as his own?

'On the fourteenth of June, Rosanna Hempel was accosted, and despite her reservations, she allowed me to help her. After years of being numb, I came alive. How is that?'

Her smile started coy and delicate, but when he bit her knuckle, a twinkle of mischievousness flickered in her eyes. Far from a blushing bride, Rosanna moved with confidence as she planted her palms on either side of his head and deftly swung herself over his body. Even after availing himself of her all night, he felt himself growing hard, his cock stiffening at every little rub and nudge as she adjusted herself into a position that suited. She splayed her fingers to shake out her hair, and the tips of her hair tickled the top of his thighs as each curl twisted and settled.

Everything about her screamed decadence. He licked his thumb and circled a nipple while his fingertips pressed at the softness of her breasts.

She nuzzled into his neck, then nipped his skin. Phineas squirmed. Rosanna sat back. Her eyes widened with shock, and she grinned in realisation. 'Are you—'

'No,' he snapped.

'You are! You are ticklish!'

With a shriek of delight, Rosanna attacked him, her fingers dancing and skittering over his sides and bare skin, light and searching in all his delicate places. He snuffled and tried to push down a spluttering laugh, but to no avail, as her brisk assault raged on. He caught her wrists and flipped them both, and she squawked and wriggled beneath his weight until he silenced her with a kiss.

'Phineas...' she muttered against his lips.

'Hmmm?'

'I like fucking.'

'I had noticed.'

'Not so much the first time. Not at the start, anyway. But after that, I liked it much more. I would like to do it again, but I am so hungry. Is that normal?'

'I have an idea.' He swung off the bed, grabbed his trousers from the floor and slipped them over his nakedness, then swiped his shirt and tugged it over his head. 'I will ask Felix to make a picnic basket so that we can eat in bed. He will be beside himself with delight.' He kissed her nose. 'And I will bring you tea. I've heard that's what men do when they adore their wives but aren't so good with the words.'

The house mumbled with the sounds of early morning, of people waking. A door creak, feet on floorboards, pipes squeaking. A busy house. A home. His slippers scuffed the stair runner. If making tea was going to become a habit, perhaps a first-floor bedroom would be best. Then he wouldn't have to walk so many stairs each day to bring Rosanna tea. On the ground-floor landing, Phineas swung into the lobby, making for the servants' staircase near the dining room that led to the kitchen. He'd made his own brew daily in the army. Surely, he could manage now.

'Morning, Babbage. Running late?'

Phineas took a few steps backwards to peer into the entrance. 'Taylor?'

His colleague was leaning against the front door. Phineas blinked twice to convince himself he wasn't still asleep. Taylor had never been to his house before. He'd never even asked where Phineas lived, nor had Phineas enquired after him. Their conversations never extended past pleasantries and the ledgers.

How had he even got inside?

Taylor sneered, then inspected his nails. 'I heard you were looking for me.'

The penny dropped. How had he been so blind, so stupidly, stubbornly oblivious?

'Pennington.' Phineas gripped the banister tighter as terror coursed through him. 'If Lord Richard has spent your money, I'll pay it directly to you. I'll pay double. Leave Rosanna out of it. She's nothing to do with him or anything else.'

Pennington chuckled. 'I'm not interested in that bumbling fool. Although he did come in far more useful than I expected. What he cost me is a small price to pay for finally cornering you.'

'If you don't want money, what do you want?' Phineas asked, even though his stomach sunk with realisation as he spoke. Only one thing was more powerful than greed.

Revenge.

'You cost me thousands of pounds in Edinburgh, but more than that, you cost me time. When the National came undone, I lost all my contacts. For years, I worked on that network. All of it was humming along. Then you stuck your nose in, and I lost everything. I found you here in this infernal metropolis, hiding away in your little bank, ruling your margins, watching the stock market, just like before. Quite good at speculating, aren't you? Most clerks can barely afford a few rooms over a shop, and yet you managed this.' He waved a finger in the air. 'I knew money wouldn't move you, but I am a patient man. I've been waiting for you to have something to care about. Something you couldn't bear to lose.' He pulled a slip of paper from his coat pocket and flipped the cheque Phineas had written for Lord Richard between his fingers. 'And now, you finally do.'

'You showed me the ledger, though... You...' The gaping size of his failure loomed before him, stretching into the grey light of the hallway. 'You showed me on purpose. Not because you wanted my help, but to make me curious. You wanted me to stay.'

'Can't help but help, can you?' Pennington scrunched the cheque, then tossed it aside. 'Let's go to the bank. I'd like you to check my figures. And when I say check my figures, I mean open the safes so that I can clean them out.'

Phineas scanned the entrance. Knick-knacks, his umbrella, so many damn ornaments—there had to be something he could use as a weapon. 'I'm just a clerk. Why would they tell me the combinations?'

'They wouldn't, and yet I'd wager your lovely wife that you still know them.' Pennington opened the door. Tepid early morning light glanced off the walls, and the hum of an awakening street filled the air. Phineas edged into the entrance and craned his head just enough to look in the direction where Pennington gestured.

Across Honeysuckle Street, before the ruin that had been Number 6, Spencer sniffed the air, then scarpered and climbed the tree beside the fence, edging along a branch that ran close by a window to Number 4. A man in a black suit dropped a cigarette, then stubbed it out with his toe. He leant against the fence and crossed his arms. The man from the park and the hallway at the Aster. He raised a finger in acknowledgement. Pennington nodded in reply.

A tap and skip came from upstairs, a few levels up. Phineas's heart contorted, its rhythm alternating between still and racing. He slunk back into the doorway to the lobby and peered up the stairs. Bare feet patted against the wood. A slip of ankle and the white hem of a nightgown skipped down the upper stairs.

'Phineas? Did you get lost trying to find the kitchens?' Rosanna giggled.

He swallowed a knot of fear. 'I'll be just a moment,' he called. 'Go back to bed.'

'I'll help you with the tea. I can't imagine you've even *been* in your kitchens, much less know how to use them.'

'For once, will you listen to me!' he bellowed, his voice bouncing up the stairwell. He sucked his next breath between his teeth. 'Go upstairs. I will bring you tea.' Would she understand the urgency in his voice? Would she comprehend what he was trying to say?

'No need to be such a grump,' she snapped as she turned and clomped up the steps. 'Two sugars and lots of milk, if you don't mind.'

As Rosanna stomped out of earshot, Phineas eyed Taylor, weighing the man's mettle, his reach, his fists. He could fight him off well enough to run, but to win? To knock him out and keep Rosanna safe? Uncertain. And even if he could get to Rosanna and get her away, what of the rest of the household? Felix and Hugh and Letitia and the singing one, that Jean... And an entire family next door. Her family. Her everything.

'You can't beat me, Babbage. Maybe if you were just you, and I was just me, you might. But you have people to look after now, and I have people who look after me.' Pennington huffed a laugh. 'She'll do better without you. Deep down, you know that.'

Phineas hung his head. His vision blurred as he blinked down the painful realisation. She would do better without him. It would always be true. And the only way to give her a free life, to keep her safe like he'd promised, was to walk away.

'How can I trust you?' he asked. 'I could do everything you want, and you'll still hurt her. You could be lying.'

Pennington strode through the entrance hall, his neck muscles tensing as he grasped Phineas's collar and pulled his face close. 'I never lie. I always keep my word.' His voice dropped to a whisper. 'That's what makes me so terrifying.'

Phineas stumbled as Pennington shoved him through the entrance and towards the door. Phineas reached for his umbrella. Pennington smirked and shook his head. 'Clerks. All the same.'

As a small outfit with a modest number of clients on the books but still holding aspirations to be mentioned in the same sentence as Barclays or the Bank of England, Empire Savings and Loans had invested in a range of security measures to keep their clients' money protected. The most impressive of these was the subterranean bank vaults which secured dozens of locked drawers and safe deposit boxes. Clients placed their precious money and belongings in a box, locked them away, and kept their own copy of the key.

The bank also had small safes in each senior manager's office, and in a space behind the clerks' rooms on the lower ground floor, they had installed two Mosler safes.

As tall as a man, with fireproof double doors and almost indestructible, they secured the necessities for the bank's day-to-day operations. New bonds, shares, banknotes that needed to be exchanged at other banks, and currency for withdrawals—they were all stored in the Mosler safes.

Keys were too fiddly and too easily stolen or lost, but a three-number-combination, spun by hand to release the lock, offered a practical means of security.

Phineas hadn't ever intended to learn and memorise the combinations. But over the course of seven years, he had noticed the flick of a wrist while assisting a senior manager to deposit a stack of bonds. Or he'd overheard one man reminding another of the number sequence, as each safe had a different combination and occasionally the older bank officers became confused. Far more than words, numbers adhered to his memory and settled into the nooks and crannies of his mind.

It had always felt like a blessing before. His capacity to calculate had allowed him to reinvent himself over and over again, to move through life unobserved and unremarked on. But as he spun the last number on the dial, heard the bolt drop, and cranked the lever on the heavy door open, a cold shiver raced the length of his spine. The blessing had turned into a curse.

The door crept open with aching slowness. Behind them, the clerks' offices stood deserted, their empty spaces gaping in the bank's early morning slumber. The most diligent and eager clerks would start to arrive at around eight o'clock, not for about an hour. There was not a soul here to question them.

Inside the safe, stacks of bonds stuffed into folders tied with string, wads of bank notes, and trays of bright gold sovereigns, fresh from the mint, filled the shelves that ran along its sides. Pennington shoved Phineas aside. He shoved the wads of paper and coins into a bag and grabbed folders with client details and bank balances. For a man like himself who could read the stories behind the numbers, find vulnerabilities and secrets in the margins, it was a life-changing haul. More than money, Pennington was shoving power into his bag.

'You have everything you want?' Phineas asked.

Pennington sneered. 'Not quite.' And with a hard shove against his back, Phineas stumbled forward, his head colliding with the sharp edge of the open door. Through a blurry veil of thumping agony, he staggered back, only to be thrust forwards again. He steadied himself against the shelves. Pennington chuckled. 'Now I have what I want.' Phineas turned and stretched out through the blur, but he was too slow.

The last thing he saw was Pennington, smug and framed in the white light of the bank, before the door swung closed.

Chapter
Twenty-four

When she found Phineas, she would wring his neck.

And she would find him. She must.

She had to tell him how stupid he was.

Rosanna paced the length of the library. Using her riding crop, she flipped the curtains open a smidge. She'd recognise Pennington's messenger anywhere. He'd bruised her cheek and torn her dress. A brute like that left an impression.

She'd been on the landing, about to follow Phineas's order to return to her room, when a blast of fury had engulfed her. Only the night before, he'd promised her a marriage of equals, and then he had asserted his authority at the first opportunity. Instead of toddling back to take her dutiful place between the sheets, she had spun on her heel, taking each step in silence as he'd taught her. She was going to follow him to the kitchens, sneak in to find him confused and fumbling, and remind him who he was married to. Three steps down and she'd heard another voice. Heard the threat and his ready concession that she was better off without him.

Who did he think he was, treating her like a helpless damsel? When she found him, she would set him straight.

Rosanna stifled a sob against her riding glove and choked her panic down. She would find him before Pennington hurt him. She would.

Felix tapped on the door. 'Mr Brown has saddled Lovelace. And I don't know if Miss Hartright received it, but we sent your message between staff, over the walls. Letitia went on a reconnaissance mission. There's the man across the road, and one on each end of the lane that runs along the length behind the stables. Only the one across the street is very attentive though. The other two—'

'Seem to think that they've got an easy job on their hands, and that a woman alone is weak and easy to bully?'

Felix smirked. 'I'd wager they're thinking something like that. I delivered a message to your brother, but I think a few others may have overheard...'

Felix jolted forwards as Johannes pushed him aside to squeeze through the doorway. In his wake, a steady stream of family followed. Elliot and Beatrice, even Ammie and Nova, all of them loud and clamouring with questions. Father brought up the rear end of the rabble. He clapped his hands twice, then again. The group settled.

'What's this I hear about Babbage needing a rescue party?' he asked.

'Pennington tracked him down and threatened me if he didn't go with him to the bank.' Rosanna tapped her riding crop against her skirt in a failed attempt to concentrate her nervous agitation. 'He's got men watching the house, and if Phineas doesn't do what he says, they're to come after me. And instead of asking for my help, he's gone off to deal with Pennington alone.'

Father gave an exasperated sigh. 'Your husband is an idiot. Other people make us stronger, not weaker. Your mother taught me that, and when is she ever wrong?'

'Never,' Rosanna said. From Johannes to Elliot to Beatrice, even the smaller children, all of them nodded, like they were believers in the only truth in the world. And maybe they were. They all made her stronger, even when all she wanted to do was scream at them and run away. 'He's not used to having people he can rely on.'

'What's the plan, Rosie?' Elliot asked.

'Any chance you can create a distraction?' she replied.

Elliot raised a hand in salute. 'Distraction is my middle name.'

Rosanna directed the family where she needed them to be. She set Ammie and Nova by the window, with the very important job of hollering as loud as they could if they saw the man across the way take more than a few steps. Beatrice paced the hallway with Letitia and Hugh, all of them claiming they had learnt how to fight on the stage, and the real thing couldn't be that much harder. Elliot slunk off home, only to return with a mischievous grin and a bag full of thin cylinders wrapped in white paper. Johannes hung about in the entrance, waiting.

Father followed her to the stables. Mr Brown had Lovelace saddled and waiting, and he rubbed the horse's flank. Her father knelt and interlocked his hands. Rosanna placed her foot in his palms, and with a jolt, he lifted her into the seat. With a fluid follow through, he rose to standing, and as she settled herself into her side-saddle, he rubbed at dirt and bits of fluff. He'd always been larger than the full moon to her, an enormous figure of determination and strength, but as she looked down from her seat astride Lovelace, he seemed older and more worried than she ever remembered him being. A thin line of grey hair tucked behind his ear.

'I want to stay married to Phineas,' she blurted out. 'We've come to care for one another. Love one another.'

'You want to—pardon?'

'If you tell me any different, I won't—'

Father raised his palm. 'You've always known your own mind. If you say you want to stay, then you stay. Don't expect us to go carolling together, but I'll tolerate the man. For you.'

'He baited you on purpose. He said friends would make him slow, but really, I think he's scared of people leaving.' Rosanna adjusted her skirt. Was it normal to be a translator between a parent and a husband? To plead a case for understanding between two people who refused to see eye to eye? 'I've never understood why you rose to it, every time.'

'He took the house on the end of the row, with the extra windows. I promised your mother those windows.'

'I'm sure she doesn't mind.'

'I mind.' Father scratched Lovelace behind the ear. 'Once Johannes has dealt with the man across the street, we'll run a back route to the bank. If you get there before us, you wait. Understand?'

Horseshoes clipped against the stones. Rosanna pressed her heels into Lovelace's side. She hung back a little in the shadows until Elise came into view. She'd dressed in a black habit, just as Rosanna had asked, and not a blonde curl showed beneath her hat, the same style that Rosanna was wearing. The men at either end of the street would see nothing more than a streak of horse and a too-confident woman.

'You have so much explaining to do,' Elise said.

'I cannot wait to tell you everything, but first we need to help Phineas.' Rosanna reached out to her friend, who reciprocated and squeezed her fingers.

'I'll go this way.' Elise nodded straight ahead. 'Then I'll ride down Honeysuckle Street to catch the other man's attention. Once both men are in pursuit, you make your escape. I'll lose my hat so that they can see their error, and hopefully run for fear of what Pennington will do to them.'

'You do know that once you start riding fast down the street, it's all people will talk about. You will never recover your reputation,' Rosanna said.

'I've often thought that a reputation is an overrated thing. Are you ready?'

The lethargic quiet of morning chirped and hummed into the expectant tension that hung between them. Rosanna, breath crumpling in her lungs, swallowed hard. She would find him. She would.

A high-pitched squeal rent the air, and then, above them, light scattered and cracked as one of Elliot's firecrackers exploded. The faint white streaks sat stark against the grey smog of a London morning. Elise adjusted her position in her seat, then threw Rosanna a grin. 'On my mark...' she whispered. A second cracker fractured the air. 'Go!'

Lovelace nickered as Elise and Starby sped out of sight. Rosanna leant forward and rubbed her horse's mane. 'You've got this, my girl.' Another crack and fizzle as one of Elliot's creations shot into the morning sky, and horseshoes echoed at the opposite end of the street. Rosanna cast a look up at the townhouses standing side by side, one which held her past, the other her future. She squeezed her knees against Lovelace's flanks, and the two of them bolted into the day.

Rosanna leant low, contorting her body to balance out the uncomfortable combination of her saddle and her speed. Around her, London shuffled itself awake in a blur as she left Honeysuckle Street behind. Carts and drays, newspaper boys and bootlicks, flower sellers and beggars fell away and like the ticking metronome of the city, Lovelace's hooves clipped against the stones.

Finally, she reached the bank. Rosanna swung off Lovelace and landed on the pavement outside, where Father and Johannes were already waiting. As Rosanna looped Lovelace's reigns to a tethering post, Father rubbed a line of sweat from his brow, and half-bent to draw a deep breath. Johannes laughed and patted their father's back, possibly enjoying his competency over Father a little more than was polite.

'It's still closed,' Johannes said. 'How can we get inside?'

'Rosie, I can't break into a bank,' Father said, his puffs easing. 'Even for me, that's too far. If we were caught, the outcome for the family would be catastrophic.'

'Mrs Babbage? Can I help you?'

'Mr Robinson!' Rosanna cried, scarce believing her luck. The young clerk had helped her make her way to the clerk's office a few weeks before. 'Are you starting work early?'

Robinson nodded. 'I've been working hard at my ledgers. I'm hoping to make my way up a little in the bank. Maybe earn a little more in wages. Mr Babbage has been ever so helpful in giving me advice.'

'Phineas came in early, but I was asleep when he left. I missed him and thought he might like a short break for some tea and a proper breakfast. Especially since my family here is available when they are usually not... Is there any chance you could show me down to his office again?'

'I'm not supposed to...'

Rosanna smiled, then swayed. 'I know he won't be cross with you. He'll be ever so appreciative. I just know it.'

'Once more won't hurt, I suppose. But this can't become a habit,' Mr Robinson said emphatically. He led the way through a side door, along a dimly lit hall, and down a set of stairs.

'Mrs Babbage...'

'Yes?'

'This is your brother. And your father.'

'That's correct.'

'Do you by any chance have a sister?'

Behind them, Lawrence growled, menacing as a lion.

'I do,' Rosanna said, the lightness in her voice betraying her fear. 'She's seventeen, and not yet debuted.'

'I am nineteen, and I haven't debuted either. That is, I mean... I'm not so good with society. I avoid it when I can,' he confessed.

'My sister Beatrice is very confident. Perhaps you can join her dramatics club?'

Mr Robinson rolled his mouth to suppress a smile. 'Perhaps I might.' At the doorway to the clerks' offices, he glanced across the room, frowning. 'He must have stepped out for a moment. He's normally at his desk right here. He works with Mr—Mr Taylor!' Robinson waved. 'Have you seen Mr Babbage?'

Fury propelled Rosanna across the room and between the desks. A flick of her riding crop wiped the smug smile from his face, and Taylor, who she would bet ten years of her allowance was not Taylor but the fiend who had started all of this, let out a yelp. 'You dare to threaten me?' She levelled her crop at his chest. 'Where is my husband?'

His hard eyes narrowed. 'Safe.'

Chapter
Twenty-five

Phineas threw himself at the door. A sharp spasm of pain radiated through his chest as he collided with cold steel, and in the smothering darkness, he knocked an elbow against the shelves.

'No!' he shouted, the word swallowed by the tight confines of the safe. 'Not now. Not like this.'

Darker than midnight in winter, shapeless and compressed, the small world inside the safe contained not even a blink of light. He raised his fist to thump against the door, but his fear dissolved into despair and sunk from his stomach, unbuckling his knees before pooling in his heels. Phineas pressed his hand against the steel, then scrunched his fingers into his palm, his nails scraping the flesh. He collapsed, huddled awkwardly in the small gap between the door and the shelves, defeated. It wouldn't matter how loudly he cried. No one would hear him. Even as the office filled, the safe would not allow a peep to escape. He could holler all day if there was enough air—and in a fireproof safe, there was not. Not to last an entire day. If they figured out where he was, maybe they'd fetch one of the senior clerks and bring him across town to the bank to dial the combination. Maybe, when they came down to fetch the money for the bank tellers upstairs, they'd open this safe and find him.

Maybe they'd get to him in time.

The little bud of hope shrivelled and died. He was too much of a realist to hold fast to such a notion. Too good at calculating outcomes and assessing situations. And the forecast for him, now...

Insurmountably bleak.

Phineas pinched his eyes tight against the sting. Goddamn feelings were a waste to him now, but he couldn't stem the pathetic flood of self-pity. How he loved her. How very much he'd been looking forward to learning how to live with her beside him. So extraordinary, so full of vitality and confidence. Worthy of so much more than a no-name bank clerk, but deigning to love him anyway.

Pennington was right—she'd be better off without him. She'd gain the chance for a proper new beginning. A slate wiped clean. After a year in black dress, she could step out into the world on her own terms. She'd create her own tomorrow. And he, who should be dead a dozen times over, would slip into the ether with the knowledge that an exceptional woman loved him. Quick as a whip, sharp and calculating, eyes like spring and skin that smelt like roses and sunshine. His enchanting Rosanna.

It was more than he should have hoped for, more than he'd ever dared to wish for. He'd experienced an eternity in an evening, forever in a day, and heaven in a sunbeam. At least he would die a redeemed man.

This would be his happy ending. A happier ending than any he deserved.

Tick.

Tick.

Like a watch, but not. Not the right rhythm. Not the right pace.

Tick.

Tick.

Clunk.

Light flared, white and ghastly. Phineas scrunched his eyes against the bright onslaught until it squeezed its way between his lids. Coughs, shouts, and clamouring voices bounced off the safe's walls. Gradually, the world shifted into focus. Someone sat before him, crouched low. Someone with dark hair and a familiar smile.

'What are you doing here?' he asked.

Lawrence tapped Phineas's cheek. 'No one fucks with my family, Babbage. I told you. Having people to care about makes us stronger, not weaker. If you plan on being Rosie's husband, you'd do best not to forget that.'

Phineas squinted, and as the fuzzy outlines sharpened, he picked out the sprawled form of Pennington, flat and comatose on the floor with a towering Johannes over him alongside someone else.

'Robinson?'

Robinson hopped from foot to foot, tight and trembling. 'I listen, sir. Just like you told me. I didn't know all the numbers, but Mr Hempel here guessed the last one.'

'Guessed?'

Lawrence winked. 'Some habits die hard.'

Phineas braced himself against the safe and heaved himself up, then slumped backwards. Lawrence reached out to assist, but as Phineas extended his own shaking palm to meet him, Rosanna shoved her father aside.

'Phineas Babbage, don't you dare do that again.' She grasped his shirt and hauled him towards her. His side creaked with pain, but when she kissed him, he found comfort in her touch and solace in her lips. She pushed him away, and he sagged again, then slid onto the floor. 'Don't you dare sacrifice yourself. Don't you ever think I will be better off without you when I would be destroyed.'

Phineas gripped his side as he coughed into a laugh. 'You *are* better without me.'

'No!' She flared with anger and hurt, her words so honest he had to close his eyes against her fierceness. 'How dare you? How dare you assume to think on my behalf? How dare you decide that I, who has had to suffer through your views on jam and your missives on boots, do not love you enough to be utterly devastated if something were to happen to you?' She grasped his cheeks and kissed him before withdrawing. 'You said I was your equal. Don't ever assume to think on my behalf. You are a stupid man, Phineas Babbage. You will not dictate to my heart ever again.' And then she flung herself at him, wrapped her arms around his neck, and sobbed against his shoulder.

He kissed her cheek and pulled her tight to counter the dark and fear that had subsumed his senses. She tasted like fresh air and honey, like days stretched naked in bed in the sunshine and nights huddled by the fire. She smelt like burning oak in a hearth and sugar-coated almonds and any other good scrap of memory that had slipped from his life. More than anything, as she shoved him away with one hand and drew him close with the other, he held tight to his Rosanna, his ferocious Mrs Babbage who met the world like a firecracker in whisky.

Why had he thought she needed to be saved, when all along, she had been saving him?

He coughed, and his chest pinched. Lord, he'd cracked a rib. 'I'm sorry,' he spluttered, then laughed, which made his whole body shake with joy and pain again. 'I won't think to protect you ever again. I swear it.'

'Good.' She settled against his chest. Phineas took another strained breath and stroked his wife's gloriously soft hair. All for him, all his own. 'But seriously, Phineas,' Rosanna chastised. 'Kidnapped in your own home. Some bloody spy you are. You will never live this down.'

EPILOGUE

Christmas Eve, 1876

Phineas set his ruler against the ledger. Readied his pen. Drew a long, crisp line.

'Not still working, are you, sir?' Felix stepped into the upper room, now converted into an office. 'It's Christmas Eve.'

'Only completing the entries for this quarter. Then I'll finish up.'

'I've set your whisky and a glass in the library, just how you like it. Are you certain you don't mind me heading out? It seems a sad thing to spend Christmas alone, with only liquor for company.'

Phineas cast a crestfallen glance at the telegram that had arrived earlier that afternoon. Owing to a shift in the weather and ice on the rails, Rosanna and Johannes had been delayed on their return from Brighton. They'd been away these past two weeks, and now she wouldn't be home for Christmas either. Phineas shrugged off his disappointment. He'd spent Christmases alone before. Better she get home safely than not at all.

'Don't fret, I'll only be having one drink. Enjoy your evening with Letitia. Best of luck. I hope she says yes.'

'How did you...?'

Phineas raised his brows. 'I always know.'

He hadn't actually known. Rosanna had pointed out to him how much time Felix spent on the upper floors and how smitten he seemed with the lady's maid. But no point in letting that fact slip. His wife was right often enough as it was. 'Don't feel as if you need to quit. A married couple will want their own lodgings, I understand, but there's always employment for you here. If you want it.'

'Thank you, sir. Fingers crossed, ey?' Felix buttoned his coat. 'Merry Christmas. Don't work too late.'

Felix left. Phineas returned to his ledgers. Across the top margin, he wrote the date, the costings, and the sale price in his smooth hand. The steady work of breaking up and selling off the individual components of Abberton & Co., of trying to recoup losses and refund shareholders, was best done in a quiet house. After he'd discretely provided the bank with everything they needed to carry out their own investigations, he'd resigned from his position. Pennington had been right about his skill at making investments and speculating. It had been a long time since Phineas had relied on his clerk's salary, and the thought of sitting in a room adjacent to the tall Mosler safes still left him unsettled. Besides, this was where he was needed. This was where he could help.

Phineas tallied the final column. He closed the book, sat back, and rubbed a hand across his weary eyes. The room had turned darker as he worked, so he lit a candle to guide his way downstairs. He walked along the hallway, papered with bright woodblock and decorated with paintings purchased during their honeymoon in Venice and Rome, into the stairwell where photographs hung frame-to-frame. A stretch of happiness filled every wall, and even though he was the only person in his residence this evening—Jean had begged time to visit her grandmother in France, while Hugh had travelled to see his parents—he didn't feel alone. That's what home was, wasn't it? A place where you never felt alone because you knew you belonged and the spirit of those you cared about remained, even if they weren't with you.

In the library, Phineas set his candle beside the whisky. He poured an inch into a glass, then eased the decanter back to stop the drip. He took a sip as he crossed the short distance to the mantlepiece, then tapped the top of the frame that held the photograph of Imogen. After he'd sent her sufficient forgeries of paperwork to pass as a woman named Mabel, she must have stopped putting off the farmer who brought her flowers. An envelope containing a newspaper cutting from the *Chelmsford Chronicle* wedding announcement column was the only acknowledgement he'd received, but all he needed. And in the unlikely event that Pennington ever saw life outside a cell again, Phineas couldn't imagine the fiend would bother to chase down the woman who'd once been his wife. Would he be full of enough fire to come for Phineas after his release? Possibly... And yet, if that day ever came, Phineas would be ready—because as much as it worried him, he would not be alone.

Phineas clinked his glass against the frame beside Imogen's, the frame that held an old calotype of his friend, the failed duke. 'Here's to you, Arley. *Joyeux Noël*.' Next, he raised his glass to a picture of Mother, the corporal, and himself as a boy. Rosanna had found the *carte postale* hidden in a book and insisted that the only relic from his childhood join the little line-up of his past. Some days, he felt warmth at seeing the small family of his memory. Others, a little sadness. And he was learning to accept that both those feelings could exist side by side. Neither needed to be put into a box just because they didn't get along.

A slight tug and a bump against his shin shook his thoughts into the room. At his feet, little baby Hazel blubbered, rocked on all fours, then rolled onto her bottom.

'Who let you in?' he asked.

Hazel looked up, her green eyes bright and happy. 'Mum mum mum,' she recited, before clapping her hands and pursing her lips to blow a *pffft*.

'You cannot spend Christmas alone,' Wilhelmina said as she entered the room. 'We also received a telegram. And we thought we'd save you the pitying invitation to dine with us by coming to you. Do you have a tree?'

Behind her, a flashing line of red coats and loud voices filled the space just outside the library door. This was what came of giving his in-laws a key. Some Hempels stomped upstairs to the front parlour that looked out over the street. Elliot stuck his head into the room. 'Did Jean leave any little cakes?' he asked, then took off before waiting for the answer, likely making for the kitchens to investigate for himself.

'I feed them. All the time. I swear it. Children are always hungry.' Wilhelmina squeezed his arm. 'You watch Hazel. Leave the rest to us.'

'I'm fine, really, I—'

'Rosanna would never forgive us if she thought we left you to spend Christmas alone. You know I'm right,' Wilhelmina called over her shoulder as she left.

There was no use denying that. And when it came to Rosanna, resistance was futile. Phineas scooped the baby up. She swayed a little, then clasped his shirt. Chubby little fingers gripped his waistcoat, and with her other hand, she poked a finger into his eye. 'Steady on,' he said with a laugh and a flinch. 'Not every Hempel needs to wage war on me.'

The house echoed with shouts, noise, and activity. He carried Hazel to the window and settled onto the seat. She pressed her palms against the glass, her eyes wide as she followed a flurry of snowflakes that dashed past the window to settle on the shrubs. A small group of people emerged from the shadows and ascended his staircase with a flip of coats and boots, shortly followed by the clap of the knocker against the front door.

'I suppose we should answer that,' Phineas said, swinging Hazel onto his hip as he made for the entry. The first shape to greet him was Spencer, who shot over the threshold in a blur of grey fur. He shook himself furiously, and little flecks of ice and snow scattered over the walls.

'It's colder than last year. How is that even possible? Hold these!' Hamish shoved a basket covered with a chequered cloth at Phineas, who grasped the handle with his free hand. The viscount turned to help his wife with her coat before shrugging off his own.

'We heard reports of the terrible weather, and that the trains were delayed,' Iris said as she smoothed her hair. 'We didn't want you to spend Christmas alone. We are so grateful for your help with the company. Papa is with Odette. She's invited Jonah and a few of their friends from the early days to play piano. She thought a small group might be nice for him to spend time with. So we thought we'd come to you.'

'How is he?' Phineas asked.

'This morning he remembered all of us,' Iris said with a tender smile. 'Today was a good day.'

On his hip, baby Hazel grasped the chequered cloth over the basket to reveal a jumble of shortbread and sugar biscuits. Her little hands clenched and released before she made a grab for a treat.

'These are mine!' Hamish said with mock outrage and snatched the basket away, then presented it again. 'Go on, have one.'

Phineas sighed as the baby crushed crumbs against his waistcoat. He turned to the door, but another gust blew in a flurry of snowflakes, bringing Petunia and Elise Hartright along with them.

'It is far too cold to sing in the park.' Petunia stomped snow off her boots and shook out her scarf. 'Besides, we heard you were alone. Which way is your new piano, Mr Babbage?'

'Upstairs, in the parlour. But there really is no need. I am far from alone now, and I was quite happy before—'

Elise clapped her hands in front of Hazel and held them out, ready to catch. Hazel, familiar with the game, pushed herself forwards and fell into Elise's waiting arms. Chattering fast, the five of them made for the stairs and ascended into the bluster and noise above.

'A party without me?' someone hollered from the street. 'I am outraged.'

Phineas stepped out into the cold. He descended the few stairs to the path and peered into the late afternoon. 'Benton Hunter? What on earth are you doing here?'

'Two years abroad, and that's all you can say? In case you've forgotten, I live here. And I'd like a proper greeting if you will, or you won't get your present.'

Phineas clasped the hand of the man who owned the townhouse at the opposite end of the row, the sole resident of Number 9, Honeysuckle Street. Had the diplomat developed some manners or at least some tact during his time away?

'I must ask,' Benton said as he gripped Phineas's hand, 'how many veins were visible on Lawrence's forehead when he found out you'd compromised his daughter in the park?'

Apparently, he had not.

The fast tap of boots, a jubilant laugh, and a lunging blur of red and white was the only notice Phineas received that Benton had not returned home alone. Rosanna launched herself at him, wrapping her arms around his neck and kissing his cheeks, his neck, his lips. Roses and sunshine, cold cheeks and warm hands—Phineas clasped her by the waist and pulled her against him in shocked delight.

'I thought you were delayed. I didn't expect you for days,' he said, when he finally caught his breath.

'We made it as far as Crawley by rail. I had just sent the telegrams when we ran into Mr Hunter, who had landed in Portsmouth and was also making his way north. He managed to negotiate passage for the three of us. It was like a Christmas miracle.'

'Shh! The last thing Benton needs to hear is that he's a—'

'Your Christmas miracle has arrived!' Benton shouted into the house, already at the top of the stairs. 'Now the celebrations can begin!'

Johannes followed suit at a steadier pace. He clapped Phineas on the shoulder, then lumbered up the stairs. Shadows danced across the warm light that shone through the first-floor windows, while melody and bubbling voices spilled onto the street. Laughing, Rosanna linked her fingers with his and took a step forwards. Phineas pulled her back.

'Before we go in, can I steal you for a moment? I think you should open your present from me without anyone around. Just let me sneak my coat.'

Moments later, hat, gloves, scarf, *and* coat donned, Phineas crept from the house to meet his wife. With a curious smirk, she threaded her hand around his elbow, and they crossed into the park together, strolling along the gravel. Lamps cast glowing yellow circles onto the path, and they walked past the sunken garden, the iced-up fountain, and the frozen pond, which was dotted with skating children and couples. Snow crunched beneath their boots. Rosanna shivered, and Phineas pulled her closer. Before the church, he slowed his step. He reached into his coat pocket to pull out the small, rectangular parcel covered in brown paper and tied with a red ribbon, and Rosanna grasped it, tearing at the wrapping. Phineas caught the paper as she revealed the long, thin box. With shining eyes, she wiggled the lid off.

But when she looked up, she was scowling.

'A portable pen? If this is a joke, it's a terrible one.'

'The vicar came to see me the other day,' Phineas explained. 'He was quite distressed. He said that when we married, in all the confusion—'

'And arguing,' Rosanna interjected.

'Yes, arguing, we did not sign the register. I promised to bring you over as soon as you returned.'

They stepped to one side to make way for a few departing parishioners, including Mrs Crofts. Then Phineas directed Rosanna up the stairs and over the antechamber, and they walked side by side down the aisle. Phineas waved at the vicar, who busied himself with the large register, muttering as he flipped through the pages. Finally, he gestured at the entry of their names made back in June.

'Are you telling me that all this time we haven't been fully married?' Rosanna whispered. 'And if we are to be properly wed, I need to sign my name?'

'Provided you want to sign your name against mine. This is your last chance, Hempel. There really will be no escaping me. *Till death do us part*. I know I am not much, but you have made me so—'

'No need to be melodramatic,' Rosanna said as she swept the nib across the page, notarising herself as *Rosanna Hempel* for possibly the last time. She underlined her commitment with a flourish, then passed the pen to him.

'I had a whole speech prepared.' He scrawled out his own. *Phineas Babbage*. 'I was going to say so many lovely things about you.'

Rosanna plucked the pen from his hands and screwed on the lid. 'We could do the kissing bit again. I don't remember that being very exciting last time.'

The vicar coughed.

'Apologies, vicar,' Phineas tucked his wife into his side. 'We'll leave you to your evening. Thank you, and Merry Christmas.'

In the short time that they'd spent in the church, the light snowfall had turned to heavier flurries. White carpeted the grass, and he breathed in air rich with pine, woodsmoke, and snow. Between two lampposts, poised at the edges of both circumferences of light, Phineas drew her close. 'I think we can sneak that kiss now,' he said. 'Before we are missed.'

'Don't you want your gift from me?'

Phineas burrowed into the small gap between her coat and her felt bonnet. 'Ever so much, but I cannot unwrap you out here. And it may not be appropriate to whisk you away from all the visitors—*HOY!*'

A flat *thunk* against the back of his head jerked him to attention. A thread of ice snaked down his back, beneath his coat. His gaze swept the park, and Amadeus jumped from behind a bush, lobbed a snowball that scuttled at Phineas's feet, then dove back behind the foliage. 'Take that, Babbage!' he shouted. Elliot emerged from the same bush and threw another snowball with much better aim. 'And that!' Another snowball came from the left, then the right. And then the left.

'There are so many of them,' Phineas said, as he crouched down and scooped up a ball of snow. 'Hempels vs Babbages hardly seems a fair fight.'

Rosanna knelt beside him, working fast to fashion a missile of her own. She stood and hurled it in the direction of her brothers. 'We need more allies. Would one more Babbage help? Although it may be some time before they can join the fray.'

'Where will we find another...' Phineas mouthed their surname, his voice contracting into shock. 'Another? A little? Rosanna, are you—'

'Having a baby. Yes. We are.' Little plumes of mist from her smiling lips made each word physical, almost tangible, and Phineas followed their path as they floated away, then vanished. His chest constricted, and the world blurred as fear and elation and shock and wonder collided. He would be a terrible father. She would be a wonderful mother. The house would be so noisy. The house would be so happy. He would try to do everything right, but there would always be so many things beyond his control, and so many things he would do wrong.

Everything would change.

'Phineas? I know life will be uncertain, but we'll manage it. Together.' Rosanna pressed her palm to his cheek. Her touch brought him into himself again. Into the cold, the grey light, and the certainty he always found in her eyes. All the words he had composed before to recite in the church... They would forever go unspoken because what he'd felt before was wholly inadequate compared to now.

Forget the neighbours, forget the onlookers, forget everyone. The only thing in the world that mattered was his wife and the terrifying, beautiful future before them. Phineas spun her into his arms and tipped her back.

'Bring the chaos, my darling. Bring the storm. For nothing could be worse than you.' And before she could argue, he silenced her with a kiss.

THE END

HISTORICAL NOTE

Please enjoy the nerdy bits, the history bits, and the random threads of research that became the heart of this story.

I didn't intend to write a book about a bank clerk. As I write this, it is almost two years since Phineas Babbage came into being. Initially the man who had annoyed his neighbour Lawrence because he gazumped him and bought the townhouse on the end of the row with the extra windows and the view of the park, I imagined Phineas as a secret agent, working as a clerk for his cover. But as I began researching spies and financial fraud in the Victorian era, he slowly told me more about himself. Over time, he revealed his backstory, one he'd been hiding through two books and a novella. The bland bank clerk brought with him the heftiest cases of a troubled backstory of any of my characters to date. I adore him for it.

Most men in the Army were not permitted to marry. However, in some cases, men were able to apply for permission to marry, and if approved, were able to bring their wives with them if they were posted overseas. While the working conditions were hard, and couples lacked anything remotely like privacy, being an army wife brought food, financial stability, and possibly a greater likelihood of keeping a husband faithful. Many children raised in the Army went on to enlist at a young age, often while abroad.

Desertion from the Army carried different punishments at different times. At the time Phineas absconded, deserters who were caught were court-martialled, often whipped, and branded with a D on their left side to stop them from enlisting again. Extreme cases carried the death penalty, but this was not common. Many deserters were transported to Australia as convicts where, after serving their seven-year sentence, they settled down to become average members of society. The branding of deserters in the British Army was abolished in 1879.

Charles Dickens, Anthony Trollope and Émile Zola, along with many other novelists of the Victorian era, all devoted plots to financial fraud and mismanagement. The emergence of the upper working classes and the middle classes created wealth, and along with shopping and consumption, extra savings could be used for financial investments. Banks and companies were under no overarching scrutiny or even government regulation. The Tipperary Bank scandal was one of many unfortunate incidents that shattered many lives. However, because I write historical romance, I wanted to give even the investors in Argonauts Trading something of a happy ending too, so while they may not have made a profit, they did, at least, get their money back.

The Married Women's Property Act of 1882 is generally considered to be the major milestone in women's independence. Before that, less successful but still significant, there was the Married Women's Property Act of 1870. This Act allowed for a limited number of financial freedoms for a woman once she married, and she could retain some control over her own property outside of her dowry. It was not retrospective, so only helped new wives, and only related to real property (land, furniture, stocks and livestock) and not cash. Wives could (in theory) keep their own wages, although I do wonder in a home within a patriarchal society how much control many women actually had. Contracts and premarital settlements could further protect women if a father or male guardian made the effort to have them drawn up. The period when Rosanna is negotiating courting and her potential married life is a complicated time, and so much of a woman's future happiness depended on the intentions of the man she married. Rosanna would have kept control of her dowry and kept her wages from Aster, but her personal savings she held at the time of marriage would have passed to her husband. She would have been vulnerable to his ongoing manipulations.

The description of the London Stock Exchange is drawn from *The Great Metropolis* (1837) by James Grant. I have done my best to put together an accurate description of the building, the behaviour of the members and the locations of offices, but some of this information is hard to pin down. The location of the tickertape machines is purely for my own convenience. The building is now a shopping arcade.

Honeysuckle Street is not, and to the best of my knowledge, has never been, a real street in London. It is drawn from the rhythm of life of the time in which I write. Modern townhouses that cater to the burgeoning middle classes line one side of the street, while older houses line the other. Dukes and earls live alongside merchants, traders, and other members of the upper crust. It is a street depicting a world in transition, constantly changing and evolving.

A Song and a Snowflake

Would you like to read about the scandalous love story that destroyed the Hartright family name?

Subscribe to my newsletter, An Old Fashioned Quickie, to receive your FREE copy of A Song and a Snowflake at aliviafleurbooks.com

A woman seeking redemption at the end of a church aisle...

Beautiful songbird Charlise Hartright is ruined.

Introverted, shy and grieving her mother's loss, she would do anything to restore the family name, even commit to a loveless match, if it means her beloved sister Elise will have a chance at finding her own happiness.

A man out to make his own name...

Sinclair McIntyre has travelled halfway across the world to pursue his own destiny. Tired of being in the shadow of his older brothers, he is determined to do things his own way to become an independent, self-made man.

A future laid out before each of them...

But with a song

And a snowflake

Everything will change.

Acknowledgements

This book was written on Wiradyuri Country. I pay my respect to elders, past and present. The place where I live, work and write always was and always will be Aboriginal land.

I am writing these acknowledgements at that point in the process following completion but before release, when I am full of elation and fear and worry and excitement—so many feelings and like Phineas, I do not always sit well with them. Thank you, dear reader, for making it this far with me. I hope you have enjoyed this story. I certainly loved writing it, especially with its slightly bonkers plot. Thank you for supporting me as an indie author. It is the readers and reviewers of independently published books that make everything possible.

As always, thank you to Rachel. You're a hilarious and ever so supportive writerly friend. This one wouldn't exist without you.

Thank you to Amber Knight for your amazing editing. It really did feel like you were sitting here with me, talking through each problem. 'Steam steam steam by the tickertape machine' is hands down my favourite editorial note ever.

Of course, special thanks to the magnificent Louise Mayberry. Thank you for reading my book as I sent it in dribs and drabs and for pushing me to tighten up those squeaky chapters. And for all the other bits in-between. You are a treasure, and I am so grateful to have you as my colleague and friend.

To Sidekick Sophie. You are still my favourite. Gold Stars for you every day.

And always to Mr Fleur and the skin-dogs. Please stop leaving your crap on my desk. Love you all so much.

About Alivia

Hi! My name is Alivia, and I write steamy romance for history lovers.

I started writing romance in 2022. At first I wanted to write short stories, but then my characters kept turning up with copious amounts of back story, demanding I help them solve their problems! In April, 2023, I published my first novel, *A Beginner's Guide to Scandal*, the first in my series, *Tales from Honeysuckle Street*.

My novella, *The Portrait Sitting*, is a Romance Writers of Australia RUBY award winning story.

I live on a farm a long way from anywhere interesting, with my husband, our four dogs, and a charismatic chicken named Persephone.

You can learn more about me, my stories and upcoming releases at aliviafleurbooks.com